Nancy Martin

NIGHTCAP

Harlequin Books

TORONTO • NEW YORK • LONDON
AMSTERDAM • PARIS • SYDNEY • HAMBURG
STOCKHOLM • ATHENS • TOKYO • MILAN

Published July 1986

First printing May 1986

ISBN 0-373-70221-3

For Marsha Zinberg, with great affection

CHAPTER ONE

AN ALBATROSS LANDED on the bowsprit of *Bobbie McGee*, just off the coast of Pitcairn Island, and Blackie Lowell, ordinarily not a superstitious man, figured he couldn't ignore the classic sailor's sign. So far, his luck had been miserable.

He was going to lose the damned race. His crew had jumped ship, the wind had been dull and Pointy Hargraves had snatched the lead position somewhere off the coast of Chile, crowing with delight and waving a champagne bottle in the sunlight like a Yalie twerp. But now Blackie had his chance to catch up; a storm was bearing down on him like a hurricane. In fact, it might very well *be* a hurricane.

The snoozing albatross took one look at the impending gale, squawked once and clumsily flapped his wings in takeoff. Blackie ran up the storm jib, tightened every screw, bolt and line on board the sailboat and crouched at the tiller when the first blast of wind hit the sails. The night sea, black as oil and churning as if kicked from below by the hideous monsters of seafarers' tales, began to heave and foam, hissing like a maddened beast. Clouds boiled overhead. Racing before the lashes of wind, *Bobbie* swooped along the churning waves, plunging faster and faster every second. Her hull groaned. Her cables creaked. Lines rapped against her mast like machine gun fire. But the wind. The wind was glorious.

Blackie flung a look over his shoulder at the storm. They ran before it like a straining kite on a taut string, but he knew that at any second the gale would attack. "Come on, *Bobbie*!" he shouted gleefully, surging with joy and thrilling to the sensations of speed and danger. Blackie began to laugh. "Let's show 'em how it's done, old girl!"

Lightning tore across the black sky, a jagged streak that splintered through the clouds and exploded on the wild surface of the ocean. Thunder rolled in one continuous blast. The storm overtook them like a pouncing animal starved for prey, but Blackie held on to the tiller and clung to the rail. He'd make a hundred miles tonight if he had the guts to ride the storm.

Bobbie danced on the rim of a gigantic chasm, then plunged over the brink and into darkness. The ocean roared, and she spun like a paper boat in a vortex. But she fought her way to the top of the wave again, gallant and determined. As the wind screamed in her sails and rain blasted from astern, *Bobbie* bucked and lunged, swooping across the sea as if hurled by Neptune himself. Freezing rain began to pelt her deck, but Blackie dashed the water from his eyes and crowed with exhilaration.

How many hours did man and boat fight the elements? It could have been two or twenty. Blackie couldn't tell. The world had become a raging, howling tunnel of blackness, and yet the small, brave craft battled her way across the vicious seas. Her master used every iota of strength, every ounce of skill, every whit of intelligence to keep *Bobbie* on course. This was life at its greatest pitch, excitement beyond measure, an ecstasy of exhilaration that outstripped any description. The hours fused into one long night of primitive battle—man and boat against the sea.

But finally the pummeling rain turned to a needle-sharp spray in Blackie's face. His vision blurred, and his arms began to blaze with the strain of unrelieved tension. At last, common sense prevailed, and he fought his way forward, staggering to shorten the sail. They'd come far enough for one night, he decided. Triumph burned hot in his chest like a victory fire for a Polynesian warrior.

As he stood on the bow and peered through the darkness, Blackie saw the feeble glow of a real fire ahead. It was a warning, no doubt, some kind of signal displayed by the thoughtful inhabitants of a nearby island. He returned to the tiller and steered around the marker. He coaxed his boat lovingly. "That's my girl, my love. Steady now, *Bobbie*. We'd better watch out for these islands. I'd hate to scratch your lovely haunches on the rocks."

She skittered like an infuriated thoroughbred when he reined her in, fighting for her head, pitching through the tops of waves and wallowing in the troughs. Suddenly it seemed as if the boat were caught in breakers.

"Can't be." Blackie stood up, clutching for his balance and looking around in disbelief. "What the *hell*?"

Rocks. Thousands of them. They loomed in his path, washed with evil serpents of foam. Geysers shot up as surf crashed against the stones. The fire hadn't been a warning at all. He'd been tricked.

Blackie swore and dove for the tiller. Frantically he heaved *Bobbie* over and sent her into a sloshing valley of waves, trying desperately to turn his precious boat away from the jagged shore that undoubtedly lay ahead. Water cascaded over *Bobbie*'s rails, and she rolled to the leeward, sails flogging angrily. The tiller started to swing and *Bobbie* faltered. Blackie prayed for a few more feet of depth and cursed his luck. Only a miracle would save them now. Then *Bobbie* plunged bow first into blackness. No escape. The keel struck sand and Blackie fell. Helplessly he hurtled across the deck, hands scrabbling for a hold. He crashed against the mast, and the boom swung around with silent, deadly force. He saw it, but ducked too late.

A blinding light exploded in his head. Then darkness.

He dreamed of South Sea islands after that, of native maidens with golden skin and flowers twined in their fragrant hair. He dreamed of luxury and pleasure, warmth and coddling in an exotic and mystical land. It was a blissful dream full of Gauguin colors. Like Fletcher Christian, he was in love with life again. A woman—a beautiful woman—forgave him, knelt over him like an angel, touched his face with her cool fingertips and murmured soft words he did not understand. Absolution, perhaps. He was alone no more. Beneath him *Bobbie McGee* rocked and rocked, gently lulling him, soothing him with a mother's rhythm.

But then the woman's fingers turned into freezing rivulets of seawater, and Blackie came out of the dream like a rocket from a cloud bank. He was soaked and cold, crawling up the sand and choking on vile saltwater. The darkness swam around him, and the earth tilted crazily. Surf creamed and hissed, bubbling around his knees like thousands of tiny living creatures. Blackie clambered onto the beach, his heart pounding, his stomach rolling. Panting, he stopped, crouched on his knees and braced his hands in the wet sand. He choked once and retched.

When he looked up, there was no Polynesian beauty smiling at him. There was, in fact, a round-faced kid with a pair of fogged-up Radar O'Reilly glasses on his pug nose and a bow tie placed neatly at his collar.

Blackie blinked once and shook his head, trying to dispel the mirage. But the boy stayed put, staring back at him with an open mouth, fascinated.

"What the hell are you lookin' at?" Blackie growled, still on all fours.

The kid gasped in fright and scrambled out of sight.

Blackie squeezed down another impulse to vomit seawater and squinted through the darkness after the boy. The glow of a respectable campfire provided just enough light to see. Amazingly, Blackie thought he could visualize even more little kids across the sand. A dozen, he'd swear, all sitting on the beach wearing tidy little schoolboy uniforms and staring at him as if he were some kind of a mermaid killer. And beside the cluster of huddled kids was a pair of legs.

Blearily he stared at the legs. Bare legs, they were. Bare *beautiful* legs, in fact. Female legs. He followed them up to a pair of gorgeous knees and some breathtaking thighs that appeared to be encased in a sopping-wet skirt. He looked up past the skirt to a soaked and nearly transparent blouse and lingered over two small, upturned breasts before taking in a thin but softly feminine throat and gazing into the wide blue eyes of a startled young woman. She was no Polynesian maiden, but she could definitely be bracketed in the beautiful category. She had eyelashes like Audrey Hepburn, pale, pale skin that hadn't been tanned yet by the tropical sun, a trembling mouth and straggly black hair that was plastered wetly against her slim head and curled around her throat.

In precisely pronounced English she said, "I beg your pardon. Are you all right?"

Blackie plunked his posterior down in the wet sand and stared at her while trying to collect his addled wits. "No, I'm not all right," he rasped when he had found his voice. "I nearly drowned out there!"

"I doubt you were drowning," she said politely. "There are barely three feet of water."

Blackie turned around and looked at the ocean. There in the shallows was his beloved *Bobbie McGee*, squatting sideways and looking like Admiral Nelson's cocked hat. Her keel was firmly plowed into the sand, her loose spinnaker flapped pathetically in the wind and the mast tilted at a seventy-degree angle. The woman was lying. At least forty inches of water sloshed around her hull. The burned-out shell of a wooden dinghy bumped forlornly against her stern.

Blackie groaned. "Oh, *Bobbie*!" He lurched to his feet and clapped one hand to his forehead in abject grief. "*Bobbie*, darling *Bobbie*," he cried, his voice breaking as he absorbed her predicament. "What's happened to you?"

A little boy piped up from behind him. "It fell over, mister. It zoomed in here and fell over just like a sack of rotten potatoes. We saw it, honest."

Blackie swung around and glared at the kids on the sand. "A boat does not fall over! She ran aground!"

"It fell over," insisted the kid with the fogged-up glasses. "And you plopped over the side and threw up in the water. We saw everything."

Blackie glared at the kid and took a threatening stride toward him. "Listen, you sniveling little runt—"

The woman interrupted hastily. "I'm very sorry you had an accident, sir," she said, mincing down the beach toward him with a pair of high-heeled shoes in one of her hands. There was a gold bracelet on her wrist, and the glitter of a necklace showed between her breasts, too. She had lost one earring, but the other flashed in the firelight. Garnet, Blackie thought. Her pristine appearance was spoiled by quarts of seawater and something smeared down the front of her shirt— something that might have been mud. Or even blood, he supposed.

She paused two yards away and eyed him, saying, "You seem to be in good health, however, and your ship wasn't damaged. The tide is just starting to come in, so you'll be able to sail it out in just a short while. In fact, I'm delighted to say that this whole incident is just what we were hoping for."

Blackie squinted at her. "Huh?"

"We're stranded," she said succinctly. "We're in a bit of trouble as a matter of fact, and we have been trying to signal for help. We sent our only boat out with a torch in it, hoping that someone like yourself would come and—"

"Wait a second," he snapped. "You mean that you set a boat on fire to lure me into this bay?"

"Well, I have to admit that we didn't expect quite such good luck, but—"

"Dammit!" he exploded. "Do you realize that you nearly wrecked my boat? And almost killed me in the bargain? Are you crazy, lady?"

She blinked, looking as prettily startled as Lady Astor discovering the wrong spoon beside her soup plate. "We didn't intend to do harm. We simply put the dinghy out to sea in hopes that—"

"You're supposed to keep signals on *land*, lady, not in bilge buckets like that!" He jabbed an outraged finger at the sad excuse for a dinghy that scraped his beautiful boat. "Signals are supposed to help sensible people like me to steer *clear* of hazards so that exactly what happened here doesn't—"

"But if you had steered clear," she said reasonably, "we'd still be stranded, wouldn't we?"

He glared at her with murder in his heart. "You're *still* stranded, your ladyship. Just who the hell are you, anyway? And what are you doing on this godforsaken island?"

The young woman paused, and the red-headed kid in the glasses clambered to his feet and came forward. "We were captured by pirates, sir," he explained earnestly. "They took us off our sight-seeing boat and brought us here."

"Sight-seeing boat?" Blackie repeated. "Pirates?"

"Harold—" began the woman.

"Let him talk," Blackie cut in, waving his hand rudely in her face. The last thing he wanted to hear was some drivel out of the mouth of a sophisticated uptight priss like this one. "Go ahead, kid. Start from the beginning."

The red-headed kid had a pudgy face and china-blue eyes behind the thick lenses of his glasses. He was probably ten years old, but he was smart, Blackie could tell. He plunged into his story with gusto and a surprisingly good command of the language. "We're students at The American School on Pago Pago, sir. That's American Samoa, you see—"

"Yeah, yeah," Blackie intervened impatiently. "Get to the important stuff."

Harold nodded and pushed his glasses up onto the bridge of his nose. "Very well, sir. This is Miss Theodopolis, our teacher."

Blackie looked at her. She didn't look like the kind of teachers he remembered having.

"Our parents are all American diplomats, stationed on Pago Pago," the kid continued. "We were having an educational cruise, you see, and our boat experienced engine difficulty. Some men came along in another boat and said they'd assist us, but they didn't. They kidnapped us instead and then had to stop here to wait out the storm. Then one of them started, well, started bothering Miss Theodopolis. He took her jacket and tore her skirt a little, and then he dragged her off the boat and threw her on the beach behind the rocks over there." He pointed to an outcrop of huge boulders. "Then he unzipped his—"

"Harold," she interrupted again, more firmly this time. There was some color on her face, too—two spots of bright pink on her cheekbones.

Oho. So that was it. A near rape on the beach. Blackie gestured with one hand again. "I get the picture, kid."

The boy swallowed hard and avoided looking at his
teacher. Just the memory of what had happened to her
at the hands of the "pirate" made him blush furiously. He didn't stammer, though, and cut short his
story. "Well, she hit him on the head with a rock and
ran off up the beach. It was dark. The other guys
started chasing her and left us alone on their boat.
Peter decided we had better run for it, too, so we got
off the boat and came onto the beach. Then Miss
Theodopolis sneaked back through the rocks and
brought us over here. The men are still looking for
us."

Looking like a platoon of miniature soldiers in their
uniforms, the rest of the boys had crept closer during
the telling of the story. They all wore navy-blue shorts,
white shirts with bow ties and blue jackets with a
multicolored emblem on their breast pockets. With
shock and fear still evident on their young faces, they
began to add bits and pieces to the tale in breathless
voices.

"Yes, those men are looking on the other side of the
island right now."

"They've got guns, too! Great big ones!"

"And that man she hit, he—"

Miss Theodopolis briskly took charge of the story.
She appeared to be formidably in control of herself.
"What all this boils down to is that we're quite desperate to get off this island. They're still looking for
us, you see, and they're armed. Won't you help us?"

Blackie looked at the group of boys. He counted
only five heads, not a dozen as he'd first guessed. Plus
the teacher. The kids would be useless weight, but she
might be slightly helpful.

He studied the tight, determined features of Miss Theodopolis before allowing his squinting gaze to slide down her figure appraisingly. She held herself stiffly under his scrutiny, as a woman trying to remain poised while staving off an attack of hysterics. She trembled, but at least there weren't tears in her eyes. Yet. She gritted her teeth to keep them from chattering. Crudely Blackie assessed her body once more. Not bad. Maybe strong enough to be useful if she didn't break down right away. Bluntly he asked, "How are you with a tiller?"

She shivered so hard that she dropped her shoes on the sand. His lingering study of her figure had unnerved her. Blinking those enormous eyelashes again, she tried to compose herself and asked, "A what?"

"A tiller, dammit! Can you sail?"

"Sail?" she said stupidly.

"Never mind. I can see your experience is probably limited to punting on the Thames. Well, your ladyship, maybe I can teach you the basics. I can use the help. My sailing partner jumped ship after we rounded the Horn, and I'm having a bitch of a time sailing alone."

She reached automatically for the youngest boy in the bunch and laid her hands over his ears to shield his tender soul from foul language. The kid wriggled until he could hear every word perfectly, but she didn't notice. Delicately she addressed Blackie. "Are you suggesting that I help you sail this ship?"

"Boat," he snapped. "She's a boat, lady. Judas, don't you know *that* much? What are you teaching these kids, anyway? Knitting?"

That did it. Miss Theodopolis drew herself up finally, thoroughly affronted. Her blue eyes flashed with sudden fire. "I *do* know," she said furiously, "that that—that *bilge bucket* of yours is barely afloat! How do you expect to get anywhere in that thing? It was a wreck even before you got here!"

Well, no one, but no one could call his beloved *Bobbie* a bilge bucket and get away with it. She might need some paint and exterior patching before she could win a beauty contest at the yacht club regatta, but *Bobbie* was a demon when it came to racing, and Blackie would not hear a word of criticism against her. He blew up. "She was nearly a wreck because of *you*, Miss High-and-Mighty! It's only a blasted miracle— and my sailing expertise—that kept me from cracking up on those rocks out there. She's perfectly seaworthy, so keep your stupid opinions to yourself."

"I only meant," said the teacher stubbornly, "that it could use a coat of paint. A little yellow trim on the edges would look nice, too, and some flags perhaps— you know, the striped ones with—"

"Women!" Blackie shouted, clutching his aching head. Somehow, in the middle of the Pacific Ocean, he had stumbled upon the Duchess of Windsor. She was every inch a lady, all perfectly mannered and mouth-wateringly lovely, but inside that pretty head was a completely inane brain. She had been nearly raped and murdered by who knew who, and all she was concerned about was a blasted paint job. Blackie groaned and spun around, putting his back to the lot of them.

"Oh, brother," he muttered aloud after a long moment's consideration. "I suppose only a hard-hearted pig would leave the bunch of you here."

Harold edged around and smiled up at him appealingly. "Will you take us, sir?"

Blackie sighed in disgust, looking down at the kid. "All right, all right. But, damn, the lot of you are going to have to work to earn your keep. Understand?" He turned and glared around the circle of upturned faces and at Miss Theodopolis in particular. He would not be bulldozed by some Archduchess of the Arctic, and he tried to communicate that in one glare.

She lifted her nose in the air and sniffed. "Very well. I suppose we haven't much choice but to go with you."

"Don't do me any favors, lady!"

She stifled her own sarcastic retort with a visible effort.

Harold smiled broadly. "Well, it's all settled, then. Sir, may I formally present Miss Katherine Theodopolis?"

She sighed explosively and stuck out her hand. Her nails, he was not surprised to note, were long and flawlessly polished with an enamel the color of pink lemonade. She looked forward to shaking his callused and grimy hand with loathing in her expression.

Blackie took her hand with exactly the same air of distaste. "Hello," he said ferociously.

"And you, sir?" Harold asked, turning to him with the good manners of a well-trained maître d'.

He grunted. "Oh, Lowell. Blackie Lowell."

Harold practically clicked his heels. "How do you do, Captain Lowell? I am Harold Pickney. And this is Peter—"

The boy never got a chance to finish the introductions. A bullet whistled past Blackie's ear and thudded against the ruined side of the sinking dinghy.

"Judas!" Blackie shouted, galvanized into action. "Let's get the hell out of here!"

CHAPTER TWO

KATHERINE THEODOPOLIS had no time to think or even to scream. Instinctively she herded her charges toward the disabled sailboat, pushing one, shoving another and finally snatching little Jimmy Monahan into her arms and plunging into the surf. The tide was coming in quickly, and already the long-keeled boat was righting herself. Katherine was hip deep in water before she reached the hull.

From behind came more gunfire and shouts.

And beside her Blackie Lowell began to curse violently. He pitched one boy after another onto the slanted deck of his boat and finally snatched Jimmy from her arms and heaved him like a sack of grain over his shoulder. To Katherine he snapped, "You're on your own, your ladyship."

Katherine wasted not an instant. When a bullet whanged off the chrome railing not twelve inches from her hand, she yelped and jumped, throwing herself onto the boat deck on Blackie Lowell's heels.

The storm had abated, and the rain was no more than a thick, stinging mist in the air, but the breakers of the incoming tide crashed repeatedly over the sides of the stranded *Bobbie McGee*. Katherine stumbled, conscious that the enemies on shore were still firing their weapons. The explosions were drowned by the noise of wind and sea. She could hear nothing else.

Except, of course, Blackie Lowell shouting.

"Put the kids below!" he bellowed, feverishly struggling with a tangle of ropes wound around a spool. "Get them out of sight!"

He was a daunting spectacle. More than six feet tall, she knew, and most of it solid bone and muscle. He wore nothing more than a ragged pair of shorts and a flapping rubber rain slicker opened to bare his broad chest, and no woman could have ignored the astounding male physique that his lack of proper clothing revealed. Katherine lay panting on the deck and stared up at him. His body glistened magnificently with water. His hair was dark and wild—uncombed like an Indian's—and at least a week's growth of beard covered the lower half of his face. It did not, however, obscure the hard line of Blackie Lowell's jaw and the wide curve of his lower lip. His brows were dark and thick, but his eyes were light. And full of rage at the moment.

"Move!" He grabbed Katherine and sent her staggering with a brutal shove. "We're going to get killed in a minute, you idiot! Get those kids off the deck!"

The boys knew instinctively where to go, and Katherine scuttled after them toward the open hatch that led to a lower deck. A meager light burned in the cabin, giving off the glow of warmth and safety. She hastened toward it. "Hurry, Harold! Stop crying, Jimmy! We'll be safe in a minute! Peter! Take him with you!"

Blackie Lowell slammed the little door before Katherine could dive through it to safety.

"Forget it, lady," he snapped above the roar of the elements, barring her retreat with his arm. "You've got to help me get this boat going, or we're sitting ducks for your pals over there."

Katherine gulped and peered up at him through the wet tangle of her hair. "Wh-what shall I do?"

He pointed authoritatively. "Go back there. See that lever? Hold it fast and don't let it shift. It's the tiller, understand? We're gonna sail her out of the sand and clear out. But for God's sake, keep your head down!"

She didn't need to be told twice. Katherine hustled along the slippery deck, shuddering with fear and cold. When a huge wave crashed over the railing and soaked her to the knees, she barely managed to stifle another cry. Blackie Lowell yelled something back at her, but she couldn't hear. She threw herself down against the tiller and grabbed it with both hands.

Blackie spun lines out and raised the sail with rapid jerks of his powerful arms. Then he caught his balance on the railing, reared back and kicked the boom over with both feet. The wind filled the sail at once, and the *Bobbie McGee* gave a heaving lurch. When the next breaker splashed against her sides, she tilted hard toward the shore.

Katherine shrieked and hung on to the tiller to prevent herself from being swept overboard.

"Keep her straight!" he roared.

Frantically she tried to right the tiller, but she wasn't strong enough. Struggling with the heavy thing, Katherine cried, "I can't! It won't move! It's—"

He bit out a horrible expletive and ran back to her. With one foot he jammed the tiller to the right and glared down at her like a furious war god. "Now keep it that way, you idiot, or we'll all be killed!"

As if to punctuate his vindictive shout, a bullet slammed into the fiberglass skin of the boat, just inches from his knee. Blackie took one look at the hole—no bigger than a silver dollar—but he let out an anguished cry. In a rage he whirled around and faced the beach. "You lousy sons of—" He raised his fist and roared out a string of ferocious foul language.

Then he dove through the cabin hatch and came back an instant later, shouldering a huge weapon.

Katherine stifled a cry of terror. The thing looked like a flamethrower.

Standing at the railing of his boat, Blackie began to jam a huge projectile down into the barrel of his gun, shouting threats that were torn away by the wind. His face told the story. He was in a towering fury.

On the beach the men who had been racing down toward the surf finally noticed the size of the weapon being trained on them. As if commanded by the same nerve center, they froze in their tracks. Blackie raised the barrel of his gun and pulled the trigger.

Katherine screamed. Flame shot out of the gun, and a huge explosion rent the air. She cowered on the deck of the boat, and the men on the beach began to run. Blackie reloaded his weapon and raised it again. A second blast assaulted Katherine's ears, and the stench of gunpowder stung her nose. On the beach an evil red glare smoldered on the sand where the projectile had struck.

Chortling, Blackie threw down his gun. "*That* ought to hold 'em!" he shouted, his eyes on fire. "Now let's show them some fancy sailing!"

He worked like a fiend, first tightening the smaller sail, then wrapping a line around his waist. To Katherine's horror, he next threw himself overboard to stand shoulder deep in the water below. His shout barely reached Katherine's ears. "Heel her over! Heel her over!"

Katherine hadn't the faintest idea what he meant, but the lever of the tiller was pushed as far to the right as it could possibly go. There was only one alternative. Fighting, she yanked the tiller to the left and wedged herself against the railing of the boat to hold it in place. *Bobbie McGee* swung sideways, her sails straining, and then—miraculously—she was free, bobbing in the rough water and nosing out to sea.

For an awful instant Katherine feared she was alone on the speeding boat.

But Blackie climbed the rope and flung himself over the side rail, giving a triumphant shout. Throwing water from his dark hair like a soaked spaniel, he strode down to Katherine and grabbed her arm. He hauled her to her feet and stuck his face next to hers. "Now go up on the bow. Hang on and watch for rocks. Point at them, so I can see, and we'll pick our way through. It's gonna be a bitch, so keep your eyes open! Got that?"

Katherine nodded, too dazed, too shocked, to speak. Tottering, she headed for the front of the boat, seeking handholds ineffectually as she went. She was weak. She was frightened. Her wet clothing clung to her like the cold suckers of an octopus. She couldn't control her shivers, and her chattering teeth sounded like the frantically clicking keys of a typewriter. But she hadn't any choice except to obey Blackie's command. She edged as far as the slanted front of the cabin and stopped, clutching the rail.

"Keep going!" he shouted. "You can't see anything from there! Go out and hang over the bow!"

She quailed, staring with horror at the surging nose of the boat. He couldn't possibly mean her to climb out onto that teeny-weeny bit of space. And how on earth did he expect her to see anything in this blackness?

"*Go*, dammit!"

For a moment it looked as if he were going to chase her out onto the bow himself so Katherine hastily found a toehold and eased around the cabin. Shaking like a leaf in a hurricane, she clamped her hand around a wire-thin rope and hung on for dear life. The ocean tossed like a sodden black beast, roaring and hissing at the delicate hull of the sailboat. Mesmerized in horror, Katherine froze.

"See any rocks?" he shouted.

Rocks? Oh! She was supposed to be looking for rocks. With difficulty Katherine knelt down on the heaving deck, anxious to stabilize herself against a dizzying wave of fear. The boat lurched and she cried out. Half blinded by spray, she peered into the night, whimpering unconsciously. But almost at once she let out a shriek. "There! Oh, quick! Go to the left!"

He obeyed, wheeling the boat hard so that it sailed smoothly past the jutting stone. Katherine held fast and forced herself to pay better attention to the waters ahead. They were in terrible danger of sinking in the shallow bay littered with treacherous outcrops of rock. She did her best to concentrate. The light of the cabin behind her helped a little. Each time a hazard loomed in the mist, she signaled Blackie. She couldn't manage her vocal cords, so she relied on sign language.

It worked. The boat edged this way and that, sometimes creeping through narrow stretches, sometimes streaking over smoother water. Once the keel scraped bottom, and Blackie cursed her roundly. After that Katherine frowned and, with the aid of the dim cabin light, strained to see every peak that thrust up from the water's surface.

Finally there was nothing to see but open water. The sailboat gathered speed, and Blackie tied down the tiller. He paced forward and adjusted the sails. *Bobbie McGee* sprang forward like a panther released from her cage, swooping across the waves in exultant leaps.

Shaken, Katherine made her way back to the curve of the cabin. The terror was over. They had made their escape. If she could only stop trembling, she'd be fine. *Act like an adult,* she told herself.

"Not bad, lady," Blackie crowed, happily working a rope into place somewhere overhead. "You were braver than I expected."

"Are we—is it safe now?"

He tied off the rope and turned to her, his white teeth flashing as he grinned. "Safe enough, I guess. Unless they've got a better boat than this, which I doubt."

She cast an uneducated eye around the small deck of the sailboat. "It's a much bigger boat. And it's got engines."

He shook his head, supremely confident. "No match for *Bobbie*. They won't catch us. Unless they're very determined, of course. You'd have to look a hell of a lot better than you do now to attract their attention, I'd say."

Katherine glared at him. So that was his style. With a smile on his face, he appraised her as if she were a prize sheep at market. Realizing that the remains of her elegant suit were hardly adequate cover for a decent woman, Katherine flushed hotly. Her blouse had been reduced to a tattered wisp of silk that clung to her soaked bra in a way that left nothing whatsoever to the imagination. Even her belly button showed. Somehow—probably climbing aboard the boat—she'd torn her skirt, too, and it laid one of her long thighs bare for his bemused examination. The wet fabric clung to each of her lean curves, and Blackie Lowell appeared to take a complete inventory. Katherine hugged her elbows and tried not to shiver.

Blackie, however, braced one hand against the rail and leaned back languidly, taking the time to look her over properly. An annoying smile quirked the corners of his mouth, and his eyelashes were lazy, but did not hide the swordlike gleam of appreciation in his gaze. He obviously liked what he saw. Katherine returned his open scrutiny with her haughtiest aplomb.

But he was not entirely bad to look at, either.

Under the scruffy beard his face was almost handsome, except for the smug expression that foretold the kind of self-satisfied male ego Katherine had not encountered since adolescence. He was tall and tanned by the tropical sun and—she had to admit—so undeniably virile that he practically flaunted his masculinity like the folds of a valuable garment. His near-naked state obviously pleased him, for it bespoke his sex better than any planned wardrobe could. He was a primitive beast. And from the look on his face, it was easy to see that Blackie Lowell was impossibly satisfied with himself.

In another era the unshaven brute who stood before her might have been a Moroccan corsair, a dastardly pirate who pillaged his way across the seven seas, or perhaps a daring explorer who battled the earth's natural hazards for the thrill of success alone. He climbed mountains and sailed oceans because they were there, no doubt. He taunted fate, cursed his luck from time to time, but did not accept defeat, she was sure.

He had enjoyed the skirmish on the beach, Katherine could see. His eyes were full of the sparkle that only adrenaline could produce.

Now, perhaps, he was looking for some reward for his hard-fought battle. Expectantly he regarded her, eyebrows cocked. He asked, "What's your name again?"

"Theodopolis," she replied coolly.

"Theo...?" He looked comically puzzled, light eyes wide, dark brows arched.

Clearly she repeated, "Katherine Theodopolis."

Shaking his head, he counted the syllables on his fingers. "Kath-er-ine The-o-do-po-lis. God's teeth, woman, that's eight syllables!"

"That's correct."

"No, no, no," he said decisively. "That won't do at all. Why, in an emergency, I'd hardly have time to spit out a name like that to get your attention! We'll call you Kate and be done with it."

He took charge of her with the effortless air of a man who was never disobeyed. As he turned away, Katherine sputtered. "Now—now, see here!" she blustered. "I admit that I've thrust my problems on you without giving you the opportunity to—"

"That's right," he said, cutting her off. "You've thrust yourself and five little problems on me, and I've got a few to cope with already. Let's make this easy, Kate, and—"

"I will not be called Kate! That's not my name. If you—"

His hand shot out and she yelped.

But he didn't hit her. He grabbed her shoulder hard and squeezed Katherine into silence. He tilted his head upward as if testing the wind, and his eyes narrowed as he stared into the night blackness astern. Alert, he demanded, "How big a boat did you say those friends of yours are sailing?"

Katherine spun around to follow his look and immediately saw the pinprick illumination of a searchlight. They were being followed. Unconsciously she shrank back against the man behind her. He was solid as a tree and warm as just-pressed steel. They stood in silence together, straining to hear the first drone of a boat engine. Anger washed out of Katherine's system as if a drain had been unstopped. Fear began to seep in once more. To herself she finally whispered, "They're chasing us."

"Just who are they?" he said behind her. "Besides being determined SOBs?"

Staring at the distant bobbing light, Katherine said, "I don't know who they are. I haven't the faintest idea."

The world had turned itself upside down. Katherine felt as if she had plummeted somehow into a different century. She was a girl again, defenseless and frightened and ignorant. Yesterday she had been a self-possessed career woman, steadily climbing a ladder of success. Now men were men, it seemed, and they proved it by manhandling her in ways she had only read about. Until today she had never felt so vulnerable, so inadequate, so afraid. Indeed, who *were* the men chasing her?

Without waiting for an answer, he thrust her away. He was captain of his ship again, leaning out over the rail to glare at the pursuing boat. "They're after us, all right. Tell the kids to douse the light. Then we'll change course and see how fast my *Bobbie* can really go."

"Why not—why don't you use that gun again?"

"Gun? Oh, the flare." He grinned down at her. "Bloodthirsty little thing, aren't you?"

"No! I—"

"It's not a weapon, Kate, it's a flare launcher. Maybe it looks like a bazooka, but now they know it's harmless. We won't scare them a second time. And if we fire it now, we'll just mark our position for them. No, we'll run in the dark. Go check on the kids. I'll handle this."

She heard the derision in his tone, but her pride was already in shreds. Glad to have the chance to hide below with the children, Katherine scuttled away from him. Cowardice felt fine.

Blackie let her go without a second look. He had work to do, and he wasted not a moment.

Once the light in the cabin went out, it took just a few minutes to tack and cut a wide swath through the choppy waves and find a new course. He could hear the faint whine of a powerboat to the south, but it wouldn't matter much longer. They'd lose his trail in seconds and never find *Bobbie* in the dark. Sailing alone in the darkness held no fears for Blackie. He loved it, in fact. But powerboaters would be too frightened to look very far or long. He set the sail before the wind and gave *Bobbie* her head. She shot straight on a north-by-northwest course and clung to it like a compass needle. It wouldn't hurt to run on the wind for an hour or two.

With the wind at his back, Blackie realized he was smiling. He didn't ponder why he found himself so pleased with the evening's entertainment. He ought to be annoyed. For some reason, however, he was delighted.

A noise caught his attention, and he glanced over his shoulder. Kate had crept timidly out of the cabin once more, her face pale and eyes round. The sky was lighter after the storm, and he could make out her features clearly by sporadic moonlight. She had a pointed chin and a too-sharp nose, but her mouth was full lipped and the color of claret. Her eyelashes, he thought, were like velvet. Though her hair was still a tangled mess, it had begun to dry and looked full and soft. It had curl, too, and he remembered the vague scent of perfume that had wafted from her. At the memory of that fragrance, something stirred within him.

"Are we safe?" she asked, her voice husky with fear.

Blackie felt the stirring sensation again, and he pinpointed the location. The whole territory between his chest and his knees began to roil. She was a good-looker, he had to admit, especially when she wasn't putting on that princess-of-the-realm act. And there was a fire to her that Blackie found particularly appealing. His grin broadened. "That depends on your definition."

Haughty again, she asked, "What do you mean?"

He swaggered toward her, feeling flush. "Are the kids okay?"

"Fine, yes." She cleared her throat and appeared to pull herself together completely. "They're terrified, of course, but not hurt. I think they'd prefer to stay inside tonight."

Maybe it was the thrill of danger, or perhaps the combination of excitement and bad weather and a long, hard voyage alone, but all the elements suddenly manifested themselves in plain, simple sexual arousal. To Blackie, Kate looked like the perfect answer to his needs, the best way to top a stormy night. She was drenched, dirty and battered, but he didn't see that. He saw her body, young and slender, her breasts aquiver, her belly smooth, her legs long enough to wrap around a man and pull him into a vortex of hot liquid pleasure. She faced him without fear, her blue eyes cold and direct, her chin firm. She was a lady with spirit.

He grasped her wrist and looked down into her face, a smile on his mouth. "Care to share the spoils of war, your ladyship?"

"What are you talking about?" Her voice was cool, but her eyes wavered.

"I just saved your neck," he said and tightened his grip on her arm. "How about letting me nibble the prize?"

Without waiting for her permission, he bent his head and found the soft flesh of her throat with his nose. A subtle perfume still remained on her skin, and he inhaled the last of it. She held herself rigidly, not refusing him, so Blackie wrapped one arm around her back, drawing her slim body against his. Her breasts felt like brands on his chest, her nipples drilling his skin like hot bits. Blackie growled appreciatively and pressed his mouth against the vibrating flesh of her throat. She was taut yet soft, warm and gloriously female. Without wasting time on preliminaries, Blackie wedged his knee between hers and relished the heat of her thighs around his own.

She gasped and threw her head back so that her midnight hair tumbled around his arm and her neck lay exposed for his better enjoyment. Laughing softly, he found the warm hollow at the base of her throat and kissed it. Her pulse fluttered wildly against his lips. Blackie dropped her wrist and laid his hand along the indentation of her waist. She was narrow there, but blossomed above and below in womanly curves. He fondled her hip, then stole higher to seek her breast with his palm.

Moving feebly, she chafed his leg with her own, inflaming him more. She arched in Blackie's arms and the words that escaped her lips were pleading. "Please—please—"

She was a seductress, hot and cold at the same time, goading him, urging him. Desire flashed in his veins, and Blackie laughed, cupping her breast and squeezing. "Temptress," he murmured, his lips against her cheek. "You're beautiful."

She braced one of her hands against his chest and pushed, dislodging his contact with her breast. "D-don't."

"Too rough?" He heard his own voice rasp. "Your ladyship wants me to be gentle? I'm not sure I can, not tonight. That's it. Touch me."

She delved her fingers through the crisp hair on his chest. Abruptly, then, she closed her grip. It hurt. "Don't," she said again, her voice stronger. "Don't hurt me. Don't make me do it again."

"What?" Blackie lifted his head and stared, trying to make out her face in the darkness.

"Please," she said, gasping, and she trembled so hard that he finally, belatedly, recognized the signs of shock. "Don't make me hit you again."

"Again?" Blackie loosened her, flooded with consternation. "Listen, lady, I'm not the same guy. Hey, I didn't mean—"

She slumped away from him so quickly that he thought she'd fainted. He grabbed both her forearms and hauled her back to her feet again. Her head lolled, then came up. Her blue eyes reflected fear, anger, horror. "He hurt me," she whispered in amazement. "He—he hit me and—and put his fingers in my mouth." Disgust twisted her features.

"Hey," Blackie murmured, revulsed and appalled by what he'd almost done to her on a whim. "Take it easy. I didn't mean to scare you."

A wave of shudders seized the young woman so that she could barely speak. Somehow she managed to disengage one hand, and she put her fingers to the corner of her mouth as if it hurt. Her eyes were huge and swimming with shock. "He made me kneel, and—and he put his fingers in my mouth. Why would he do that? Why...?"

"It's okay," Blackie said, though he had the feeling he was talking to a zombie. She was crazy with shock, that was it. "It's over now," he said.

She wagged her head, pawing at her mouth with her fingertips to get rid of a bad taste, a horrible memory. "I had to hit him. I didn't have a choice. He fell on me, and—and he was so heavy! There—there was blood everywhere. He soaked me with it." With an unsteady laugh she asked, "How much blood is in the human head, class?"

"Listen," Blackie soothed, aware that she'd been through a terrible ordeal and that he'd only made it worse, "I'm sorry about what happened. Maybe you'd better go to bed and sleep it off. My bunk's in the forward cabin."

She staggered out of his grasp then, pressing both hands to her mouth. "No," she said, shaking her head and mumbling against her hands. "No, no, don't touch me. Don't kiss me. Don't make me do it again."

CHAPTER THREE

THE NIGHT WAS BAD. When Katherine woke, the fragrance of morning coffee wafted in the air, and for a snoozy moment she thought she was snug in her bed at the house in Pago Pago. The nightmare was over.

Then she sat up abruptly. Wet, clammy clothing, smelling of saltwater and fish, clung to her skin. Her hair reeked, too, and felt sticky in her fingers. What in the world...? Reality swam into perspective then, and she remembered where she was. *Bobbie McGee* moved smoothly as a swallow. Rhythmic waves slapped her sides.

Katherine hugged herself. She hadn't been dreaming. Every horrible, disgusting event had been very real. Her brain reviewed it all: the boat faltering, the apologetic captain reporting engine trouble, the arrival of the second boat and relief turning to terror. The leering men—three younger ones and the old man. They'd teased the boys and slapped them. Then one—what had they called him? Toals? Tolb? He wanted some real fun, he'd said, grinning at her through piggish eyes. His hands had felt greasy on her arms, she remembered. Katherine buried her face in her palms. She'd killed him for it, for fouling her mouth, hurting her body, humiliating her before boys who were too sensitive, too impressionable. Abruptly she felt a retch start in her throat.

She quelled it. She forced herself to forget. With eyes closed Katherine made the memories drain from her conscious mind like filthy bathwater. No one could accuse Katherine Theodopolis of being weak.

She opened her eyes and determinedly looked around. The forward, or sleeping, cabin was no more than seven feet long and only four feet across at its narrowest point. Again she forced herself, this time to make note of details. The bed took up all but two square feet of the cabin and consisted of nothing more than an unforgiving foam mattress and two cotton blankets, both damp. Two latched cabinets lined the walls on either side, a firmly shuttered window made up the third and the door—a meager bit of wood locked in place by a flimsy clasp—finished the cabin. There were less than forty inches of headroom over the bunk. Luxury? Not a bit. It was, however, Blackie Lowell's bed.

She'd almost forgotten about him.

Tensing, Katherine listened for his voice. Where was he? From somewhere above she could hear the ebb and flow of conversation. She clambered to the door, preparing to go up on deck. Where were the boys? She had to find out what was going on.

One look, however, into the small mirror that hung on the back of the door stopped her. "Good Lord!"

She was a wreck. Her hair hung in a harridan's nightmare, curling in stiff ringlets around her shoulders. Mascara ringed her eyes so that she looked like a blue-eyed raccoon, and there was no trace of her lipstick. Her blouse was torn from one shoulder and two buttons were missing so that a generous display of her lace bra was bared to the light of day. When she tried to gather the blouse over herself, another button popped and skittered across the mattress. There was blood on her blouse.

She plopped back onto the bed in dismay and stared down at her ruined clothing. The slit in the seam of her skirt had reached to midthigh, and the fine linen had been spoiled beyond rescue. She didn't dare appear before the boys in bloodstained clothes. "Now what am I supposed to do?"

Her voice bounced eerily in the small space, and she looked up automatically, wondering if those on deck could hear her talking to herself. No doubt Blackie Lowell already assumed she was crazy.

Blushing, Katherine remembered the events of the previous night. Good grief, the man probably thought she was a first-rate crazy woman. She'd been an absolute idiot with him, thankful to be safe in his arms one minute, then babbling in hysterics the next. Or was she confused? Maybe Lowell had tried to hurt her, too?

No, no, someone had been gentle with her, she remembered. It had to have somehow been the roughneck sailor. And she'd actually felt grateful. How embarrassing. Katherine assured herself that the moments she had spent in Blackie's embrace had simply been the culmination of a harrowing day. He'd have to understand. She'd been in shock, that was it. Of course. She'd acted foolishly, yes, but surely he'd understand that she hadn't been herself, wouldn't he? She'd suffered a terrible ordeal. Naturally she hadn't

been in full command of her common sense on deck
last night.

She'd be dignified today, Katherine assured herself. "Yes," she muttered aloud. "I'm a lady, and he's
going to treat me like one!"

But another glance at her clothing assured Katherine that Blackie Lowell would think she was anything
but a lady.

There was a shirt hanging on a hook just above the
door. She seized it joyfully. The fabric was soft with
age, but at least it was not in tatters. She tugged the
garment down and discovered a perfectly wearable
pair of shorts, too. In moments she had stripped off
the remains of her blouse and the sorry excuse for a
skirt. Her underwear was still damp, but she was willing to suffer. Under no circumstances would she face
him without a bra.

Pushing her hands through the sleeves of Blackie
Lowell's shirt, Katherine was relieved to find that it
was amply large and dry. It had once been a white
button-down man's dress shirt, but the sleeves had
been hacked so that they barely reached her elbows.
No matter. The shorts were not quite clean, but they'd
do. They were huge on her waist and therefore fell
comfortably around her hips.

She pulled her hair back and tied it with a strip of
red satin torn from the lining of her skirt. With the
mascara wiped from around her eyes, she looked almost human.

The outer cabin was empty. Katherine noted the
jumble of blankets on the floor, along with a few of
the boys' sodden jackets. The square footage was
small, but every inch of *Bobbie McGee*'s interior had

been put to good use. She entered the galley as she exited the forward cabin. The kitchen space was hardly large enough for two adults to stand in, but it was perfectly serviceable. Katherine noted an apartment-sized stove complete with oven, a double sink, a pint-sized refrigerator that was tucked under the counter, and another appliance that she thought was a dishwasher, but actually turned out to be a trash compactor. Above the appliances louvered cupboards contained supplies, no doubt. She did not stop to investigate.

The main part of the cabin was perhaps eight feet wide with padded benches on either side. A table with fold-out leaves was propped up out of the way, but it obviously opened to seat perhaps six adults comfortably. Both overhead and beneath the benches were latched cabinets for storage. The layout reminded Katherine of American travel trailers used for camping.

Beside the hatchway that led to the deck, Katherine saw a complicated-looking computer console with plenty of dials, switches and blinking lights—a modern navigation system, probably. There was a radio microphone plugged into the electronic gadgetry. A rack for charts lay within arm's reach above, and a fold-down chair was tipped against the desk surface below.

Although the below-deck quarters were not as plush as those of the luxury yachts that occasionally docked in Pago Pago, this boat did boast all the essentials for relatively comfortable living. And—bless boatbuilders everywhere—there was a bathroom. The head, she supposed it was called. Katherine locked herself inside the tiny space and found a toothbrush. It had to be Blackie Lowell's, but by that time she couldn't have cared less. Using as much Colgate as possible, she brushed her teeth twice, hoping to erase the foul taste that lingered in her mouth. Afterward she scrubbed the rest of her skin so clean that it stung and glowed.

Feeling a little improved, Katherine cautiously let herself out of the empty cabin and into the sunshine.

The sun was blazingly bright, magnificently golden and delightfully hot. Not a single cloud marred the azure sky. The ocean was just two shades darker and sparkled like rough-cut diamonds as sunlight danced along the swells. A breeze teased the air, smelling warm and fresh. With eyes closed Katherine took a deep breath of that air and held it.

When she opened her eyes again, she met the unblinking, openmouthed stares of five little boys. They sat cross-legged on the deck in an orderly circle, holding coffee mugs in their pudgy hands and looking up at her as if she were a complete stranger. They were awestruck.

Above them, leaning casually against the railing and wearing nothing more than a brief pair of snug khaki shorts, deck shoes and an appreciative, lazy-lidded smile, relaxed Blackie Lowell. His feet were crossed at the ankles as he lounged beside the tiller. The sun glanced brilliantly off his golden shoulders and glowed on the solid contours of his naked chest. He looked every inch the pirate master of a renegade privateer, right down to his self-satisfied smirk. Beneath his lashes his eyes were crystal gray and seemed amused by the astounded silence of her pupils.

"You've struck them dumb," he said, saluting her appearance with a coffee cup. "Good morning, Kate."

The boys blinked in unison, and Harold Pickney found his tongue first. "You sure look *different*, Miss Theodopolis."

"No doubt I do," she said briskly, stepping up on the deck to join them. "My clothes are ruined, so I took the liberty, Mr. Lowell? I hope you don't mind."

Blackie's gaze skimmed the billowing white shirt she wore and fell to admire her legs. Taking his time, he moved up her body. He made no pretense of studying the clothing. By the light of day, he appraised her figure, narrowing his eyes like a connoisseur. If he harbored any misgivings about the moments they'd spent in each other's arms, he concealed them admirably.

With a smile he drawled, "I don't mind at all, Kate. You're welcome to share anything of mine."

Including my bed. He didn't say the words aloud, but he didn't have to. His face conveyed the message perfectly.

Katherine endeavored to stare him down with her coolest expression, hoping to wipe the grin off his face. She would not stand for jokes. He didn't blink, though, and looked more and more cheerful with each passing second. The man was crude.

Brusquely Katherine ended the pregnant silence. "Well, I can see you've met the boys. Are you getting acquainted?"

"Just starting," said Blackie, and he let his gaze fall to the uniformed lads at his feet. "I was just saying that I'm not exactly crazy about kids in the first place. How do you manage to tell them apart?"

"They're individuals," Katherine said swiftly. She hoped he had the brains to see how frightened the boys were. "You remember Harold, of course."

Red-headed Harold Pickney smiled brilliantly up at Blackie, and the sun bounced off his glasses.

"Oh, yeah." Blackie gestured again with his cup. "And this one's Peter, I understand."

Peter Dodd maintained a stiff posture. He was the oldest of the group at thirteen, but he had not quite determined how a grown boy should act. He had taken refuge in an aloof attitude that infuriated the younger boys, but seemed the safest bet for Peter. His father had died many years ago, and his mother was a State Department official on Pago Pago, a strict, cheerless woman who took her job seriously and left the raising of her son to the educational system provided by the government.

Bluntly Blackie asked, "What's your last name, Pete?"

"D-D-Dodd, sir," the boy replied, backsliding into the stuttering speech that had plagued him throughout his youth. Just the authoritarian presence of Blackie Lowell was enough to send him into a tremor of repetitions and bring a hot blush to his normally pallid complexion. "P-P-Peter Dodd."

Blackie nodded and transferred his attention to the next boy in line. He pointed. "Who are you, kid?"

The little boy was paralyzed.

"Jimmy," Katherine supplied. "That's Jimmy Monahan."

"Let him speak for himself," Blackie shot back. "Where're you from, Jim?"

Jimmy was blond and small boned, with a narrow face and shy blue eyes that made him appear younger than his seven years. He smiled almost constantly, however, a nervous habit. He ducked his head timidly and mumbled something too softly to hear.

"What?" Blackie barked and leaned closer, expressing amazement at what he thought he'd heard. "You're from *Siberia*?"

"No!" Jimmy giggled, having been goaded into speaking properly. "*Sel*ma! Selma, Alabama."

"Oh, a Rebel, huh?" Blackie grinned. "Okay, you two." He pointed his chin at the Kuransky twins. "I suppose you're Frick and Frack."

"N-n-no," Peter said, speaking up for the twins. "They're—"

"Shut up, Pete," Blackie interrupted. "Every man does his own talking on this boat."

But the Kuransky boys were too shy, too overwhelmed, perhaps, to say a word. They just smiled nervously.

When they didn't answer, Blackie shrugged. "Okay, it's Frick and Frack, I guess. Frack, jump up and let Kate have your coffee. You don't seem to be drinking it very fast, so let her have it. We're short on supplies."

The boy did as he was commanded, getting obediently to his feet and pacing across the deck with careful steps. Tongue-tied, he handed a nearly full cup of lukewarm coffee to Katherine. She accepted the offering, murmured her thank-you, then sipped the drink. Realizing suddenly how empty her stomach felt, she drank thirstily.

While she gulped coffee, Blackie surveyed the group and tried to remember who was who. Pete with the stutter, Harold the whiz kid, Jimmy the baby, Frick and Frack. He would remember. And Kate. He wasn't likely to forget her, certainly.

She looked amazingly good this morning. The kids had been startled when she'd arrived on deck in bare feet and one of his shirts. No doubt she had them thoroughly in awe at school. They probably worshiped her, putting her on some kind of pedestal where beautiful women and straitlaced teachers ought to go. She would give them a glance for a reprimand, no doubt, and they'd melt through their desks. But this was a side of their teacher that they hadn't imagined before. Her change into man's clothes, her lack of makeup and perfectly coiffed hair and the bruise that had started to show on the corner of her mouth brought the kids up short. They had seen her assaulted by a strange man, and the memory was very fresh.

Blackie could see them all reassessing her from the corners of their eyes. Suddenly she was a woman to them. A flesh-and-blood woman like any other.

Well, he corrected himself, not *quite* like any other. Ordinary women didn't have perfect legs. Or waists so narrow and breasts so pert that even a man's shirt couldn't spoil her silhouette. And most women looked like hell when they got out of bed in the morning, didn't they? But Kate looked good enough to, well, to take back to bed. As she drank her coffee, he could see her slender throat move, and he longed to go over and touch her there. Vividly he remembered that her skin felt just as soft as it looked.

Last night he'd made a regrettable mistake. He'd wanted to throw her down on the deck and take her lustily under the night sky. Damned if he didn't feel like doing exactly that right now, too. But she was back to acting like the Duchess of the Deep Freeze, and it might take weeks to thaw her again. If he'd played his cards a little better, he might be sharing his cabin with her even now, enjoying a little morning wake-up recreation.

She didn't look as if she were in the right mood now, however. She drained her coffee cup and closed her eyes briefly as if savoring the taste. Then she collected herself and turned her gaze on him directly. He'd seen the look before. Teachers used it to get a student's absolute attention. He liked her spirit, all right. She was not the kind of woman to give up under the worst of circumstances. Speaking clearly, she said, "I think that all of us owe you great thanks, Mr. Lowell, for—"

"Blackie," he said, settling back to listen to her speech.

"I—" She caught herself. "Very well," she said, obviously deciding to play along for the moment. "Blackie. We owe you thanks for helping us last night."

Harold broke in avidly. "Shall we give the captain a hip-hip-hooray, Miss Theodopolis?"

"No, Harold," she said, calm as lake water. "We're going to discuss the future. Mr.—Blackie," she addressed him again, "I'm very concerned about notifying the boys' parents of our whereabouts. We have been gone for much longer than we intended, and I'm certain that the captain of our cruise boat has returned to the island and told our people what has happened—"

"Our people?" Blackie repeated. "What people are those?"

She blinked her velvet eyelashes and said, "Our families, of course."

"*Your* family?" he pressed. "Or theirs?"

For an instant she almost looked flustered. "Why, theirs, of course."

"You aren't married?"

"No," she said, "I—"

"Thank you." He regained his own unruffled demeanor. "That's all I wanted to know. You were saying?"

Her cheeks began to show some color. "Mr. Lowell," she said sternly, "I am requesting that you radio the nearest island at once and report our well-being. My students have—"

"Already done," he said simply and passed his cup to one of the twins at his feet.

"Already...? What did you—"

"I talked to Pago Pago this morning," he explained. "They know you're fine, and they're gonna start looking for that boatload of criminals who kidnapped you. It's all taken care of."

"Oh. Well. Thank you." She looked disgruntled that he'd already done them another favor. "Then I suppose you'll be taking us back to Pago Pago now."

"Are you kidding? Hell, no."

"What?"

"You heard me."

She stared. "Where are we going? What direction are we heading?"

"Not in your direction," he retorted, "that's for sure. That's out of my way."

She looked magnificent for a moment. Her spine went straight, her shoulders shot back and she braced her legs apart as if taking a stand for a fight. Ah, a lady with real courage, a worthy opponent. With blue flame in her eyes, she challenged him. "Do you know exactly in which direction you *are* going, Mr. Lowell?"

"Now, Kate," he cautioned with amusement, "don't get ugly."

"I demand that you return us to our homes."

Enjoying her impotent rage immensely, he said, "Listen, your ladyship, I'm not out here for a pleasure cruise, and I'm not running a taxi service. I'm in a race."

"A race!" Harold cried, practically rubbing his hands together with delight. "What kind of race, Captain?"

Blackie grinned. The kid had potential. "It's a match race, kid. A challenge between me and a friend of mine, Pointy Hargraves. We're sailing from New York to Taiwan."

"That's China!" he exclaimed, eyes huge behind his thick glasses.

"Well, at least your teacher gives you some geography in between the knitting lessons. Yeah, it's China. Pointy and I have a bet to see who's got the better boat. His *Nightcap* is practically a luxury liner, and *Bobbie* here, well, she can sail circles around anything afloat. Only Pointy won't believe me. I have to prove it. I can't very well lose, can I?"

"Oh my, sir! Your honor is at stake! That's peachy!" Harold was in ecstasy. "Are you winning now, sir?"

Blackie frowned when reminded of his own current dilemma. "Uh, not exactly. I'm a hundred miles behind, in fact. You see, my crew got unhappy and left me, so without her I'm making the trip solo—"

"Her?" Kate interrupted.

Blackie's grin returned. She looked appalled by the potential influence he could have on the boys. "Yeah," he said expansively, "a lady friend of mine. We had a—a difference of opinion, so she took off, and I'm sailing alone now. But if I don't show my stuff in the next few days, I'm finished. So I *won't* take a detour and go back to Pago Pago."

"But—" she sputtered. "But—"

"Look," he said swiftly before she could explode, "I'm headed west and I've got to stop once or twice to get supplies, so I can drop you off. My last stop before China is Guam, but—"

"Guam!" she cried, goggle-eyed.

"So what's wrong with Guam?"

"That must be a thousand miles from here."

"Three thousand," he corrected smugly.

"Three thousand miles!"

"Nautical miles, yes, at least that. Why? Forget your seasick pills or something?"

"Of course not! I—I'm just, well, I'm shocked that you won't step a short distance out of your way to help us."

"I didn't *want* to help you in the first place, lady."

"We certainly don't want to be trapped here with you, either. I insist you let me radio Pago Pago at once. I'm sure they will send a rescue plane for us."

"Don't be so sure. Rescue planes don't land on the ocean, and a helicopter can't come this far. Hey, *they* suggested I take you all the way to Guam. Believe me, I'd rather be rid of you long before then, too."

"What about the Gilbert Islands?"

"What about them?"

As if pressing her advantage during a tournament debate, she said quickly, "We must have to sail directly past the Gilberts to get to Guam, correct?"

"Yeah, sure, but—"

"Then you can drop us off there, and we'll find our own way back to Pago Pago."

He put up both hands in surrender. She had figured out the same plan he'd come up with hours ago. "Okay, okay," he said. "We'll shoot for the Gilberts if that will make you happy. You can call home from there and tell everybody I dumped you and the seven dwarfs. They'll have to send a plane then."

Her face froze before the glow of triumph entered it. Stiffly polite, she said, "Thank you."

"Until then," he growled, "stop bellyaching and we'll all make the best of a bad situation."

Her eyes popped with rage. "I am *not* bellyaching. I'm simply concerned about these boys and how I'm going to get them home."

Blackie shrugged. To him, the boys looked enthralled, not the least upset about their parents. He said, "You can try swimming back to Pago Pago—if you want to take your chances with the sharks, that is."

She glared at him. "Are my chances any better with you?"

He laughed then. Clearly there was no danger of this one doing something foolish—like falling in love with him during the trip—and yet she was obviously capable of providing hours of enjoyment. He was going to relish tormenting her. Oh, she was going to be a pleasure.

Harold sat up on his knees, his pink face glowing with excitement. "What about provisions, sir? Are we going to be forced to survive on coffee for days? Or— or maybe consider cannibalism?"

Blackie liked the kid better and better every minute. "Don't get overanxious, Harry. Suffering isn't all it's cracked up to be. I've got enough food, I think, especially if we do some fishing to supplement my stores. The accommodations aren't going to be too comfy, though. This voyage was intended for two people, not five. Two affectionate people, in fact."

Harold missed the innuendo and snapped his fingers. "*Treasure Island*!"

"Huh?"

Excitedly the boy explained himself. "In *Treasure Island* the sailors sleep in hammocks on the ships. Couldn't we do that? Make things to hang and sleep in the air?"

Stroking his chin, Blackie murmured, "Well, we could try it, I suppose."

"And we could help you sail, sir! Stand watch, climb the rigging, man the oars—"

"There aren't a-a-any oars," Peter said.

"Could we, sir? Could we help? We'd try ever so hard to please you, sir."

Blackie looked at the five little faces turned up to him, and he felt a funny sensation creep up his spine. All five boys were pale and skinny, pathetically interested in their predicament, but clearly unable to fend for themselves in anything resembling a crisis. Their idea of excitement was probably reading *Treasure Island*, not sailing or climbing or racing. Eagerly, hopefully, they gazed up at him, their eyes full of a hunger that Blackie understood very well indeed. They longed for challenge, for danger, for life.

How could he deny them? Even more to the point, how was he going to give in without looking—heaven forbid—like a good-natured softie? Above all, Blackie intended to play his crude routine to the hilt. So far it had worked perfectly.

He made up his mind about the right technique and manufactured a stern frown. "I don't stand for laziness, you know."

All five boys nodded vigorously.

"And I won't take any lip from any kid, either!" he threatened.

Again five simultaneous nods.

"And anyone who disobeys an order," he continued dangerously, "gets galley duty for a week!"

"Yes, *sir*!" Harold piped.

"Yes, s-s-sir!" Peter echoed.

Blackie stood up and clasped his hands behind his back, glowering down at the boys on the deck. "All right, men, we've got a long voyage ahead of us. We'll share hardships, I have no doubt. But if we all pull together, we'll have a safe landing for ourselves and our womenfolk. Are we a team?"

Together they chorused, "Yes, sir!"

"All right!" he snapped. "Then go below and get the place shipshape. Fold up those blankets. Bring all the wet clothes up on deck to dry. In a few minutes we'll get some breakfast. Now get moving. And take off those damned ties while you're down there!"

The boys leaped to their feet and scuttled off the deck, pushing each other to get into the cabin first. They were excited, but still too repressed to chatter or shout. Like sheep they crowded into the cabin and disappeared.

KATHERINE HELD HER GROUND when the boys were past and glared at Blackie. She was angry. "Womenfolk?" she repeated. "*Women*folk?"

He grinned and strolled toward her. "That's what you are, right? If I remember correctly from last night."

"Keep your distance," she commanded, backing away from him instinctively. He was looking like a pirate again. "And let's get a few things settled between you and me right now."

"Sounds good," he agreed, taking her wrist in his hand. "I'd like to get settled with you as soon as possible, Kate."

"For starters, let me go."

His grip was effortless. And unshakable. The man was made of steel, she was certain. His arrogant smile gave Katherine the urge to swing a slap at him then and there.

He must have seen the impulse in her eyes. He grabbed her other arm and held Katherine hard, pushing her back until her bottom made contact with the railing of the boat. Behind her the ocean sloshed, but Katherine was aware only of a more immediate danger. She gulped. Blackie wore very few clothes. And the shorts he did wear could not disguise the physical response to her proximity. When he pressed against her, Katherine immediately stopped writhing. The last thing she wanted to do was inflame him further. She froze.

His face was inches from hers. His smile curved in delight, and his eyes sparkled with adrenaline.

"Now look," she said and was glad to hear her voice sounded surprisingly strong. Determinedly she did not look at his bare chest, for that would have been her undoing. "I won't put up with this," she said. "These boys are going to get a very full education as it is, without adding human biology to the curriculum. Let me go at once."

"But you're such a sight for sore eyes, Kate."

Tartly she inquired, "Were you using these charming methods of seduction on your girlfriend? Is that why she jumped ship?"

His grin didn't waver, but Blackie loosened one of Katherine's arms and lifted one forefinger to touch her under the point of her chin. "She was unprepared for the rigors of sailing, that's all. And the galley facilities didn't meet with her approval, since cooking is her thing. Lovemaking was not the cause of her departure. Trust me on that, Kate. Or try me."

"Thank you," she said shortly, holding his gaze icily, "but I'll pass up that offer."

He tipped his head with skepticism. "You were anxious enough last night."

So he was going to bring that up. Obviously, he had no idea how she felt. "I was in shock last night," she corrected. "I had a—a bad day, Mr. Lowell. I'm sorry if I acted foolishly. I didn't know what I was doing. That sounds like a cliché or—or some kind of freshman excuse, but I wasn't—it's just that on the beach before you came, I—"

Blackie interrupted. "Did you ever fall off a horse, Kate?"

She looked up at him warily. "What?"

"I'm serious." The expression in his eyes was anything but serious, however. Settling himself on the rail, he folded his arms and began to tell a story with the soft-voiced gentleness of a benevolent parent. "Once upon a time when I was a kid, I wanted a pony more than anything. I really did. Every Christmas I faithfully wrote to Santa asking for that damned pony. Finally I got my chance to learn to ride one summer, and, of course, I fell off the first day. My instructor told me to get right back on, or I'd never ride again."

He had lulled her into relaxing. Blankly Katherine asked, "So?"

"So I got back on," he said simply, smiling at her with a demonic gleam starting to shine in his gaze. "And I ride all the time now."

"But what does that have to do with...?" Katherine stared at him. Suddenly outrage began to build inside her breast and she exploded. "You're not actually suggesting... You really want me to... After what I've been through—almost raped by a maniac— you expect me to...?"

"Exactly," he pronounced, grinning broadly. "Let's go make love, Katie. Right now. Unless we administer the back-in-the-saddle theory, so to speak, you might never again—"

"Blackie Lowell," said Katherine, turning on her heel, "you are an unspeakable pig! For a moment I mistook you for a human being."

And then she couldn't control herself. Katherine faltered in midstep, hiccoughed once and felt a dam burst inside. Her self-control was washed away in a deluge of emotion. She knew all too well what had occurred in the hours before Blackie arrived and rescued them, and he'd managed to dredge up all those memories. Horribly she began to cry. The storm of tears came in ugly, humiliating sobs, blinding her so that she couldn't take a step.

"Hey," he began, startled. Awkwardly he said, "Hey, steady there."

She shook her head back and forth, unable to check the tears that poured from inside. Stumbling, she tried to hurry away from him. "I—I'm sorry. This—this isn't like me."

The deck moved and Katherine lost her balance. Blackie caught her just before she fell. He did not let go of her arm, and she swayed for a moment, too embarrassed to look at him, too shaken to pull free. "I—I'm sorry," she said again. "I hate to cry."

"Oh. Well. It's all right," he said gruffly. He cleared his throat. "Maybe I've been, uh, callous. About what happened last night on the beach before I came along. Did, uh, did he hurt you?"

She managed to shake her head again, but didn't look up, not wanting him to see her face. "No," she whispered. "He didn't—I wasn't raped, if that's what you mean. It's just—I've never felt so—so helpless like that."

The memory swam up around her like an ugly monster from a murky swamp. The brute strength, the panting, the screams choking in her own throat, her mouth wrenched open. The man's stubby fingers against her tongue. Katherine began to shudder uncontrollably.

Without a word Blackie took her in his arms. His body absorbed her tremors. He held her gently, one arm wrapped around her back so that he eased her head onto his shoulder. Not realizing exactly what she was doing, Katherine melted into him, glad of the support, thankful of some human compassion. Blackie stood silently and held her.

After several hard racking sobs, Katherine got a grip on her composure. Her face felt hot, and she was terribly embarrassed. Good Lord! This was no way to act. And in the arms of a loutish sailor. With an effort she stopped her tears.

"That's it," he coached. "Now take a couple of deep breaths."

She obeyed, easing out of his embrace. Katherine wasn't sure which was worse—her memory of the night before, or the fact that she had actually bawled in Blackie Lowell's arms. She hated being out of control. Stiffly she stood back from him.

He said, "Feel better now?"

"No," she said shortly, still trembling. After all, she was still confused about the events of the previous night. Had Blackie tried anything? This sudden, out-of-character niceness was hard to believe. He was up to something. "I'll recover," she said. "And I'd be happy if you'd mind your own business until then."

"What?"

She managed to get her hand free and faced him, nose in the air once more. "I can handle myself from now on. Please stay away from me."

His gray eyes snapped with anger. "Excuse me for being human! Look, this isn't such a big deal, so don't—"

"Not a big deal!" Katherine repeated hotly, emotion rushing into her chest.

"Well, it's not like you got raped or something. He probably took one look at that squinched-up pickle face of yours and lost all—"

"How dare you say such a—"

"If he didn't actually *do* anything," Blackie burst out, "there's no reason why you can't pull yourself together and act like a normal—"

"I don't care what he did!" Katherine shouted suddenly, losing control. "Damn you, I care what *I* did!"

"Huh? What are you talking about?"

"I killed him! Don't you understand?" Katherine heard herself shriek, "I hit him on the head and killed him, you idiot!"

CHAPTER FOUR

LORD! KATHERINE had had no intention of admitting what had happened on the beach, not to Blackie Lowell—not even to herself. She gulped and wished to heaven she could snatch back the words. He stared at her. Before he could control it, a wave of emotions crossed his face. Shock, grave understanding, then, briefly, pity.

That was too much. If he'd just been surprised by her emotional explosion, that would have been okay. But he felt sorry for her.

She tore away from him and headed for the cabin and the boys. She'd rather die than discuss her feelings on the subject of murder. This brute would never understand. Parading naked before him would be easier than explaining the anguish she felt. Self-control was the answer, of course.

Katherine vowed to stay in command of herself. It was the only way to cope. She would stay busy, stay out of Blackie's way and manage somehow to keep her sanity.

First order of the day was breakfast. After consuming a surprisingly filling meal of a prepackaged concoction he called gorp, Katherine cleaned up the worst of the mess they had made in the cabin, and the boys assembled on deck, prepared to absorb every word Blackie spoke. They stripped off their shirts and unconsciously began to mimic his postures, his walk, his ease in handling everything he touched.

The boys adored him. It took only a few hours, but they worshiped him like a god. Katherine saw immediately that it would be a lost cause to try to undermine Blackie's growing rapport with her students. He was bigger than life to them.

On deck he gave them each a length of line.

"We'll start at the beginning," he said, standing over them on the small, crowded deck of the boat. "Tying knots. Everybody paying attention?"

They chorused affirmatively.

He looked at Katherine, who was hanging around to make sure he didn't corrupt the boys. His eyes glinted, for he knew exactly what she was worried about. "Your ladyship," he chided, taunting her, "where is your line?"

She managed a cold smile. "I thought womenfolk were excluded from this lesson."

"Tch, tch," he said. "You feminists can certainly hold a grudge, can't you? Your choice: tie knots with us, or go take inventory in the galley."

"I know my place," she said wryly. "I'll go to the kitchen."

"Galley," he corrected as she went by, apparently unconcerned by her departure. "Okay, men. Take the ends of the line in your hands. Watch, please. Make a loop with this end. That's it. Frick, what the hell are you doing?"

"How can you tell I'm Frick?"

Blackie glowered down at the boy. "You are, aren't you?"

"Yes," said one of the Kuransky twins. "But how can you tell us apart?"

"Because I'm brilliant. Now what are you doing with that line?"

"It's a noose," said Frick, and he giggled. "A noose for hanging."

Katherine paused in the hatchway and turned back, ready to put a stop to the boy's nonsense at once.

But the other boys got into the spirit too quickly for her to protest. They all tittered nervously, and Peter said, "I b-bet a rock's a quicker way to d-death."

"Especially," added Frick, "if Miss Theodopolis throws it."

Again a chorus of silly laughter, out of control and foolish. Katherine froze, and her heart seemed to stand still for one awful moment.

Blackie saw her face, of course. The boys were turned so that they were unaware that she could hear, but Blackie knew and saw her expression.

He snapped, "Shut up, you idiots! I don't have training wheels for this boat anymore, so pay attention to the lesson and save yourself from drowning later."

Katherine fled through the hatch.

In the cabin she tried to calm down. She had to make herself busy. Determinedly she began to slam through all of the latched cupboards, looking through the supplies Blackie kept arranged so neatly there. As she searched, Katherine became increasingly appalled by the skimpy supply of food. There were hardly enough provisions to sustain one person for a week, in her opinion. A few cans of tuna, some plastic bags of gorp, a dozen foil packets of dehydrated eggs, some peanut butter, that was it. Another cabinet revealed a Tupperware container of fresh fruit, mostly shriveled apples. The oranges were stamped with the Sunkist logo, but looked the worse for wear.

Katherine opened the last cupboard and stared. Inside she saw eight cans of chocolate syrup.

She was still staring at the cans when Blackie swung himself through the hatch. Katherine whirled around to face him.

"Well?" he asked, ignoring her startled reaction to his arrival. "What's your opinion of the supply situation?"

"I think," she replied tartly, closing the cupboard door, "that you're a chocoholic. And the rest of us are going to starve."

"Starve?" He strode back through the dinette toward her, tipping his head so that he didn't bump it on the low lamp fixture suspended from the ceiling. "Are you kidding? You'll all be fat by the time the Peace Corps picks you up."

He was teasing her, she saw, but she was in no mood for games. He made her nervous. Had he seen how close she was to losing her marbles this morning? Did he intend to drive her to that point, pressuring her while she was weak?

"Mr. Lowell," she said seriously, "just how long is this voyage going to take?"

He braced his shoulder against the galley cupboards and relaxed. "Ten days."

"You're sure?"

"Maybe fourteen," he corrected with a shrug and folded his arms over his chest. "Don't panic about the supplies. We're going to fish. The boys are stringing the line right now. Besides, you haven't looked everywhere. Your bunk sits over a pullout freezer.''

"It does?" she asked in honest surprise, forgetting her discomfiture momentarily.

"Sure. Have a look."

He wasn't kidding. Katherine propped open the door to the forward cabin and crouched on the floor. She pulled out a long drawer, and a cool mist clouded up around her face. The freezer was full of food, mostly things that could be boiled in the plastic bags they were stored in. Katherine saw plenty of vegetables, several loaves of whole wheat bread, even frozen waffles and what was undoubtedly meat wrapped in white freezer paper. Immediately she was relieved. Supplies were plentiful. Shipboard life had come a long way from the days of salt pork and biscuits, she thought. Her memories of how Captain Bligh's crew on the *Bounty* suffered did not compare to the vast selection of foods in Blackie's freezer. They weren't going to starve at all.

"See?" he said behind her. "You had no faith in me, Kate."

She ignored his crack and closed the drawer. "All right," she said, getting to her feet once more and keeping her cool. "A sailor's life isn't so bad after all, I see. The boys might actually enjoy this voyage."

He grinned. "My thoughts exactly. Even you might enjoy it."

She eyed him warily, suddenly alert for danger.

"Take it easy," he said. "I only meant that you might use the time to sort out what's happened."

"I don't need to sort out anything," she began.

"I saw you up there a minute ago," he interrupted curtly, cutting her off. "The kids were just jagging around. No harm intended."

"No harm done," she said stiffly.

"No?" He regarded her with tranquillity. "Are you all right?"

So he had seen how upset she was. Katherine bristled. "I'm fine, of course. I haven't—"

Blackie reached out, and when he touched her hair, Katherine could not finish her sentence. Her voice died with her courage. Very gently his fingertips brushed the wisps that had escaped her makeshift ponytail. It was a possessive gesture, she thought dimly, as if he were proving that he could touch her whenever he chose to. "You bolted off the deck," he observed, "like a scalded cat."

"Well, what do you expect? Those boys are sensitive young men from very good families. I didn't want to embarrass them while—I just . . ." She took a deep breath. "You know, it's your influence that has them joking around in such bad taste."

His gray eyes widened. "*My* influence?"

"Certainly." The best defense was a good offense, and once Katherine got her wind up, she was in fine form. "I've got a responsibility to those boys up there, and I don't want them exposed to—to your kind of behavior. I hope you respect that."

"My behavior is perfectly natural. *Your* reaction is unbelievable. Do you expect them to ignore what they saw last night?"

Hoarsely she said, "They'll understand. The boys are intelligent and sensitive. I just don't want to expose them to any unpleasantness, if I can help it."

"Quite admirable," he said, terse and unfriendly. "You're putting their mental well-being before your own, your ladyship."

"Of course!"

"But what about yourself? You think ignoring what happened to you back on that island will make it go away?"

"We don't need to talk about that incident," she said quickly, hoping fervently he was not going to drag up something she thoroughly wished to forget. "Can we drop this, please?"

"Sure." He shrugged, then smiled, full of charm. "There are other ways to overcome a bad experience besides talk. When you're ready to put it behind you, let me know. I'll be glad to do my part."

She glared at him. His taunts did not please her. In fact, the man deserved a smack across his smirking face.

Unfazed and cocky, he turned away and walked through the dinette to the computer terminal. Standing before it, he flipped a switch. Then he found a ring-bound notebook on the overhead rack, pulled it down and dropped it on the counter, preparing to make some notes.

At a distance he looked safe enough, preoccupied by his work and temporarily off guard. Swallowing the last of her misgivings, Katherine said bravely, "I do have a few requests to make."

He did not look up from his notebook. "Requests? That sounds ominous."

"Not at all. Just a few rules to establish."

He glanced up with a quick grin. "Rules, huh?"

Coolly she said, "First, there is the matter of segregation."

He glanced at her again, eyebrows high. "Between the sexes, I presume?"

"Yes."

"Don't worry." He looked away and nonchalantly sat down at the chair in front of the console. Flipping through the pages of his notebook, he found a clean sheet and pulled a pencil stub out of a slot in the desk. "There's room for a couple of the boys to sleep on these cushions, and we'll string some hammocks for the rest of them in here. I'll take the floor. You can have the bunk at night when you're not standing watch."

Katherine advanced as far as the table and asked, "Standing watch?"

"Everybody has to pull his or her weight," Blackie reminded her. With the short pencil he made a scratching notation in his book. Raising his voice to lecture-room volume, he said, "In order to earn privileges like privacy, food, water and whatever else makes you happy, each one of us is going to shoulder some responsibilities. Otherwise, we have chaos. A little work won't kill you, your ladyship, and it ought to be good for those boys, too."

She took a deep breath, but decided it would be childish to inform him that she had already decided to shoulder her share of the work aboard the boat. "All right, agreed," she said. "Next, I'd like to request some changes on your part."

Still sitting, he looked at her with lifted eyebrows. "Changes?" he inquired carefully.

"Yes." She eyed him coolly, standing a safe six feet from him. "Your speech, your behavior, your attitude, even your personal habits, if you don't mind my saying so, are going to have a profound effect on the boys."

"My personal habits?" he repeated with one of his unholy grins starting. He threw his pencil down and tipped his weight back in the chair, devoting his full attention to her with his hands linked behind his head. "Exactly what are you referring to, my dear Kate?"

"Spitting, for one."

"Spitting?"

"Yes, you were spitting into the water after breakfast."

"So sue me!" he objected, sitting straight again. "I don't like raisin stems. When I find one, I spit it out."

"And every one of the boys imitated you within the next fifteen minutes." Once she got her steam up, Katherine felt brave enough to press her point. "Spitting is a reprehensible habit, and I won't return these boys to their parents if—"

"Okay, okay." He put up his hand in surrender. "Spare me the etiquette lectures, your ladyship. What else?"

"Language," she said promptly. "Some of the words that come out of your mouth, sir, are not fit for mixed company."

He grinned. "Okay, I won't swear when you're within earshot."

Hotly Katherine said, "Look, if you won't take this seriously . . ."

"I'm *not* going to take this seriously, as a matter of fact." His grin disappeared. He got to his feet and towered over her. His voice rose, this time without the bite of good-humored sarcasm. "I'll take your advice when it suits me and not before. I am *not* one of your pussy-whipped students," he snapped, "and I won't have a female tell me what I can and cannot do aboard my own boat!"

"I am only thinking of the boys' well-being."

"Fine. That's your job. But it's not mine. I'm not going to go around playing David Niven in a smoking jacket for the benefit of five runny-nosed boys who—"

"Their noses do not run!"

Blackie laughed harshly at that. "Why not? They're too well-bred or something? C'mon, Kate! Those kids don't need to be sheltered from me. They could use a good look at the real world, though, and you're blocking the view."

"Are you accusing me of being overprotective?"

He stuck his nose down to her level. "Bingo."

"These boys are my responsibility. I'm their guardian, and I've got to think of what's best for them."

"Maybe you don't *know* what's best for them."

"I suppose you think *you* know?" she demanded, arms akimbo, glaring up at him.

"Maybe I do. All I know is that I'm not going to put on an act for them—not now when our lives may depend on what they learn about this boat and how to sail her. It's my responsibility to get us all to the Gilberts in one piece, and I'm going to do it the only way I know how. So you can take your requests for changing my language and my attitude and my personal habits, Miss Priss, and go—"

"That's enough," she commanded before he could make an uncivilized suggestion.

"No, it's not enough," he shot back sarcastically. "But since I did agree to watch my mouth in mixed company, I can't say exactly what's appropriate right now."

"You are," Katherine began angrily, "an unspeakable—"

"Pig. I know, you said that once already. I admit it. I *like* myself this way."

She met his glare with an equally ferocious look of her own. She matched his sarcasm, too. "How you can stand yourself is beyond my comprehension, Mr. Lowell. My Lord, the smell *alone* is enough to attract sea gulls!"

"What smell?"

"Your smell!" she flung at him. "Captain Lowell, *you* need a *bath*. Desperately, in fact! I don't know why I'm so worried about your influence over the boys. In another two days they'll be driven away by your stench!"

A half second of dead silence greeted that accusation. His murderous expression darkened.

Then, abruptly, Blackie exploded into laughter. He threw his head back, rocked on his heels and roared.

No further insults came to Katherine's mind, and he appeared to be unable to make a verbal comeback, so she decided to execute a stalking exit. She pushed past him and stormed out through the hatchway and up onto the deck. She slammed the hatch behind her for good measure. He was rude, obnoxious and coarse. He was beneath contempt. And she was stuck with him.

Of course, Blackie's last view of Katherine was a pleasantly diverting look at her backside. Her legs were fantastic, he'd told himself all along, but she had a very attractive bottom as well. Rounded, without flab, and the muscle that joined her hip with her thigh had not blurred yet. She was taut all over, he'd bet. Very nice.

He turned back to the computer, grinning and shaking his head. He'd like to touch her, he thought to himself. Yes, smoothing his hands up and down her thighs made a very nice mental picture. And the look on her face would be priceless. Taming a hot-blooded female might be just the thing to keep his spirits up.

Maybe he'd take a bath, after all. There might be benefits.

CHAPTER FIVE

UNFORTUNATELY for her sense of pride, Katherine knew nothing about sailing. If she had, she could have wowed him with her abilities. But she had been born and raised in Ohio, and her experience with boats was limited to outboard powerboats used for teenage waterskiing parties on Lake Erie.

Sailing *Bobbie McGee*, she discovered, was a complicated business light-years from puttering on freshwater lakes. There was much more to sailing than running up the sails and sitting back to let the breeze blow through your hair. So Katherine was forced to control her temper and behave as if Blackie Lowell were in charge. She hated being subservient to a man like him, but there was no alternative.

Blackie set about teaching the boys how to sail, and Katherine relegated herself to watching the fishing rods with Jimmy. The older boys—barefoot and shirtless—learned to scamper from bow to stern, pointing out the parts of the boat as Blackie called out the names. Grudgingly Katherine had to admit he was a good teacher.

Soon he had them changing the tension on some of the lines and shifting the sails to execute the tacks. He was strict and yelled mercilessly at the boys if they made mistakes, but he laughed with them, too, and once coupled his brusque commands with a hilarious story of his first sailing attempt, a tale of disaster that ended with him swamped and sinking off Cape Cod. The boys laughed uncertainly, not sure how to respond to this guffawing sailor who called them rude names and demanded absolute efficiency without question.

"Harold!" he bellowed when the boat made a wide sweeping tack and the breeze filled her sails again. "Get your fat rump off the railing, you idiot! Do you want to fall overboard?"

Harold scuttled off his precarious perch just in time, for the boat heeled and zoomed off again. He looked frightened at Blackie's murderous frown but a moment later he had a sheepish grin on his round little face. Perhaps he was pleased to have been singled out for attention.

The boys stayed in their assigned positions even during lunch, which consisted of cheese sandwiches that Katherine served. As she handed out the food, she saw that her students were barely able to contain their excitement. Their eyes gleamed as they never had before in any classroom, and both the Kuransky boys even forgot to say thank-you. They all responded to her questions with the standard "Yes, Miss Theodopolis," but Katherine realized that she had been usurped as the center of their universe. Their eyes were glued to Blackie.

During the afternoon, while the tropical sun beamed down upon the rolling swells of the ocean, *Bobbie McGee* surged northward. They caught sight of land twice, but kept sailing without stopping.

In the late afternoon Katherine went below and searched through the stores for an appropriate meal. At least she could make herself useful below deck, and she didn't have to look at Blackie Lowell's smirk all the time, either.

Her cooking abilities were nearly on par with her sailing skills, so she chose a canister of dry soup makings and a muffin mix—both with simple instructions printed on the boxes. Jimmy, the only boy who was too cowed by Blackie to speak to him, was her assistant. They mixed the dry soup with water and added some frozen chicken legs. While it simmered, they made muffins and then straightened up the cabin. When Blackie came down to investigate, they were busily trussing some blankets into sleeping hammocks. Jimmy shyly climbed into one finished product to show it off.

"Not bad, kid," Blackie told him. "You used the knot we talked about this morning."

Jimmy nodded, smiling.

"Hmm," murmured Blackie, and he frowned as he studied the rope more closely. "Not bad at all. I'll want you up on deck tomorrow, Jimbo, no excuses. I can use an extra sailor. Let her ladyship dirty her hands below deck."

Katherine sizzled.

"And you," he said to her, "had better be careful with the stove. Shut off the gas when you're not using it. I don't want my boat blown up, please."

"I'm not stupid," Katherine retorted.

He shrugged. "We'll see. You want the boys down here for dinner?"

Controlling her urge to shout at him in front of Jimmy, she said calmly, "Yes, send them down in shifts, if you like."

Mockingly he saluted. "Aye, aye, your ladyship."

The boys were practically too exhausted to eat, but their appetites gained momentum, and they consumed the soup almost before Katherine could ladle a cup for herself. Against her better judgment she reserved a portion for Blackie. It might work to her advantage to starve him, but that ploy would be too obvious. When Peter and Harold went on deck to relieve him, Blackie came down and casually took his supper without speaking to her. While he ate, he questioned the Kuransky twins about their interests.

"Music," said one of the boys finally, when they realized that Blackie was genuinely curious about how they spent their spare time. "We're going to be musicians."

"What kind of music, Frack?"

The twins were delighted by their new names and responded eagerly. "Well, sir, we like Mozart, of course, but we really find Bach more challenging."

For a moment Blackie looked as though his soup did not agree with him. "Mozart?" he repeated, staring. "At your age?"

"Yes, sir!"

"Haven't you heard of The Rolling Stones? David Bowie?" He shook his head. "Bach, huh?"

"Oh, yes, sir. Would you like to hear us play?"

"Well, sure, Frick, but—"

The twins scrambled off the bench and dove for their blazers, which had been neatly hung on hooks near the hatchway. They came up with shining faces and harmonicas in their hands.

Blackie burst into laughter. "Harmonicas? You're gonna play Bach on those?"

The boys plunked down on the benches once more and tuned up. In a moment they were briskly buzzing their way through a Brandenburg concerto, accompanied by Blackie's chortling laugh. Halfway through the piece he stopped them.

"Hold it, hold it! Those gizmos were never meant to play that kind of stuff, Here, listen to this for a while. Let me know when you can play it."

His computer terminal included a tape player for cassettes, it seemed. He opened a drawer and found a tape that suited him, and soon the first thumping strains of a blues tune filled the cabin. Blackie turned up the volume until the hull vibrated with the sound.

"There," he said triumphantly over the noise. "*This* is harmonica music!"

He was right. As the twins listened spellbound, their tight frowns were clues to Katherine that they intended to learn the tune and play it for Blackie as soon as possible.

LATER, WHEN NIGHT HAD FALLEN, Blackie gave orders. "You can sleep tonight," he told the boys, "but in a few days when you've learned something useful, you'll take turns standing watch. I've got to sail at night if I'm going to beat Pointy to China. Now, everybody line up for the head. Wash up and get into bed. Lights out in half an hour."

He let the boys herd themselves toward the bathroom, elbowing each other to get better positions in line, and then Blackie turned up the music again and strode back to Katherine, who was still busy in the galley. The level of music prevented their conversation from reaching the boys' ears. It was time to confront her.

Blackie began to toss leftover muffins into a plastic bag. Unceremoniously he said, "You're going to have to learn some sailing, too."

Drying the pot she'd used for the soup, Katherine regarded him wryly as he put away the leftovers with the matter-of-fact air of a helpful husband. The image didn't quite fit with his bulky sweater, tattered shorts and the scruffy red bandanna he had tied pirate-style around his head to keep the salt spray out of his hair. He looked like a man's man, all right, and his suggestion that she learn to sail struck Katherine oddly. "I thought I was supposed to stick with women's work."

He grinned and tossed the muffins into a cupboard. "That won't last, if I'm any judge of character. Besides, if something happens to me, I'd feel a little more comfortable knowing that another adult could handle *Bobbie*."

"Would you trust your precious boat with anyone else?"

"No," he said frankly, "but I won't have much choice if I'm dead, will I?"

Annoyed, she muttered, "Oh, for heaven's sake!"

He laughed. "If I'm fish food, you'd be on your own, your ladyship."

"Don't joke about it!" she burst out suddenly. Heaven knew why, but her poise broke. She'd been tense all day, and the minute she was alone with the man, she fell apart. Trembling, she cried, "Death is not funny!"

It only took an instant to regain control. But Blackie looked at her, clearly surprised by her sudden vehemence and the rigid way she stood before him. Awkwardly Katherine turned away, embarrassed and angry.

Blackie had read her expression. Wisely he chose not to dish out any sympathy. Instead, he began to grin devilishly. "Why, Kate!" he mocked. "Would you miss me?"

"Of course not." She forced her voice to sound normal again and finished drying the soup pot. "You're needed here, and we can't get along by ourselves, that's all. Naturally, I don't want anything to happen to you."

His smile was broad as he lounged against the cupboard where the pot belonged. "Once I deliver you to the Peace Corps, you wouldn't care if I drowned, would you?"

She sniffed, pretending complete disinterest in his welfare. Opening the nearest cupboard, she made room for the clean pot beside the cans of chocolate syrup. "Just don't do it while the boys are watching, that's all I ask. As you know, I want to spare them any unpleasantness."

He laughed and reached across her. Opening the cupboard, he retrieved the soup pot and put it in its correct spot. "I think you'll be surprised how well these kids can cope with unpleasantness, Kate. They're not the defenseless little children you think they are. At least they won't be for too much longer."

"Now, see here, Mr. Lowell," she began firmly, facing him again in the small space. "I would appreciate it if you were more circumspect about what you teach my students."

"Don't start that junk again," he warned easily as he reached for an apple from the container on the counter. Buffing the apple peel on his sweater, he said, "These kids could use a walk on the wild side now and then. They've been sheltered too long already."

"Mr. Lowell—"

He cut her off. "I refuse to play by your rules, Kate, so you might as well play by mine. I'll bet you're longing to anyway." He smiled at her curiously. "Can you really be such an uptight priss as you seem? Or are you hiding a different kind of woman behind those pretty blue bedroom eyes?"

Stiffly she said, "What you see is what you get with me, Mr. Lowell."

He bit into his apple and shook his head. "If that's true, I'll be disappointed," he said around his mouthful. He swallowed and gestured with his apple. "May I have the use of my cabin for a few minutes? It's going to get damned cold tonight, and I want a change of clothes."

Living in such close quarters was definitely a disadvantage. Katherine stepped aside so he could gain entrance to the forward cabin. Attempting to be civil, she asked, "When do you intend to stop for the night?"

"Stop? Hell, lady, you don't win races by stopping for the night."

"But . . . I mean . . ."

"I sleep off and on," he said, leaving the cabin door open and rummaging one-handed in the compartment over the bed while he munched the apple. Again with his mouth full, he said, "But the key to single-handed sailing is vigilance. If I don't want to end up in Peru, I have to get up every hour or so to check our course."

She edged to the open door. "You do that every night? Really?"

"Yes, really." Through shrewdly narrowed eyes, he glanced down at her, his smile playing suspiciously on his mouth. "Why? Disappointed? Did you want to invite me into bed tonight to keep you warm?"

"No," Katherine snapped, her eyes blazing with anger immediately. Abruptly she turned away from the forward cabin and walked away, head high.

Blackie grinned. Biting into his apple, he felt a chuckle rumble up from inside. He loved to see her eyes flash.

He had to admit that he didn't mind having her around. In fact, having a crowd on board his boat didn't annoy him as much as he'd thought it would. After two weeks of complete solitude after what's-her-name left in Rio, it was almost pleasant to have someone to talk with, someone to torment. Besides, his own thoughts were often unsettling after a day or two of brooding, and he rather appreciated the diversion provided by Katherine Theodopolis and her boys. Kate especially. The boys were fun, but Kate provided challenge. Perhaps tonight he'd mull over a strategy where she was concerned.

The boys went willingly to bed, though there was some squabbling over who was allowed the privilege of sleeping in the four hammocks. Blackie issued orders, though, and everyone was soon peacefully tucked in with blankets. Katherine disappeared into the forward cabin and did not show her face again.

After making himself a cup of coffee, Blackie went up on deck. He liked to check the stars at night. Like most modern ocean sailors, he relied on the computerized navigation system, but he preferred to make sure of his course the old-fashioned way each night also. It was as if he were giving his brain some exercise and double-checking the machinery's accuracy, too. Tonight, as he expected, *Bobbie McGee* was right on course.

Blackie dug his notebook out of his pocket and slid off the rubber band he kept around it. Religiously, he made notes every night, composing a kind of captain's log for himself. Not only did his writing keep track of where he was, but also, Blackie admitted, it helped organize his thoughts. The log had become a journal of his private reflections.

Tonight, though, he had a hard time deciding what to describe. For the first time on the voyage, he was tempted to write about another person, not just the boat or the weather. Katherine Theodopolis was on his mind. Something about her appealed to him. Not just her body, either, he thought, though it was very nice indeed. Her spunk was attractive, too. Other qualities niggled at him as well—the fear in her eyes that she couldn't control, for one. He laughed at himself. Judas, was he starting to feel protective? That was a bad sign.

Or worse, did he see some of his own feelings reflected in her expressions?

Before he could roll that thought around in his head sufficiently, Blackie's solitude was interrupted. Oddly enough, he hastily stuffed his journal out of sight when he heard the cabin latch click. Why he felt sneaky, he wasn't sure.

In any case it wasn't Katherine who came up on deck. It was Peter, the oldest boy, the one who stuttered.

"Everything okay?" Blackie asked roughly.

"Y-y-yes, sir." Peter timidly crept up on the deck. "I c-couldn't sleep, s-so I thought I'd bring up s-some more c-coffee for you, sir."

Blackie softened inside. He held out his mug and watched the boy's careful lip-biting concentration as he poured from the pot. "Thanks, Pete," he said when the job was done. "You going to stay up here a while?"

Peter almost smiled, and his eyes looked joyful before he caught himself and cast down his gaze. "Y-yes, sir, if that's all r-right with you."

"Sure." It was pathetic to see a kid get so excited about spending a little time with an adult. Blackie was sitting against the rail, and he gestured at the place next to him. "Come join me. The rest of them asleep?"

Shyly Peter slid to the spot on the rail and leaned there, holding the coffeepot handle in one hand and balancing it with his forefinger under the spout. "Everyone's as-s-sleep, I think. Jimmy cried, but M-Miss Theod-dopolis talked to him."

Conversation with one kid was much harder than talking to the whole bunch of them, Blackie discovered suddenly. What was he supposed to discuss with a thirteen-year-old wimp? Blackie tried to come up with a good topic, but his imagination failed him. Before the silence stretched too far, he said quickly, "Well, Jim's young. He's not used to being away from his mama, I suppose."

"Oh," Peter began, "he's away from his m-mother a lot. His p-parents got divorced. H-he's still having a hard time gettin' over that. He c-cries a lot."

"Hmm," said Blackie, feeling increasingly uncomfortable. "That's tough."

"M-Miss Theod-dopolis has been a big help, though. She's kind of t-taking his m-mom's place."

Blackie's attention sharpened. "Oh?"

Peter nodded, looking out at the dark ocean, unaware of his audience's increased interest in the subject. "She's been going with M-Mr. Monahan for a few m-months now—since the divorce."

"Going with him?" Blackie repeated. "What d'you mean? Are they getting married or something?"

"I think s-so, sir. M-Mr. Monahan asked her, and she—she's been extra nice to Jimmy lately—especially since they're f-fighting over who g-gets to k-keep Jimmy."

"Hmm," said Blackie, thinking over the information. He hadn't expected her to be attached to anyone. Kate was good-looking, though, and a smart woman. She had polish, too. She'd make a good diplomat's wife. All the right manners, all the best social skills. An ambitious diplomat with a wife like her at his side could do some pretty slick entertaining, which was always important in foreign ports. Yep, Kate would be a first-rate diplomat's wife. It was a wonder she wasn't married already, since she had to be thirty years old, at least. What the hell was the Monahan character like? And why, Blackie asked himself, was he so concerned all of a sudden?

Peter spoke up. "My parents aren't d-divorced. M-my father died. H-he's been gone a long time, though."

Blackie jerked his thoughts back to the present and looked down at the boy. "What?"

"My d-dad," said Peter. "He's g-gone. My m-mother didn't marry again yet."

"Oh," said Blackie.

Peter kept staring at him, his eyes surprisingly direct with purpose, as if sizing Blackie up. Finally he asked, "Are y-you married, sir?"

Blackie grinned. He couldn't help himself. "No, I'm not married, son."

Peter's gaze didn't waver. "M-maybe you'd like to m-meet my mom, sir. She-she's really pretty."

Blackie smiled down at Peter. So the kid was a matchmaker. Gently Blackie said, "Sure, Pete. I'll be glad to meet your mom someday."

Uncertain suddenly, Peter added, "Of course, m-mom's not as pretty as M-Miss Theodopolis."

"Well," said Blackie before he thought things through carefully, "I don't know anybody as pretty as Miss Theodopolis. Do you?"

"N-no, sir," said Peter loyally. "She's wonderful," he declared with heartfelt sincerity. He struggled with an inner thought and finally blurted out, "D-do you like her, sir? E-even if you yell at her sometimes?"

Blackie shrugged. "Sure. I like her just fine."

Peter frowned. "Sh-she's upset, though."

"I seem to affect most women that way."

Peter didn't smile. He shook his head. "N-no, it's that m-man. The one who t-tried to hurt her before she hit him on the head. He yelled at her, too. She was s-scared of him, and h-he hit her, and—and—Well, it w-was b-bad." Just remembering, Peter began to shiver. "She—she's not herself anymore, sir. She—she's s-sad and worried."

"She'll be all right."

Peter shook his head again. "Y-you don't know her, sir. M-Miss Theod-dopolis is always happy and—and so much fun. She—she's not herself at all right now. She's upset about what that m-man did to her."

Blackie looked down at the uncertain boy and tried to decide exactly what he could say that might help allay the kid's anxiety for his teacher. Explaining the psychology of rape to a kid didn't sound like a good idea at all, and Blackie certainly did not want to find himself in the position of discussing the difference between lovemaking and violence. "Pete," he said finally, in the hope that he could at least put the boy's mind at ease, "Miss Theodopolis had a bad experience. It's not the kind of thing that any of us men are likely to understand completely, but she'll get over it, I'm sure. She's tougher than she looks. All we can do is try to be nice to her for a while."

Peter looked doubtfully at him sideways. "Y-you yell at her."

Blackie laughed shortly. "Is that what this is all about? You think you've got to protect her from me?"

"W-w-w-well," Peter began quickly, stuttering more horribly than ever before. He was frightened as a rabbit, but he steeled himself to finish what he'd started.

"It—it's not right f-for her t-to be scared, sir. It's m-mean and n-not fair."

Silently Blackie clapped Peter on the shoulder. The kid was right, after all, and he'd been brave about standing up to him. "You're all right, Pete," Blackie said. "Kate didn't deserve what happened to her, and she doesn't deserve the rotten business I've been giving her since then."

"N-no, sir."

"I just figured I'd razz her out of her bad state of mind, but maybe that's not the best way to handle it. I'll try to be nicer to her from now on."

Peter looked relieved for a moment. Then another problem struck him, and he drew a long breath. Looking up at Blackie, he asked, "W-will they hang her, sir?"

Startled, Blackie asked, "Hang who?"

"M-Miss Theodopolis. For killing that m-man."

Things were complicated indeed, and the kids were not missing a trick. Obviously, Peter had spent a lot of time thinking over the situation. Blackie said kindly, "Peter, don't worry. Miss Theodopolis won't get into trouble. She's got you and me to look after her now, right? We'll take care of her."

"Y-you and m-me, sir?"

"And the rest of the fellows. She's in good hands, I promise."

Doubtfully Peter said, "I—if you say so, sir. It's a b-big problem, though."

Blackie patted the boy's thin shoulder again. "Not for long. Listen, I think you'd better go back to bed. We've got a long trip ahead of us, and I need every sailor in tip-top shape, especially if we've got to outrun the law. So go down there and get a good night's sleep. That's an order."

Peter smiled again, looking shy but not quite so timid as before. In fact, he almost saluted. And for once he did not stutter. "Yes, sir!"

Alone again, Blackie shook his head and smiled grimly at the stars above. The kid was right. They had some big problems.

He stayed on deck for a couple of hours, enjoying the quiet, watching the sky and turning things over in his mind. He hadn't solved anything by midnight, when a huge yawn reminded him of the need to sleep. Blackie went below to make a bed on the floor of the cabin.

But he had just begun when the opposite door was jerked open from within.

Katherine flew out of the forward cabin, her face white, her eyes wild with fear.

Blackie halted. She saw him by the green half-light of the computer terminal and clapped both hands over her mouth to stop a scream. She choked and just barely managed to stay quiet. Alfred Hitchcock couldn't have made an actress look more terrified. Gone was her unflappable poise, her aloof sophistication. She wore the oversize shirt and nothing else, but seemed unaware of her long bare legs. Her head was obviously spinning.

Blackie crossed to her at once, mindful of the sleeping boys around them. "What's wrong?" he demanded softly.

She couldn't speak, but stayed plastered against the doorjamb, disoriented and full of dread. Flinching from his voice, she tried to get a grip, but her eyes showed that too much terror raged inside.

"You all right? Something happen?"

She shook her head, and her throat worked convulsively. Trembling, she managed to whisper, "A—a dream."

"That's all?" He reached for her forearms and took them in his grip. "Just a bad dream?"

Katherine fought him instinctively, like a terrified animal. Gasping, she twisted herself out of his hold, and he let her go as if she'd bitten him. She backed up against the doorway again and would have ducked inside and slammed the door, but Blackie got his hand braced against it just in time. He held the door open. "Easy, easy," he soothed, half wondering if she were in shock. "I won't hurt you, Katie. Calm down."

The sound of her name seemed to penetrate her fear. She took a big breath and closed her eyes, as if counting in her head. Finally she expelled the air and said huskily, "Just a dream. I—I'm sorry. I was scared there for a minute and—and I didn't know where I was."

"Claustrophobic?"

She shook her head, opening her eyes once more. They were full of tears, a sight that jarred Blackie, since he'd gotten used to her cool act. Her icy composure had been shattered completely. He let go of the door and took a quick backward step.

She said, "It was the dream, that's all. That man was here, I swear he was. And—and he bled so much!"

Blackie's bewilderment cleared. She'd been reliving the time on the beach, the moments when she'd been assaulted, thrown to the sand and set upon by a man she didn't know. Though her conscious mind could repress what had nearly happened to her, it was obvious that her less-vigilant subconscious was not going to forget the ordeal of a near rape and murder. Why else would she have fought so hard to escape his grasp? She was afraid of the same thing happening again. Even now she was checking the shirt for bloodstains, tugging at it with her hands to look down at the fabric.

Blackie's heart went out to her. Gently he said, "It's all right now. It wasn't real."

She swallowed audibly and then realized she was crying. Hastily she dropped the shirt and wiped her eyes with her hands. "It *felt* real."

"You're safe," he said in the same tone as before. "Want to leave the door open for the rest of the night?"

Katherine jerked her gaze up and stared at him as if realizing for the first time who he was. Her blue eyes widened and glassed over again. She shook her head quickly. "No," she whispered, easing backward into the small cabin to be alone again. Before closing the door, she said in a small voice, "I'll be all right now. Good night."

Blackie looked at the closed door for a full minute, debating about what he ought to do. Not a sound came from the cabin, but he wondered if Kate were crying in there. She was clearly petrified. Should he have offered more comfort? Taken her into his arms?

No, he was willing to bet she'd have hysterics if any man put a hand on her just now.

CHAPTER SIX

KATHERINE FELT LIKE A FOOL. She couldn't understand herself. Suddenly a woman who prided herself on being calm and self-possessed could not sleep for longer than a few minutes before the hideous dreams began. She couldn't control it. What was *wrong*?

Night after night it happened. Afraid to sleep yet exhausted, Katherine tossed in the bunk until her body's needs finally overcame her willpower and she slept. The dream returned and she woke in panic, only to start the cycle again. Gray circles beneath her eyes became testament of her sleepless nights. Each morning her face in the mirror looked more drawn. Yet she could not sleep. Her brain was too busy.

Fortunately there was work to do during the day. Like the boys she threw herself into the routine of the boat, forcing herself to learn new skills so that she wouldn't have to think about what she'd done. Though she hated to admit it, she began to rely on Blackie's constant pressure for perfection. He wanted things done right, and striving to please him gave Katherine something to concentrate on during the daylight hours.

Blackie taught the boys about sailing. He worked them hard, and though Katherine did not spend her hours running back and forth across the deck at his command, she did learn hundreds of facts about boats and the ocean. At night Blackie gathered the boys around the table to examine the ocean charts, explaining the currents and their location. Katherine washed the dishes and listened to his voice, just as mesmerized by what he said as the boys were.

She liked the astronomy lessons best.

One night he dragged them all out on the deck to see the stars. The constellation of Orion caught the boys' fancy, and Blackie ended up sketching a figure of the mythical hunter in his notebook while telling the Greek legend. He began easily, bent over his drawing while he spoke, then caught himself and began to stumble over his words. He finished the tale abruptly, saying simply that Orion died and was made into a constellation. Over Peter's head Blackie glanced at Katherine with a look that was almost an apology.

Katherine knew the story of Orion, of course. The lusty warrior had raped his lover Artemis, who turned around and killed him.

Before the boys could see her reaction, she slipped off the deck and allowed Blackie to continue the astronomy discussion without her.

By day, thank heaven, there were hundreds of tasks necessary to sustain the lives of seven people aboard one little boat: food had to be prepared and equipment tested repeatedly, not to mention the constant vigilance needed to ensure their safety and forward progress. Katherine begrudged Blackie one virtue: he never made mistakes. He knew how to sail a boat, all right, and not once did *Bobbie McGee* run into trouble. Every waking minute Blackie knew exactly the conditions of the ocean, the direction of the wind, their course, the weather, even where every member of his crew might be. He was not going to lose a single kid, if he could help it. She had to respect him for that.

And miraculously not one of them was seasick. Once when she found herself alone with Blackie on the deck with no idle conversation to keep them both distracted from the uncomfortable tension that existed between them, Katherine remarked to him how surprised she was that none of the boys complained of nausea.

"Quick!" Blackie exclaimed in agitation. "Knock on wood!"

Katherine almost laughed. He grinned at her, but she turned away before her answering smile appeared. She felt odd speaking with him sometimes.

The biggest problem faced by the crew of *Bobbie McGee* was—ridiculously—sunburn. The boys were painfully burned from the beginning, and their skins peeled repeatedly. The first-aid kit included a small tube of zinc oxide ointment, which lasted only two days. With no supply of sunscreen available, Katherine finally consulted Blackie in desperation.

"Baking soda?" he suggested when they stood together in the galley trying to come up with an idea. "Isn't that supposed to be good for sunburns?"

"I think it's most effective when you take baths in it, and we haven't got a bathtub."

He ran his hand through his dark hair, frowning at the open cupboard doors. "You've tried shortening?"

"Mixed with almost everything we've got. I've run out of ideas, and the boys can't go much longer before one of them gets truly sick."

Blackie nodded. The sun was far too intense for their tender, pampered skins, and short of confining all of them to the cabin during the daylight hours, there didn't seem to be an answer to the sunburn dilemma. "How about just a paste of shortening and flour?"

Katherine looked at him doubtfully. "Would they wear something like that? Smeared all over themselves?"

Blackie grinned, gray eyes alight. "If I tell them to do it, they will."

He was right, of course. The boys would follow him into the jaws of hell, no doubt. But flour paste? Katherine shook her head wryly. "I doubt that, Captain."

He was undaunted. "Care to make a bet? They'll wear it if I do."

Katherine laughed impulsively. The mental picture of the boys smearing goop all over themselves was funny, but Blackie doing it also was too amusing to resist.

"What about it?" he demanded. "Want to bet on it?"

"A bet, hmm? I've already taken your shirt, you know."

He grinned. "Good point. I haven't got anything left to wager, have I?" His gray eyes sparkled, and his smile was genuine. For a quick moment they were allies.

Katherine returned his smile, aware that they had somehow reached an unspoken truce. At times Blackie Lowell didn't seem so rude as he had at first. Or as sarcastic. Could he be hiding a drop of good breeding behind that beard of his? And what kind of rough-cut sailor could remember the tales of Greek mythology at the drop of a hat? These days Blackie was almost kind to her. And his off-color suggestions were few and far between.

He couldn't resist occasionally, though. "How about," he suggested slyly, "if we bet on the shirt you've already got? If I get the boys to wear this greasepaint, you give me back my clothes."

"And go around naked?"

"Suits me. How about it?"

"Don't get your hopes up," she advised tartly, resorting to her cool lady-of-the-manor routine. He seemed to dislike that side of her personality intensely, and it always got a reaction out of him. "I don't take gambles. Anyway, you're not going to get those kids to smear such stuff all over themselves. They're more civilized than you are."

"We'll see," he promised, "about that."

Blackie accepted her challenge. And he won, of course.

In the end he convinced the boys to play albino aborigines, and Katherine's well-behaved young gentlemen joyously daubed themselves with the war paint she had made. Most hilarious of all was Blackie. He got into the act and took the role of their warrior leader.

For days they whooped and jeered at each other, playing the game endlessly while Katherine watched in amusement. The role-playing helped the boys come out of their shells, she decided, which seemed to be Blackie's goal. Every day they grew noisier, brasher, braver.

Peter, the oldest boy, developed a special relationship with Blackie. He followed the man constantly with his eyes, and sometimes—shyly—he imitated his hero, ordering the younger boys and displaying a keen interest in the weather, the sea and the sky. He had found his ultimate role model.

On Sunday Blackie swung *Bobbie McGee* into the waters off a very small, deserted island. It was so small, in fact, that high tide would submerge the land entirely. No trees grew there, and only a few birds stood on the sand.

"Why are we stopping, Captain?" asked Harold, always the inquisitive one.

In answer, Blackie stripped off his shirt. "It's Sunday, men. We're going to take baths and get cleaned up. If your parents showed up today, they wouldn't recognize a single one of you."

He was right. In less than a week the boys had been transformed astonishingly. No longer were they a collection of pale faces dressed in sedate uniforms and polished shoes. They were a barefoot mob of hooligans, wearing no more than their navy shorts and bizarre headdresses torn from towels, sheets or blazer linings. Because of a dwindling water supply, bathing had been forbidden, and they were all in dire need of soap and water.

With yells of excitement, the boys began to rip off their clothing. It looked as if Blackie had every intention of joining them.

As he wadded up his shirt, Blackie laughed at Katherine's startled expression. "Why don't you swim on *that* side of the boat, Kate? We'll take this side and leave you alone."

"You're kidding, aren't you?"

"Of course not. We're going to look great, and you'll be grungy if you don't take a bath, too." He threw his shirt over the wheel and started to shuck his shorts. "Come on. I'll put the dinghy out for you. And there's a tube of shampoo in my bunk somewhere. Think of how gorgeous you'll look after you've washed your hair."

Before he stripped naked before her, Katherine bolted for the cabin.

She heard the boys dive overboard, and soon they were splashing gaily in the water near the boat's hull. A louder *kerwoosh* signified Blackie's dive, and the boys whooped in delight. The temptation was too great. After finding the tube of seawater shampoo, Katherine ransacked the head for soap and was elated to discover Blackie's little-used razor. He'd never know, so she took it and tiptoed up on deck, steadfastly resisting the temptation to look at the cavorting boys and their fearless leader. She took off her shirt and shorts and dropped them on the deck. In panties and bra, she dove neatly over the side.

The clear water was cool, but wonderfully refreshing. Katherine plunged under the surface and came up, tipping her face to the sunlight. It was dazzling and warm. Against her skin the ocean felt crisp. She swam a few strokes to the rubber dinghy and dropped her shampoo and razor into it, then flipped onto her back and kicked idly, spouting saltwater like a whale. Laughing at herself, Katherine began to take great pleasure in her bath.

Legs first. Using the shampoo, she lathered one leg and shaved it awkwardly. Fortunately, the razor was dull and there was no risk of a bad cut. After scraping her other leg, she threw the razor back over the side of the rubber dinghy and swam out a few more strokes to wash her hair. Happy, she lathered it and scrubbed vigorously. She rinsed it with a shallow dive, then came up and repeated the process. When she'd finished, she wound up and hurled the shampoo over *Bobbie McGee*. As the splash sounded, she heard the boys yelp, then Blackie's authoritative voice as he ordered them to start washing their hair. Judging by their cries and his laughter, Katherine supposed that Blackie dunked them each personally.

At last the boys began to play a game of football in the shallow water, using the tube of shampoo and scrambling through the surf to make touchdowns. Katherine swam lazily, only half listening to their shouts and giggles. She was enjoying the swim too much to put an end to it.

A nearby splash brought her head up, though, and she looked around with trepidation.

Blackie surfaced and threw spray from his hair. He grinned, treading water effortlessly. "Feel better now that you're clean?"

"I'd feel better," she snapped at once, "if you'd go back to where you came from. You're not dressed."

His expression hardened to match hers. "Can't hide anything from you, Miss Theodopolis, can we?"

"Go away."

"Don't order me around, please. I'm not one of your little boys."

"So I see," she remarked and tried to avoid the burlesque implication by not glancing down his body through the crystal water.

"Why, your ladyship! Was that an off-color remark?"

"Of course not!" Furious with herself for blushing, Katherine said, "Leave me alone, damn you!"

He stopped swimming. "Judas," he exploded, "I can't imagine why your looks and your body are wasted on such a cold, stuck-up bitch!"

Katherine opened her mouth to protest and caught herself. Good Lord, Blackie was right. There was no earthly reason why she couldn't loosen up a little. She was being a bitch when he'd done his best to make her happy. An apology was in order, but the words didn't come. She was afraid of what he might do with one.

His frown was profoundly disgusted. Whatever banter he had been ready to exchange with her evaporated. "I give up!" Growling, Blackie commanded, "Stay out here until I call you, got that? I'll herd the troops back on board. Give us time to shower off the salt and get dressed."

"O-okay."

"And don't go anywhere," he ordered. "Don't be an imbecile and wander off."

"I won't," she promised, then started, "Blackie..."

But he had already dived under the boat and disappeared again.

He was angry.

Katherine swam and lectured herself. She ought to be able to trust Blackie by now. He was trying to be nice in his own way, and niceties did not come easily to a man like him. He was trying to be human, after all.

He wasn't so bad, not really. He liked to play the bad boy, taunting her and yelling at the boys. But

Katherine suspected that he was merely playing a role. There had been too many clues that suggested Blackie wasn't as awful as he pretended. Did an ignorant man use words like imbecile when he meant stupid?

No doubt having a woman and children aboard his adored boat was tougher on him than it was on them. Katherine could at least be polite once in a while.

She heard the boys clamber back aboard *Bobbie McGee*. With towels wrapped around themselves, they waved to her, calling her name. Katherine waved back, noting that a week before her students would never have risked seeing her in her underwear. They were changing, all right. They were braver, spunkier. And she hadn't been the one to teach them those qualities.

Blackie brusquely ordered them to go below to rinse off the saltwater. Without a look at her, he disappeared with the boys, wrapping a towel around his hips.

Alone in the water, Katherine floated on her back, eyes closed. She was going to have to pull herself together and be one of the boys. They were actually enjoying the trip. Couldn't she loosen up, too?

She wasn't sure why she stopped floating. A sound, maybe. A wisping touch, perhaps. Abruptly, though, Katherine put her head up and looked around.

"Oh, my God," she murmured, forgetting her musings.

Sharks. Their fins slashed the surface of the water with barely a ripple. Not a dozen yards away, the fins circled back and forth, coming closer. Closer.

"Don't panic," she said aloud. "Don't thrash."

She began to swim slowly, smoothly. Her whole diaphragm tensed, for she wanted to call out. Somehow, though, she couldn't do it. Fear of alerting the sharks? Perhaps. Were they that sensitive? She didn't know and she didn't look back to find out. The dinghy was no help. *Bobbie McGee* bobbed only yards away. Katherine struck out for the boat.

Suddenly a shadow fell across her, blocking the sun. Someone on the boat. Then it was Peter's voice that cried out. "M-Miss! H-h-huh-huh-hurr-hurr-*Blackie*!"

She wasn't sure how close the shark was getting. The rope ladder splashed down and hit her on the head, and she grabbed it. Simultaneously a pain like fire ripped down her calf. She didn't scream, but lunged up the ladder in one hand-over-hand leap. Peter grabbed her shoulders and pulled. Together they tumbled onto the deck, gasping, terrified. But safe.

Katherine sat up first, panting as if she'd swum a race. Her vision blurred, but she was alive. Peter sat up also, untangling his legs from hers. His breath came in heaves, too, and they stared at each other, faces blank, eyes huge.

An eternity might have passed. Then Peter glanced down at Katherine's bra, and the spell broke. His expression cracked. He blushed and almost smiled, and Katherine felt a mindless grin start on her face, too. Perhaps on account of nervous shock, they both started giggling, softly at first, then in great gasps. Katherine reached out and caught Peter's hands. He crawled over willingly and hugged her.

That was how Blackie discovered them, sprawled half naked on the deck, holding each other and laughing like idiots.

"What the hell?" Blackie started angrily. "Peter! I thought I told you to wait until—" He broke off, swore once and pointed at the deck. "Whose blood is that?"

Katherine disengaged herself from Peter and wiped the tears of laughter from her eyes. She looked down at the deck and her own leg. "Oh," she said stupidly, "it's mine, I guess."

"*Yours*? For God's sake, what kind of dumb trick did you pull now?" He braced his fists on his hips and glared down at her. "I told you to—"

"D-don't yell," Peter said. "It b-bit her."

"What bit her?"

Peter couldn't manage to speak. He pointed.

Mystified, Blackie went to the railing and looked down. He must have seen the circling sharks immediately because he reeled back and bit out a sharp expletive. He wheeled on Katherine then and stared at her. "You... Those things... How did..."

"Peter helped," she said simply. "I'm fine."

Blackie cursed viciously and snatched up the shirt she'd left on the deck. Roughly he wrapped it around her shoulders. "Peter," he said swiftly, his face set in a scowl of determination, "go get the first-aid kit. Tell the rest of them to stay below, got that? I don't want the bunch of them milling around up here. Kate—"

He picked her up in his arms. Katherine hadn't a second to protest because he snatched her up so fast. She clutched at his shoulders instinctively, gasping. Easily Blackie hefted her onto the stern seat and laid her down on the cushion, legs extended. While he worked, he kept up a stream of curses. "Of all the nitwitted, numskulled, moronic... Out there by yourself and attracting those garbage-eating jackals! What a blasted fool!'' He adjusted the cushions, muttering more abuse. "What a stupid fool thing to do!''

And Katherine smiled.

"What are you grinning about?'' he demanded finally, catching sight of her face. "You're actually looking pleased with this. What's so funny?''

"You,'' she said. "Why are *you* angry?''

He flushed and snapped, "I'd like to chew your little rump from here to Japan, lady! What were you *doing* out there? And why the hell didn't you shout for help?''

"It wouldn't have done any good. You were too far away, and I didn't have time. I just started swimming.''

He slammed his fist on the seat. "I told you not to get too far from the boat!''

"You said no such thing,'' she objected, struggling to sit up again. "You told me to stay away from the boat until you called for me, and Lord knows how long *that* would have been. I think you *wanted* me to get eaten out there!''

"I did not!'' he retorted. "I just didn't want you prancing around here in the altogether with these impressionable kids hanging around. Haven't you got enough sense to keep your clothes on when—''

Suddenly she was gloriously angry, exploding inside as if all the fireworks in Disneyland had ignited. She faced him and blew up. "Dammit, *you* told me to go swimming, and *you* told me to stay out there until the boys were inside. It's *your* fault I was bitten, and you're yelling at *me*! Is that fair?''

"You're damned right I'm yelling at you! Where are your brains, woman? You've been walking around this boat in a daze ever since I picked you up."

"I've been upset, blast you!"

"Well, how bloody long are you going to stay upset, for crying out loud? This is ridiculous! You endangered your own life—not to mention my sanity—by paddling around out there—"

"What has my life got to do with your sanity?"

"You nitwit!" he exploded. "What the hell am I supposed to do if you get yourself eaten? You expect me to baby-sit these rug rats by myself?"

"I don't believe it! For days you've been playing Peter Pan with those boys and pretending I'm some wicked pirate who's around to spoil your fun, and now you're complaining that—"

"*Somebody's* got to look after them while you do your imitation of a—a patrician zombie!" He jammed his forefinger against her chest and threatened, "But if you go and get yourself swallowed by a shark, lady, I-I'll murder you with my bare hands!"

"You couldn't murder me," she snapped. "I'd already be dead."

"Dammit!" he shouted. "You are the most exasperating female I have ever had the displeasure of stumbling over!"

"And you," said Katherine, "are a self-centered, egotistical bull! Are you going to look at my leg? Or am I supposed to bleed to death while you rant?"

His look was lethal, and it took great self-control for him to bite back a retort. He glared, than grabbed her ankle with his right hand. His fingers clamped into her skin, but Katherine willed herself not to flinch. She held absolutely still while he examined the wound. Katherine ignored the process and, congratulating herself on managing to maintain the appearance of calm, she began to button her shirt. Inside she felt absurdly triumphant. For a moment there she'd actually had him on the defensive for once.

"It's bleeding," Blackie reported tersely. "But it's not bad."

"He just wanted a taste," she responded sedately. "To see if I was worth the effort."

Blackie sent a cross look directly into her eyes and visibly refrained from making a crack. He went back to studying her calf, using his grip on her ankle to rotate her leg. Perhaps hoping to jar her, he said bluntly, "I can actually see the teeth marks, you know. It must have grazed you with its mouth open."

"Spare me the details, please." Calmly she asked, "Will you have to sew anything?"

That startled him. Blackie had not expected her to be so brave. He looked at her face once more, and his grip on her ankle became gentle. "No," he said, anger draining away. "I don't think so."

"Good. Then clean it out, if you would, and put a bandage on it." Katherine kept still in spite of the sudden impulse she felt to withdraw her leg from Blackie's grasp. When he was angry, she hadn't minded, but now she felt peculiar. His left hand lay firmly on her unwounded leg, holding her in place, and his right hand was discovering how smooth her just-shaved skin was. All of a sudden Katherine was aware that he was a man—a young and virile man at that—and she was a nearly naked woman lying on a soft cushion while he touched her bare legs. She swallowed and kept her chin up.

Blackie met her gaze with his, eyebrows rising as amusement entered his expression. He sensed the change, too, and became conscious of their positions and his hands on her body. Carefully he laid her wounded leg in his lap and smoothed his palm up to her knee, openly admiring the slender length of her thigh. Then Blackie expelled an unconscious but demonstrative sigh—one of longing, Katherine had no doubt. Like a shifting sea breeze, the mood of sexual tension changed, increasing, piquing, titillating.

Before he could say a word, she interrupted him. "Don't you dare make an apology."

His grin began to flicker. "What makes you think I was going to?"

"Because it's the kind of strategy you'd use. If you apologize for yelling, then I've got to accept, and we'll be on even ground again, and you'll start acting like a man."

"Like a man?" he inquired carefully.

Katherine could not maintain her glare. No amount of effort could hold back her smile. "You know exactly what I mean," she lectured, eyeing him askance. Inside she felt excited, bubbly, alive again. How could danger have affected her this way? She was happy suddenly, amused and pleased to be with Blackie. Pleasantly she inquired, "Are you going to hold both my legs until sunset? Or may I sit up?"

He smiled wickedly. "Maybe you'd better lie down. And I'll play doctor."

"Do you still remember how? Considering your last patient jumped ship?"

"Even after this long stretch of abstinence, I think I can remember enough." He started to laugh. "Shall we try?"

Wisely Katherine disengaged her wounded leg and swung it to the deck. "I don't think I want to be a guinea pig. Peter," she called, avoiding Blackie's grin, "have you found the box?"

On cue Peter thumped up onto the deck, puffing and red-faced. Against his chest he hugged a blue metal box with the Red Cross symbol on the lid. He dropped to his knees beside Blackie. "Are y-you all right, M-Miss?"

Katherine tousled the boy's fair hair and grinned. "Fine, thanks to you. Care to lend a hand once more?"

"Sh-sure," he said eagerly. "What do you n-need?"

"Patch me up," she said. "Mr. Lowell's forgotten how to play doctor."

CHAPTER SEVEN

STARING AT THE BLANK PAGES of his journal that night, Blackie vowed that he would never understand how the average female mind worked.

Kate had perked up after she'd been bitten by the shark. At dinner she had smiled and even laughed occasionally. Maybe all she ever needed to get her confidence back was a chance to prove that she had courage. While he and Peter had cleaned out her wound and taped bandages over it, she never hinted that she might be in pain. Peter had been sickened by the sight of her torn flesh, and even Blackie himself had felt a twinge. But Kate never blinked.

Blackie, however, was surprised by his own reaction to the incident. He couldn't eat his meal. He couldn't even work up any enthusiasm for chocolate sodas. Though he'd rather die than admit it aloud, he'd been scared out of his wits by the shark incident. The thought of losing Kate so gruesomely actually made him feel ill.

Alone on the deck that night and chewing the end of his pencil, Blackie began to wonder if the circumstance of living so closely with a woman and five little dependents was having an effect on him. Could he, after all these years, be feeling a genuine sense of responsibility for someone else? A few months ago he'd have denied the possibility. Now, though, he wasn't sure. At dinner he had caught himself watching her the way a moth studies a candle's flame. She was mesmerizing, and yet a part of him knew she was dangerous.

Weather prevented him from examining the issue further. With a look at the sky, Blackie put his notebook away. He'd only had time for a quick inspection of the dinghy he'd had the boys bring back in after Katherine's mishap when a storm caught *Bobbie McGee*, swooping down the way a screaming eagle dives on a defenseless rabbit. She ran for a while, but the seas became too heavy. Huge rollers slammed her hull, and Blackie was forced to put up the storm jib. All night he stayed on deck, with only an occasional trip down to the cabin for a cup of coffee and a check with the electronic navigation system. He didn't mind the lack of sleep since the older boys, now capable enough, had spelled him during the good weather nights. Blackie was well rested and rather enjoyed battling the elements by himself.

By morning, though, he was tired. The rain had seeped down the collar of his rain suit, and his sweater was wet. He was cold and hungry, too, and the weather looked more grim than ever.

Katherine came up on deck at first light. She wore his spare rain slicker, and her black hair whipped her face. She stared at the huge waves and driving rain with obvious shock. She hadn't expected the storm to look quite so frightening.

Blackie grabbed her arm just above her elbow and shouted above the wind, "It's not as bad as it looks."

"It looks horrible," she shouted back. Her face was pale, but when her eyes lifted to his, they weren't frightened—not the way they'd been frightened before. She caught her balance like an expert sailor and produced a packet from inside the slicker. "Do you want any breakfast?"

He grinned and accepted her offering. "Terrific. What is it?"

"Dehydrated egg sandwich. No bacon, sorry. I'm afraid to cook much—it's so rough." She cupped her hands to yell, "Pan won't stay on the stove."

He pretended to be horrified. "No coffee?" he cried, eyes wide.

She grinned. "I'll see what I can do."

As she turned to go, Blackie caught her sleeve. Maybe he didn't want her to go, or maybe he just wanted to see the look on her face when he touched her. When she glanced back, her expression was calm. It was good to see her this way—almost friendly and normal. Conversationally, he asked, "Boys awake?"

Katherine nodded. "All sick. Nobody's hungry but you. Want me to send Peter to help? Might take his mind off his stomach."

The sky was black with roiling clouds, so Blackie shook his head. "Too rough. Maybe later."

Katherine nodded. Then she patted his shoulder like a comrade and said, "Hang in there. I'll bring coffee when it's ready."

She made several trips up on deck that morning, mostly to bring him things. Once he asked her to stand watch while he hurried below to check the course. The cabin was crowded with groaning boys and littered with towels and pots and damp cloths that Katherine had used to take care of them. She had her hands full, he realized. Blackie was glad to get out of the sick-room and back up on deck again.

She wasn't shaken by having been left alone to man the boat. She'd never admit such a weakness, of course. But by the relief in her eyes, he could tell that she was thankful he'd returned so promptly.

Over the noise of the storm, she asked, "How much longer?"

He pantomimed a big shrug. "Can't tell yet. Hours, at least."

"Are we close to a safe island?"

He shook his head. "Better off out here anyway."

"But you're tired!"

She was sincere, he could see. Her blue eyes were worried, and he felt a kerthump inside his chest. Having her on his team was very nice indeed. Blackie shook his head, though. "This isn't bad."

"If we weren't here, you'd be doing this alone."

He nodded, laughing at her. "That's right. This way is much better. Kids throwing up in my cabin and a fickle female to keep me fed. I'm in heaven."

The crack wiped the smile from her face and, back to her old self, she snapped, "Just don't fall over-board, please."

Chagrined, Blackie didn't stop her from leaving that time.

The afternoon was long, but at five o'clock the sky began to lighten once more. Peter went on deck for a while, but he was white-faced and upchucked over the rail. Blackie didn't have the heart to make him work. Nothing was going to help the boy forget his seasick-ness. Harold came next, but he was even worse than

Peter. Later Katherine bundled up Frick and finally Frack in the spare rain gear so that each of the older boys had at least some time on deck.

Finally she went back herself. She squinted at the sky like a pro. "Any better?"

"Much," Blackie shouted back. "It'll be clear by sunset."

She looked unconvinced and turned to him. "Jimmy wants to come up. Can he?"

Blackie thought over the request. Jimmy was not just smaller than the other boys. He was less agile, less coordinated. The youngest boy was so light that in rough weather he was liable to fall overboard like a Styrofoam cup.

Katherine urged, "He's dying to come out with you. And he's been the least sick of any of them."

He studied her face closely. She liked the little Monahan boy. Maybe she liked him a whole lot better than the other kids in her charge. Was it because she was soon going to become his stepmother? Blackie remembered his conversation with Peter about Kate's relationship with Jimmy Monahan's father. He'd almost forgotten that she had a life away from the boat, a love life, at that. Absurdly, Blackie felt an urge to deny her request, to punish the kid for his father's interest in Kate.

Growling, he said, "You like that little runt, don't you?"

With surprise she replied, "I like them all. So do you."

He grunted, feeling surly suddenly, as well as tired. And he didn't want anyone to think he was capable of kindness. It was much better to be thought of as a complete SOB.

"I know you like them," she went on briskly. "Lord knows why you pretend to hate everything. You wouldn't talk to the boys the way you do if you didn't like them. May Jimmy come up or not?"

He scowled. "Might as well suffer through all of 'em. Sure, send him up."

Blithely Katherine turned away without remarking on his anger. How much had she figured out, he wondered?

Soon Jimmy climbed out of the cabin, wearing the much-too-large rain slicker with the sleeves rolled ridiculously around his skinny wrists and Blackie's own New York Yankees baseball hat on his head. Kate must have been hunting through the cupboards. Jimmy's smile was shy, but it was a smile nevertheless. None of the other boys had felt like moving, let alone acting cheerful. At once Blackie felt guilty for wanting to spoil the kid's fun.

He jerked his head. "C'mon, Jimbo. You can help me tack."

Jimmy scampered out into the rain and obeyed Blackie's every command. And the boy soon demonstrated a knowledge of the boat that surprised Blackie. He hadn't realized how much of the sailing lessons the little kid had picked up.

He should have been more careful, of course. He should have watched the boy and cautioned him. But Blackie was bone tired and didn't think.

Jimmy scrambled out onto the bow just at the wrong moment. A rogue wave hissed nearby and crashed over the railing. Jimmy screamed, grabbed a line and fell.

Blackie jumped for him. The kid clung like a monkey to the line and dangled out over the water for a heart-stopping instant. Then Blackie grabbed the slicker in one hand and a handful of Jimmy's hair in the other. He hauled back with every iota of strength he had left, and the two of them crashed onto the deck. Jimmy twisted, clutched Blackie around the neck and hugged. "Daddy!"

Blackie couldn't see a thing. He wrapped one arm around the crying boy. Instinctively, blindly, he swiped his other hand around to get hold of something, anything.

Another wave just then would have swept them both overboard. Headfirst, Blackie slithered helplessly aft, bumping his head and deafened by the storm and Jimmy crying in his ear. "Daddy! Please, please, Daddy!"

Then somebody grabbed Blackie by both shoulders. With that little bit of grounding, Blackie managed to wedge one leg along the cabin and the other against the rail. Katherine seized Jimmy by the scruff of his neck and hauled him loose. Together they tumbled backward onto the deck, safe.

Blackie somersaulted and landed feetfirst on the deck. He bent to help them up. But Katherine stayed on the deck, cradling Jimmy in her arms. The boy sobbed in hard chokes, his face squinched tightly.

Katherine raised her blue eyes to Blackie. "I think he's hurt."

She was right.

Blackie carried the boy below for an immediate examination. It didn't take more than a quick glance to discover that Jimmy had broken his collarbone when he fell.

In the forward cabin Blackie and Katherine looked grimly at each other over the prone and snuffling little boy. Katherine's eyes were direct, full of anxiety and concern. She looked toward him for the verdict, even though she obviously knew the truth herself.

Softly Blackie said, "It's busted for sure, but at least it hasn't punctured the skin." He asked her, "Any ideas?"

Katherine sighed. She perched on the edge of the bunk near the boy and touched his hair. In spite of the loud slap-slap of the ocean on the other side of the hull, her voice was quiet. "I broke the same bone when I was a child. The doctor taped it, put my arm in a sling and gave me aspirin, that's all. I don't think there's anything more we can do for him."

Crouched on one knee beside the bunk, Blackie studied the boy's pinched face. "It probably hurts."

She nodded. "Yes, I remember that part very well."

Blackie had a hard time imagining Kate in pain. She kept everything—emotion, hurt, even pleasure—tightly within herself. Though she'd just saved both their lives, she wasn't ruffled a bit.

A concerned frown lay between her delicate brows, though. She was worried about the boy. Sympathy came easily to her, he saw, when other emotions did not. Gently patting Jimmy's hair, she said, "We'll just have to do our best to keep him comfortable. He can sleep in this bed. It's less likely to jostle his shoulder. I'll start him on aspirin. What can I use for a sling?"

"There's a folding bandage and some tape in the first-aid kit. I'll get it."

In the cabin the older boys were round-eyed and frightened. Blackie decided they all needed to get their minds off pain and accidents. He issued orders succinctly. "Pete, you and Harry take the rain gear and go up on deck. The weather's clearing, but keep an eye out for squalls. Frick, get this place shipshape. Frack, get some coffee on. On the *double*, men!"

The boys moved as if their lives depended on it.

Back in the forward cabin Blackie handed a pair of scissors to Katherine and dug a roll of tape out of the first-aid kit.

She looked at the scissors blankly. "Aren't you going to do it?"

"Tape him?" He returned her startled gaze. "Hell, no. You do it."

"No, no, I can't do anything like this! I might hurt him." Hastily she thrust the scissors back at Blackie.

He pushed her hand away. "*I* might hurt him. You do it."

"I don't want to do it!"

He drew a deep breath and gave her a hard stare. "Kate, neither one of us *wants* to hurt the kid, but I'm a rank amateur at this stuff. Don't make me beg. Take care of it, please."

She bit her lower lip and gazed back at Blackie with wide, helpless eyes, but he was not to be moved. Just the thought of causing little Jimmy any more pain made him blanch, though he wasn't about to admit it. Purposefully he snapped on the reading lamp over Jimmy's head and then cut a length of tape and handed it to her. Katherine accepted the stuff, and after setting her teeth, she began to apply the tape across Jimmy's broken bone to hold it still.

With Blackie working as her nurse, she managed quite well in the end. Her hands were steady, gentle, but firm. Jimmy never whimpered. Blackie didn't know which of the three of them was more relieved when the job was done. He suspected it was himself.

Katherine gave Jimmy one aspirin with a drink of water and tucked him into the bunk with a dry blanket. As she returned the aspirin bottle to its place, she discovered something interesting in the depths of the drawer.

"Perfect!" she exclaimed, lifting out a silver flask and shaking its contents triumphantly.

Blackie had pressed back against the doorjamb to leave. But she grasped a handful of his sweater and pulled. "Sit down," she commanded.

Blackie obeyed her teacher's tone of voice without thinking, sliding into the spot on the bunk beside Jimmy that she had just vacated. Before he knew it, she was pressing a cup of brandy into his hands. Blackie looked into the cup and was surprised to find it nearly full. "Isn't this too much for him?"

"It's not for Jimmy," she replied, standing over him with a no-nonsense look in her eye. "It's for you. Drink it up. You're exhausted. I'll be right back."

No time to object. She left, and Blackie looked down into the liquor. What a temptation. He checked his watch and discovered that he hadn't slept for more than thirty-six hours. A brandy would taste like ambrosia.

It would also put him out like a light. He gazed longingly into the cup, salivating. What the hell.

Risking a sip, he closed his eyes and heard himself groan with pleasure. It tasted better than ambrosia. It was heaven.

"Sir?" Jimmy asked in a small voice. "Are you all right?"

Blackie leaned back against the pillow and opened one eye only. "Fine, kid. Go to sleep."

"But the light's on. I can't sleep with the light on."

Blackie snapped off the overhead light, leaving just the reading lamp to illuminate the small space. He tipped the shade so that it did not shine on the kid's face, then relaxed into the pillow again.

"Thank you, sir."

Blackie grunted affirmatively and took another sip of brandy.

After two minutes the silence was broken again. Jimmy whispered, "I'm sorry I fell, sir."

Blackie couldn't answer right away because he was yawning. In a mumble he replied, "Don't worry about it, kid. Could happen to any of us. Go to sleep before you start getting sore."

Jimmy rustled under the blanket. "May I have a drink of that, sir?"

He did not feel like sharing. Besides, Kate would give him hell. "S'not for kids, kid."

"It's brandy, isn't it? My dad gives me brandy on special occasions."

Well, who was he to argue with parental wisdom? The kid might leave him alone if he went to sleep. Blackie passed the cup to Jimmy, who drank a full inch of the stuff without a gasp. With both eyes open, Blackie took a closer look at the boy. At seven he was a boozer. With a contented smile Jimmy subsided into his blanket once more, sighing. Blackie shook his head and closed his eyes again. Just resting them, of course.

Once nestled down again, Jimmy said, "Sir?"

"Hmph?"

"Will you stay with me for a while?"

Blackie couldn't move if he'd wanted to. He mumbled something back and dimly remembered someone taking the empty brandy cup from his limp hand. Kate, probably. She tucked him in and whispered good-night in a voice that sounded like warm honey. He thought a strand of her freshly washed hair wisped across his forehead as she bent over Jimmy, and he cracked one eye open enough to see her body silhouetted in the lamplight, the too-big shirt billowing around her slim torso like gauze. She had a great figure—slender but not boyish, taut but not hard.

If he'd been strong enough, he'd have reached up and put his hands on her waist, maybe even smoothing them upward to cup her breasts. They were just the right size, one for each palm. But he wasn't strong enough to move, and she drifted out of sight, leaving behind just the mildest fragrance of soap and something else that was uniquely hers.

He didn't remember anything after that—except for long black sleep that changed into a wonderfully erotic dream.

CHAPTER EIGHT

KATHERINE HATED to wake him. Even Blackie's scruffy beard couldn't hide how exhausted he looked. Standing above him, she saw how the harsh lines of his face were softened in sleep. No, Blackie wasn't as tough as he pretended. Asleep, he looked almost gentle. She wished she didn't have to wake him.

And when she tried, it was a major effort to get him back to consciousness. She shook his shoulder and finally, rather than calling to him and risk waking Jimmy, she pressed a cool washcloth to his face until his gray eyes flew open. Blearily, he focused and saw her.

The first words out of his mouth were, "What's wrong?"

"Nothing's wrong," she assured him, swiftly putting her fingertip to her lips to quiet him. Beside Blackie, Jimmy moved restlessly in the bed, but did not wake.

Blackie sat up on one elbow, giving a quiet grunt that signified aching muscles, and glanced at the boy. "He okay?"

"So far, so good, I think. You were both snoring to beat the band."

He didn't respond to her gentle tease with anything approaching a smile. In fact, Blackie avoided her gaze and looked grumpy as a bear roused in January. Katherine decided that she must have interrupted a disturbing dream. Blackie looked quite disgruntled at her presence. His scowl was menacing. It must have been some dream, all right.

He rubbed his hand across his eyes. Voice thick, he asked, "What time is it?"

"Midnight—no, no, don't panic." With both hands laid on his shoulders, Katherine held him down on the bunk. "The boys and I have kept watch just fine. Don't worry about your darling boat. We're wondering about where we are, though. I thought you'd want to check our course."

He nodded, pushed her hands away and swung his long legs to the floor. Katherine saw that his khaki trousers were encrusted with salt and his sweater was stiff, but he noticed nothing amiss. "Right. Let me up."

Katherine didn't give way, but stood firmly in his path. "On one condition."

He glared up at her, squinting against the single feeble light that slanted through the open door from the galley. "What condition?"

"That you promise to come back here and sleep some more."

Blackie gave a short, snorting laugh. "No argument from me. Watch how fast I can do this. Stay here and look after the kid."

He left, shouldering his way out of the small cabin and striding through the cabin to the hatch. In the half-light from the galley, Katherine sat down on the edge of the bunk and touched Jimmy's forehead. Cool. He wasn't running a fever, but shifted in the bed, as if hurting. Katherine dug another aspirin out of the pocket of her shorts and found the cup of water. She roused Jimmy and urged him to take the medicine. The boy barely woke, but obeyed her, then lay down again. After covering him up, Katherine stroked his hair and whispered reassurances until he fell asleep once more.

She sat with Jimmy until she heard Blackie vault down through the hatchway. She adjusted the extra pillow and straightened the blanket, preparing to leave.

He ducked through the doorway in the act of stripping off his sweater. There was no room to squeeze past him to get out of the cabin, so Katherine stayed on the bunk and waited. When Blackie's head emerged from the sweater, his dark hair more tousled than ever, he shot a glance down at Jimmy. "He still all right?"

"Restless," Katherine reported, putting her hand on the child automatically. "I just gave him more aspirin."

"Another slurp of brandy wouldn't hurt."

Katherine jerked her gaze up to Blackie. "Brandy!" she whispered. "On top of aspirin! You didn't make him drink that whole cupful?"

He gave her a disgusted grimace and began to unfasten the buttons at the collar of his cotton, rugby-style shirt. "Hell, no. He asked for a sip, so I gave him one. He likes the stuff. It helped him sleep before. Don't worry, I drank the rest."

Katherine was silent for a moment. She had jumped to the wrong conclusion and should probably apologize. Why was he in such a rotten mood? He'd probably snap her head off if she said she was sorry.

By way of making amends, she asked gruffly, "Would you like another cup?"

Again Blackie's laugh was short. "No, thanks. I'd do my Rip van Winkle imitation for sure." He pulled a green plastic orb out of his trouser pocket and tossed it to Kate. It was an alarm clock. "I've got to get up again before morning. Set that for me, will you? Give me three more hours of sleep."

Frowning, Katherine applied herself to setting the timer on the small clock. Half to herself she said, "I don't know how you manage to sail a boat all by yourself this way. No sleep, only occasional cold food and all that coffee . . ."

"It's not so bad. Usually I don't have to worry about hurt passengers." He turned his back to her and opened a cupboard door. In one easy motion he pulled his shirt over his head and threw it onto the shelf.

He was naked to the waist, and Katherine couldn't help but ogle his bare back. Although Blackie could stand erect in the galley, the ceiling of the forward cabin was slightly lower, and he was forced to stand with his head tilted to one side. He didn't seem to care. The small sleeping area, however, was not intended to house more than two people at the most, and Katherine experienced a breathless instant of claustrophobia. Blackie was so tall and his shoulders so wide that he seemed to take up all the available space.

Blackie was larger than life in more than one sense. Not only was he brawny like Orion the hunter, but his personality seemed almost mythical sometimes, too. He was a big, demanding man, given to raucous humor when it suited him. But there was something else. Besides an occasional glimmer of compassion, she sometimes detected an almost haunted look in his eye. There was gentleness, too. She had not forgotten the way he treated her when she needed help. His foul-mouthed shouts at the boys did not disguise the fact that he was growing to enjoy their companionship. Exactly what kind of man was he?

But the muscle of his back was beautifully con-toured, and his flesh curved so neatly downward that Katherine forgot her claustrophobia and her musings and found herself mesmerized by the place where his back disappeared into the low-riding waistband of his khakis. Oddly enough, an impulse to touch him there, to lay her hand against the golden warmth of his skin, seized her. *Heavens,* she thought, linking her fingers together sternly, *he'd think I've lost my mind.*

Above her Blackie said, "You and the boys did all right out there. We're still on course."

"That's a relief."

He located a towel in the rubble of his cupboard and used it briskly on his hair. "We're running well, in fact. The storm did us a favor. We'll hit the Gilberts in just a couple of days at this rate." Casually he let the towel hang around his neck while he dropped his hands to his pants. Then, without a flicker of mod-esty, he unfastened them, dropped the zipper and proceeded to shuck off his khakis as if he were alone.

Katherine held her breath and stared. To her great relief he stayed in his jockey shorts. Nevertheless, she held herself motionless as a rabbit.

Unconcerned by her presence or that of the sleep-ing child on her other side, Blackie sat down on the edge of the bunk between Katherine and the cup-board. He kicked off his shoes, then finished pulling off his pants and hung them on the hook. From the cupboard he drew a clean pair of socks and his second pair of khaki pants, which he shook out vigorously and examined for crusts of salt. Then he began to dress again.

Any woman would have looked at him, of course. And sitting just six inches away in a cabin she ruefully considered hardly big enough in which to breathe deeply, Katherine told herself she had no choice but to gaze at the male specimen beside her.

Blackie was ruggedly built, not just tall but knit with long, taut muscle. She noticed that the backs of his hands were badly nicked, and one of his wrists was chafed from nylon line. The sun had tanned his back and shoulders, naturally, but his arms were an even darker coppery shade. His hair was probably brownish black, but a summer of sailing had richly tinted it with streaks of burnished mahogany. Across his chest, down his belly and even slightly around the back of his neck, a fine coat of golden-brown hair dusted his skin—crisp looking and rather tantalizing. How might it feel? Even his smell—a sensory combination of saltwater and manly hard work—was strangely enticing to Katherine.

He braced one leg over the other and bent forward to tug on the first of his once-white wool socks. When he assumed that new position, Katherine noticed a long purplish-white line that marred his skin, running lengthwise down his hip and curving around toward the back of his thigh. At a point just behind his kneecap was a second scar, an exact L shape.

Before she could stop herself, Katherine put her hand out and touched his knee. "What's this from?"

He glanced. "Looks like hell, doesn't it? I broke my leg when I was in the service. Still has a steel pin in it."

"You were in the service? You mean the army? Really?"

Having heard real surprise in her voice, he threw a wry grin over his shoulder. "Do I look more like the French foreign legion type?"

"A little, yes," she said honestly. "Wait, I'll bet you were in the navy."

He nodded, finishing with one sock and turning his attention to the other. He rolled it neatly with his thumb and fingers before tugging it onto his foot. "Yep. Two hitches during Vietnam, navigating on an aircraft carrier. Except I broke the leg on leave in Tokyo."

Katherine grinned. "Misbehaving?"

He smiled, too. "How'd you guess?"

"Woman's intuition."

"A woman's intuition broke my leg, too. In a red-light district that still haunts my dreams from time to time. Then I broke the same leg a few years later. That's what really messed it up. I can predict the weather by this leg. Don't need a barometer. How's *your* leg by the way?"

"Oh, it's fine," Katherine said quickly. "Really."

Blackie grunted.

Katherine eased back against the pillow, watching him finish with his clothes. Jimmy stirred beside her, sighing, but she laid a hand on his side, and the boy went back to sleep without a murmur. The sound of the ocean outside the boat was rhythmic and pleasant. In the other cabin she could hear the faint breathing of the other boys. As always the smells of coffee and saltwater mingled in the air, tickling her nose with a kind of familiarity she had come to enjoy. As shipboard nights went, this was peaceful. Even Blackie was so accustomed to the way things had evolved that he could undress within a yard of her without a second thought. *Bobbie McGee* was snug.

Keeping her voice low so as not to disturb Jimmy, she said, "You know, I don't think I've ever lived so closely with anyone as we have with you in the last week or so."

He made an affirmative noise, that was all.

Softly Katherine said, "I don't know a blessed thing about you."

With typical irony he shot back, "Maybe we'd better keep it that way."

"I'm curious," she confessed. "What do you do for a living?"

"For a living?" he repeated, sounding amused as he put a leg through one leg of his pants and then the other.

Katherine grinned at his back. "Why the sarcasm? Are you a fabulously wealthy playboy who spends all his time racing yachts?"

"I used to be a fabulously wealthy playboy," he corrected, standing up to pull on his pants and zip them. Turning to Katherine decently dressed once more, he added, "Now I'm a relatively poor playboy."

He was kidding, she could see. Even though he was tired, Blackie had enough energy to smile. He brushed his hair back by raking his fingers through it and then prepared to climb onto the bunk properly. On hands and knees he said, "I came from a moneyed New En-

gland family, Miss Kate, and I've squandered the
family fortune with my wicked ways."

She was surprised. "Really?"

"Yes, really."

Katherine stared at him uncertainly, not sure what
she should believe. "You were rich and you blew the
money? Come on, you don't strike me as the frivolous sort."

"Oh, no, I'm not frivolous. I spent it on purpose. I
gave it away. I disposed of it sensibly." Blackie lay
down on his back and cradled his head in his hands.
His long frame was relaxed, his hard thigh aligned
with hers. Looking at Katherine, he smiled and added
succinctly, "I didn't want the money."

"Didn't your family object?"

"My family is dead," he said gently. Then, seeing
her automatic recoil, he went on, "There's no need to
apologize. They've been gone a long time. Except for
my younger brother, who is alive and kicking and
amassing an even larger fortune out of his share of the
Lowell legacy."

Katherine felt awkward and ashamed of herself and
tried to regroup. Curiosity was known for killing cats
and embarrassing young women. She should have
known better than to pry into his private life. "I'm
sorry," she said stiffly. "I didn't mean to drag up
anything unpleasant about your family. I apologize."

He shook his head. "You were on the verge of being
human for a minute. Don't go into your Amy Van-
derbilt routine just because things got a little personal, all right? My parents and my sister were killed
back in 1969, so I've had plenty of time to get over it."

"They were killed?" she repeated, half afraid to hear the rest, but unable to stop the question.

He nodded. "In a military coup in South America."

Katherine couldn't help herself. A truly civilized woman would artfully change the subject and move on to safer territory, but she was too intrigued to stop the flow of information yet. She pulled her legs up and hugged them, resting her chin on her knees to watch Blackie. "Tell me," she said.

Simply he tilted his head back, looking at the ceiling and appearing to be emotionally unaffected by the tale. There was just enough light to see his expression, so he kept it calm. "My father was stationed in South America for years while I was growing up. I was educated in Argentina for a while, in fact, and my mother taught school on military bases all over the continent. When Ross and I went Stateside for prep school, my parents moved on to another country—one that wasn't quite so stable. The government collapsed, and they were caught in the wrong place at the wrong time, that's all. Shot cleanly, no torture, thank God. My sister was killed in her bed as she slept, so there was some comfort in that. Still, it was—" He stopped suddenly and finished by saying with his most casual tone, "Well, it's long over."

Although every muscle in his body seemed to be relaxed, Blackie gazed at the ceiling for several moments without expression. Then, as if summing up, he said, "My father was a diplomat."

"A—" Katherine was caught off guard. "With the State Department, you mean?"

"Yes."

Quickly Katherine sat up straight. "Then—why, you had the same kind of childhood as these boys have!"

Blackie's eyes were lazy lidded as he watched her, but he couldn't conceal his smile. "Yes, Kate. I grew up just the way your students are—shuttled from one post to the next and spending most of my time with government-issue teachers like you while my parents made the rounds. I'm sorry to say that my teachers weren't exactly like you particularly, but—"

"Why, you son of a gun!" she exclaimed softly. "*That's* why you're so concerned about their welfare."

"What's that supposed to mean?"

"You've taken them under your wing and—and insisted that I stop babying them. You make them work hard, and you've given them something that's new—an attitude about their place in the world, I guess."

He tipped one eyebrow, amused. "Let's not get melodramatic."

"I'm serious. You've been teaching them all this macho stuff—how to sail and fish and treat each other like men, not sissies, and—"

"I never said they were sissies."

"Well," Katherine said stoutly, "they were until you came along. I can see the difference in them already. Peter, especially. Why, he—"

"Now, Kate," he cautioned gently. "Let's not blow this out of proportion."

She eyed him then, trying to decide whether to ask the question on the tip of her tongue. It escaped by itself. "Were you ever like them?" she asked.

"A sissy, you mean?" He grinned. "Sure, I was, but I'd never admit it in a crowd. Oh, hell, every boy on earth thinks he's inadequate. Most men think so, too, underneath it all. I'd like to see these kids outgrow that stuff as early as possible. They need some self-confidence."

"You're right," she said thoughtfully. "That's exactly what they need."

He closed his eyes and yawned. "They'll get it."

"Thanks to you." Katherine smiled and shook her head in disbelief. "I figured there was something unusual about you."

"Unusual?" He opened one eye suspiciously. "What d'you mean?"

"You see yourself in these boys and want to do something to help them. Why, Mr. Lowell, could you possibly have a soft heart underneath all that armor?"

He snorted. "Don't push your luck, Kate. This isn't going to turn into *True Confessions*."

With a grin she said, "All right, but tell me a little more, at least. I'm dying to hear your life's story. Did you finish prep school?"

"Of course," he shot back, laughing and bristling at the same time. "Do you think I'm some kind of uneducated slob?"

"Occasionally," she replied lightly, taunting him with a smile. "Did you go to college, too?"

He grinned, eyes sparkling. "This will blow your mind. To see the expression on your face, I can't resist just blurting it out. I went to Harvard."

"Good grief!" She abandoned her poise. *"You?"*

He chuckled at her expression. "Sure. Modesty forbids me to point out that I was also named to the dean's list all four years. Graduate school, too, but of course I wouldn't dream of saying so—"

"I don't believe it! What major?"

"Promise not to scream? Art history."

She had to clap her hand over her mouth to stop the scream he'd predicted. Nothing had prepared her for this part of Blackie's background. "Art?" she finally squeaked, laughing. *"Art?"*

"Specializing in primitive stuff—mostly Mayan, Incan, that sort of thing."

"Naturally, after your upbringing in South America."

He nodded. "Now I'm interested in the Far East. There have been some terrific discoveries in the last decade that—"

"Wait, I can't digest this all at once. It's too hard to believe. What do you mean, now? What are you doing?"

"For a living?" he inquired archly. "Besides yacht racing, you mean? I buy and sell things. Not much. Just enough to keep me in sailing canvas and dehydrated eggs, but—"

"You're an art dealer?"

He shrugged and readjusted the pillow so that he could see her easily. "Something like that. I go looking for things, and I buy what I like. Eventually I sell the stuff. To collectors, mostly. Sometimes I get commissions to hunt for certain objects, but I like poking around on my own the most."

"And you don't need money desperately like the rest of us," Katherine teased, "so you can indulge yourself."

"That's it," he agreed, "in a nutshell."

She sat Indian style and cupped her chin in her hands, studying Blackie's face with a new perspective while he talked. There were many things she might have guessed about Blackie Lowell, but this past history was hard to fathom. Indulgently she asked, "How did you get started?"

"Sailing? Or buying stuff?"

"All of it."

He inhaled deeply, puffing out his cheeks, and blew out again. "Oh, I've sailed all my life, but the dealing—I've only been doing it for four or five years now. After graduate school I worked in the real world. You know—house on Long Island, take the train to work in the city, nine to five, weekend gallery openings, all that stuff."

The mental picture of Blackie dressed in a three-piece suit with his Burberry raincoat over his arm while he waited every morning at the train station was amazing. Katherine just couldn't associate his face with the image of a cultured art dealer. "What made you give up the city life?"

"Ah," he said and sat up on one elbow abruptly, reaching for the brandy bottle. "That's another story. For another time."

Roadblock. No entrance.

His expression closed like a trapdoor over a secret chamber. She'd never seen it happen before and she respected it. Blackie reached across the bedclothes to touch Jimmy's forehead, checking for fever, perhaps.

There was no need to do it, but Blackie had wanted to move, to change the conversation before it touched something he preferred to keep well hidden. Katherine saw it at once. The glib pirate had his demons, too, it seemed.

She wanted to question him, but instinct stopped her. No, Blackie would not answer, she was sure. She knew what kind of emotion could change the human face to stone. The next chapter in his story was one he did not intend to tell. At least not yet.

She would obey his wishes, she decided. Sighing, Katherine shook her head. "Well, you certainly bowled me over. I never expected the pirate to have a noble background."

He looked amused again and screwed the cap back on the brandy bottle without taking a drink. "No?"

"Not for a minute. I figured you were probably a drug runner or something. You don't look the least blue-blooded."

He rubbed his chin reflectively. "I'll have to shave soon."

"What's your real name?" she asked suddenly.

"Blackie," he said at once. "I've always been."

"On your birth certificate?" she probed, head tilted.

"Oh, that," he said and looked moderately modest. "For formal occasions I'm John Blackford Lowell."

"John Blackford? Goodness, any numerals after that mouthful?"

He shook his head. "I'm the one and only. My brother is Ross Kirkland Lowell II, though."

"And where's he?"

"The Big Apple. Most of the time, anyway. He does a fair amount of globe-trotting. Half the reason I'm competing in this race is for him."

"What d'you mean?"

"Pointy, my competitor, is one of the senior partners in Ross's firm, a firm that is made up of sailors, not just lawyers. Ross made a boast about *Bobbie McGee*, and Pointy declared that his boat could beat anything afloat. Well, he had recently decided to take a short holiday from the practice of law—he'd lost a case that was pretty important to him, you see. We had determined it was time to find out who had the better boat, and the race got a lot longer than once around Long Island. To uphold the family honor I'm supposed to win."

"What's the prize? Money? Or is that too mundane?"

Blackie laughed. "A little, yes. Just the rush of winning, my dear. That's all."

"And the fun of competing. A trip to China, a voyage-long tryst with your girlfriend plus the pleasure of beating your friend and the excitement of sailing treacherous seas in a small boat. You love it."

He smiled. "I plead guilty."

The man wasn't anything she had thought he was. Well, perhaps she had guessed some of it, but the truths he revealed were hard to swallow. He was a combination of contradictions. Blackie was full of the kind of common sense usually associated with a common man. Though he had endured an expensive education, the experience that was etched in his face had not been attained in a classroom. He was a man of action, not of explanations, Katherine decided, and pampered rich boys didn't act like that.

"Blackie," she said after a moment, "you've been around this world a few times, haven't you?"

"Haven't you?" he countered, just as lightly.

Surprised, Katherine said, "Me? Heavens, no."

He decided to argue with her. "You're working on Pago Pago for the State Department. That's not exactly life in suburbia with 2.2 children, a dog and a station wagon."

"Well," she said, ready to admit her lack of pedigree finally, "I come from humble beginnings."

He smiled slightly, as if he'd known all along that her ladylike demeanor was an act. "Where?"

"Ohio. Shaker Heights, which is a suburb of—"

"Cleveland. I know." He grinned. "No wonder you picked Pago Pago."

She laughed softly and held Blackie's sparkling eyes with her own. "You won't get an argument from me. I hated Ohio, truly, and I decided I didn't want to be like the people I knew there. I bought my way into a Swiss finishing school when I was fifteen, and I haven't been back since."

"What about your family?"

"What about them?"

"They still living?"

"Oh, yes." She stretched out her legs and wiggled her toes. With a cautious sideways look at Blackie, she said, "My father is a junkman."

"A . . . ?"

"Well, they call it the scrap metal business, and he makes a fortune at it, but it's junk, pure and simple. My mother tries to spend the money as fast as he makes it—buying everything with bad taste. She specializes in polyester in loud colors, no kidding. They're very rich and flaunt it more and more every day, I understand."

His eyes were direct but puzzled, his head tilted. "You understand? You don't know?"

She regarded her knees. Carefully Katherine said, "We're ... estranged."

"What the hell does that mean?"

Uncomfortable suddenly, she explained, "It means we don't speak. We don't get along. I left home and never looked back, and they haven't come looking for me, either. Our household was always, well, I guess you could call it tumultuous. Money doesn't always buy class, believe me. I grew up with hot tempers, fistfights among my brothers—I've got three and each one of them is a big Greek thug. I couldn't wait to put all that behind me. So now I'm here. Go ahead and tease me now. Her ladyship isn't a lady at all. Everything I do is a big put-on. I come from a big, tacky family in Cleveland."

"You never speak to them?" he pressed after a silent moment, ignoring his chance to taunt her.

Katherine shook her head. "Not in years."

"And now?"

"Now?" she repeated blankly.

"Are you going to call them when you get back to Pago Pago?"

"Why? They won't know I've been missing."

"I was thinking," he said carefully, "that you might want some support after what's happened to you."

"Oh. That."

Katherine felt her heart suddenly flip-flop inside. For a few hours she'd almost forgotten the events that had taken place before Blackie Lowell sailed into her life. She looked away from him and murmured, "You're referring to what I did."

"Hitting a would-be rapist on the head with a rock? Yes, I think you'd want to get something that traumatic off your chest, especially if you killed him."

Katherine looked down at her hands. No matter what she did, she couldn't forget the circumstances that had landed her aboard *Bobbie McGee*. Her voice quivered. "Oh, I killed the man, all right. I'm almost positive. He seemed very dead to me."

"Assuming that's true," Blackie went on, "wouldn't you like to have someone to help you through—"

Katherine objected swiftly. "Oh, I don't want my family to find out about this! They'd be so horrified and I couldn't face it! Their little girl in such . . . No, I don't want my family to know. I don't need anyone, in fact. I'm fine. Just fine."

Her insistence did not convince him. Blackie snorted. "Don't lie to me," he commanded, tapping his chest. "I'm the one who sleeps on the other side of that door, you know. And I'm not deaf."

Staring at him, Katherine felt her cheeks get hot.

He didn't flicker an eyelash, but continued, "I hear everything. You toss around in here all night. You sleep less than an hour before I hear you cry out like it's happening all over again. The boys have heard it, too, so—"

"Oh, don't!" She covered her face with her hands. "Please, I want to forget what happened."

"Kate," he said and moved up on his elbow again, "nobody expects you to go through that experience and not be affected by it. For God's sake, you're allowed to feel rotten."

"I don't like it," she declared, clenching her teeth. "It's time to put it behind me."

"Who says? Look, you've been playing some kind of role since I first met you—Lady Katherine, the cool, sophisticated woman who doesn't crack under pressure. I've seen you put on the mask. A shark just about took your leg off, and you acted as if you'd been scratched by a thistle. It's admirable, kid, but you can't keep that stiff-upper-lip routine going forever."

"That's the way I am," she said.

"Bull," he retorted. "You'll make yourself crazy. Believe me, trying to forget is just going to make things worse in the long run."

"What do you expect me to do?" she demanded harshly. "Beat my breast and wail until I've let it all out? Sure, isn't that what all those melodramatic Greek families are supposed to do when trouble strikes? I can't do that! It's not my nature anymore to—to—"

"I've seen you cry. You pretend you don't, but—"

"Oh, that's nonsense." She rolled off the bunk, determined to put an end to the discussion. "I hate soul-searching and dwelling on things that can't be helped. I tried to leave that behind. Leave me alone. I'll be fine."

Blackie moved as quickly as a cobra and caught her wrist in his hand. Before Katherine could stand up, he stopped her with a painful grip.

She gasped and twisted instinctively.

He pulled her back onto the bunk, mindful of the boy sleeping on the other side. "Don't run away from this."

"I'm not."

Reasonably he said, "I'm no shrink, but I think I know what's going on here. You're trying to pull yourself back together in record time. Don't do it for my benefit, or for the boys, all right? Not even to prove that you're not like the folks back home. You don't have to be cool as Joan of Arc every minute. That just makes the nightmares worse."

"How do you know?" she challenged, feeling angry.

"Because," said Blackie, letting her go, "I've been there."

When he released her wrist, he did not lie down again. Not teasing any longer, Blackie glanced away from her. In a softer voice he repeated, "I've been there."

Almost afraid to ask, Katherine said, "What does that mean?"

He shrugged and shook his head quickly, as if wishing he could take back the words. "Nothing. No, something, I mean, but— Oh, hell, you're the first person I've ever said this to." Abruptly the explanation came. "I've been in the same place you are now, that's all. I've had the stupid nightmares every night and tried to figure what I did wrong, what I could have done differently, but none of that helped. Only time made a difference, Kate. That's what I've learned."

"Was it something that happened in Vietnam?" Katherine asked, matching the quiet intensity of his voice.

He gave a huff of harsh laughter and threw his head back to stare sightlessly at the ceiling. "Nothing that simple. That I could have coped with, I think. No, Kate, I killed my wife. My wife and my child."

CHAPTER NINE

SHE SAW PAIN IN HIS FACE, and this time he couldn't mask it with a tough remark or cocky laughter. Blackie's eyes were the color of winter ice, and the stubble of his beard did not conceal the tension in his jaw. Even his body—usually fluid and effortlessly relaxed—was taut as a drawn bow after his confession. Katherine reached for both his hands without thinking, only knowing that she wanted to comfort him.

When she had linked her fingers with his, she whispered, "Blackie, I'm sorry."

He twisted under her hands and caught her forearm firmly, almost painfully. "Don't," he warned. "Sympathy at this point makes me furious."

"That kind of anger may be a way of hiding more, well, volatile emotion."

He snorted and pulled away. "Look who's talking."

"All right, all right," she soothed anxiously, "I admit I'm an uptight prig sometimes. But you—Blackie, I never imagined that you carried this kind of pain inside."

He would not look at her. Instead, he sat up and swung his long legs over the edge of the bunk. He wanted to leave.

The intimate exchange had been too much for him. He was going to go up on deck to be alone the way he did every night. Suddenly Katherine understood a hundred things she'd noticed since she'd climbed aboard *Bobbie McGee*. Blackie was in exile. He was punishing himself, perhaps. He was alone by choice. And just as the barrier between them was starting to open, he intended to close it firmly.

Katherine laid her hand on his arm. She couldn't let him leave like this. "Will you tell me about it? What happened?"

"What does it matter? It's over now and—"

She gave his arm a gentle shake and interrupted. "You didn't really kill them, did you? It couldn't have been murder."

Blackie glanced at her over one shoulder. His look was sharp, but sullen. "What makes you so sure?"

She tried to smile, but it didn't quite work. "I know you well enough to guess. Was it an accident of some kind?"

Blackie sighed and bent his head. Finally he said, "Yes."

"A car?"

He nodded, then ran his fingers through his hair. "I was driving," he muttered. With a terrible hollowness in his voice, he continued, "It was eight years ago, on a hell of a night, raining, sleet, ice on the road. I was in a hurry. I should have stopped."

"If the weather was bad—"

"I won't blame the weather," he cut in harshly. Without regard to the sleeping boy nearby, he said, "I won't blame the car, or anything else for that matter. It was my fault. We smashed up on a bridge, went over the abutment and into the water. My wife died on impact, and our daughter . . . she drowned.''

Katherine nearly cried out. She pressed the palms of both her hands against her mouth to hold back the sound. Blackie had had a little girl, a daughter. His voice had changed when he said the word, and Katherine could see how much the child had meant to him. An onrush of emotion hit Katherine as if she'd been hurled against an impenetrable brick wall. What a cruel trick fate had inflicted on the blithe spirit of Blackie Lowell.

"It was a lousy night," he went on, his voice under control once more. Though he didn't look at Katherine, he still addressed her. "We were anxious to get home, so we kept going. I'd driven that stretch of road hundreds of times, of course, and I knew where the bad patches were. I should have known to stop and wait out the storm. I should have—"

"Oh, please," Katherine begged, her voice unsteady. "Don't do this to yourself."

Curtly Blackie said, "It was my fault, Kate."

"It was an accident!"

Challenging her logic, he swung around and demanded, "Judas, is that supposed to be consolation?"

He gripped the edge of the bunk to keep from vaulting up. She could see his knuckles whiten and the muscles in his arms tense, as if Blackie teetered on the verge of a much more violent outburst. There was self-contempt in his gaze, and an anger that would be hard indeed to control, had it not been aimed inward.

Blackie felt guilt as heavy as her own, Katherine realized. There was no way she could talk him out of the way he felt. He'd had too many years of mulling over the circumstances not to understand all the angles, and she would only alienate him by arguing. And the last thing she wanted to do just then was make things worse for Blackie. Katherine looked away from him, toward Jimmy, who slept unawares. She tried to summon outrage at what life had dealt Blackie, but only sorrow and, yes, pity filled her. Afraid to let him see her reaction, she avoided his gaze.

"I'm sorry," he said abruptly, his voice sounding quiet and uncharacteristically intimate in the small cabin. Though they were eighteen inches apart, the distance suddenly seemed much less. So quietly that he might be murmuring in her ear, he said, "Sharing this kind of problem only makes both of us uncomfortable. I shouldn't have snapped at you."

"Don't apologize," Katherine said dully, wishing she had never brought up the subject. Inside her an ache throbbed so powerfully that it felt as if someone were inflicting an injury.

Blackie cleared his throat and moved his hands to his knees. He sat still. Perhaps he counted to ten, for in a moment he sounded almost normal once more. "I suppose the whole point of this nasty business is that I know what you're going through."

She nodded. "Yes, I think you do. Only what you have is worse."

Blackie turned to her. "Don't make this out to be more unpleasant than it is, please," he said. "I've had time to get over it, believe me. A few years of drinking too much followed by some clean living on this boat..."

"Even so, will you ever be over it?" Katherine asked, glancing up.

Blackie met her look and held it. If he had been about to smile reassuringly, the decision to do so evaporated. For a moment they were united in communication, passing unspoken messages on the same wavelength. The air crackled, Katherine was sure, and something queer moved inside her chest—her heart turning over, maybe? Or was it the impact of understanding?

Blackie managed to smile then, lamely perhaps, but it was a smile nevertheless. "No," he said, "I don't honestly think I'll ever be over it. Thank you for not insisting that I should try." With a one-handed gesture that came close to being a caress down her arm, he went on, "You won't forget what you did, either, Kate. But it should get easier to cope with after a while. You'll reach a point of accepting what happened."

"You've accepted what happened to you?"

"That's right. The nightmares don't bother me quite so often anymore. And—" he faltered, then said in a rush, "and I can see a little kid on the street now and not have to—to duck into the nearest phone booth while I pull myself together."

Katherine gulped—only it sounded like a sob, and she had to turn her head away so he wouldn't see how powerfully his admission affected her. Blackie reached and grasped her hand as it lay on the blanket between them.

Squeezing, he managed to convey a steadiness that was comforting. As though he commanded her, Katherine composed herself.

They regarded each other. Blackie didn't blink, and she finally ventured a small, hesitant smile. "Thank you, Blackie."

He frowned slightly, puzzled. "For what?"

"Helping," she explained inadequately. "It can't be easy telling this story, just—just to help me. You've been—you're a good man."

He tried to grin. "You haven't always thought so."

"Maybe not, but, well, gradually I've come to see a side of you that I wasn't sure existed at first."

"Have I been an unspeakable pig, your ladyship?" he teased, his eyes starting to lighten once more, his thumb tracing a circular caress on the inside of her elbow.

"Yes," Katherine replied with no hesitation. "You've been a foulmouthed bully from the moment you crawled up the beach to me, but tonight—" She stopped and tried to think of a way to express what she was feeling. Blackie might laugh, or worse, mock her for her female sentimentalism. Struggling to find the right words, she could only sigh.

Blackie said, "If it makes any difference, my opinions have changed a lot, too, Miss Theodopolis. Ever since the afternoon the sharks nearly got you, if you must know the truth."

"Oh," Katherine began nervously, "that wasn't as bad as you think."

"It wasn't, but it could have been."

She shook her head, smiling. "I'm much too sour even for shark taste buds."

"You're not sour," he countered at once. "You're a beautiful woman, Kate. Not just a pretty face, but good inside, too."

She was startled.

"Don't look so surprised," said Blackie, amused. "I've seen more than you think. You're not the bitch you pretend to be half the time. I just wonder why you hide that goodness all the time?"

Katherine shook her head. She wasn't good. She was bad. She was a murderess. Swallowing the urge to tell him that, she murmured only, "I could ask you the same question, couldn't I?"

A genuine smile appeared then, looking natural on Blackie's sensual mouth. The tension drifted off the planes of his face as though blown by a westerly wind. Still holding her arm, he lay back down on the bunk, watching her face. His eyes flickered, reflecting amusement and something else. "So we're alike?"

"Maybe so."

He nodded once. "In lots of ways."

The caress came then, a delightfully slow brushing along her arm, across her hand, out her fingertips. Katherine moved to prevent him from slipping away completely. Once her own slender hand was firmly enclosed in his, she gripped him hard, not wanting to withdraw. The touch felt too good.

Perhaps Blackie felt the same way. He scanned her eyes, looking for the things she could not say. The intimacy in his gaze was too much suddenly, and the moment faltered, as though hands on a clock had been stopped for an instant. Katherine felt as if she were an open book and Blackie could read her soul as if it were a printed page. Her heart skipped a painful beat.

The message was so clear in his gaze that he might have shouted the words. He wanted to kiss her. Blackie even moved, bending forward, trapping her arm to hold her still. Hovering for an instant, he waited for a sign of assent from her. His eyes were smoky. He wanted her.

Not yet, cried a panicky voice inside her head. Katherine couldn't imagine allowing anyone to touch her mouth yet. Not anyone. The last man to kiss her had left such a horrible imprint that she did not want Blackie to taste what might be left on her lips. It would spoil everything.

So Katherine tried to pull away from him and pretended she had not seen his intention. "I—I should go and let you sleep. You're exhausted and Jimmy is out like a light." Her laughter was weak, a mere shiver of nervous amusement. "It's amazing we haven't awakened him, but of course with the aspirin and the liquor... I'll just go out with the other boys, and you can have the bed for once. It's your bed, after all. I'll just—"

"Kate," he said, holding her hand so she couldn't escape. He understood, she was sure. He knew exactly what her fear was. Coaxing, he said, "Stay with me."

"Stay?" Round-eyed, she protested swiftly, "Here? Oh—"

He was relentless, pulling Katherine until she knelt awkwardly above him, her heart pounding wildly. Blackie shifted, moving back against the wall to make a space for her. "Stay here tonight. You're tired, too."

"I can't possibly—"

"Shut up," he said gently. "You owe me this much. I've bared my soul to you, and we won't be able to look each other in the eye tomorrow if we end things this way. You know that, don't you?"

"Blackie—"

"Don't be so suspicious. It's a perfectly innocent request."

Desperately she began, "But Jimmy's here and there's hardly room enough for—"

"We'll manage somehow. Don't worry. Haven't I demonstrated at least a few scruples when it comes to corrupting minors? You're perfectly safe."

"I *know* I'd be safe, I just—"

"Trust me," he said. "We'll be tiptoeing around each other again if we part company right now."

"Blackie—"

"I'm right, aren't I?"

"Well, maybe, but—"

"Then stay." He looked straight at her, zeroing in on some weaker-willed part of her brain.

She sighed unevenly. Then, even as she lay down, Katherine protested feebly, "I shouldn't be doing this."

He laughed softly.

Katherine turned on her back and looked uncertainly at the man beside her. Blackie lay on his side, head propped on one hand, legs extended. For once, however, his grin was not that of a dastardly pirate. He looked almost trustworthy.

"We really won't be able to look at each other tomorrow, will we?" she asked.

"Not without feeling very embarrassed," he agreed, straight-faced. "Deep dark secrets always affect people that way. So sleep with me tonight and we can be embarrassed about something else instead."

Suppressing the urge to laugh, she said, "That makes sense in some perverted way."

"Good." He reached for the blankets and began to pull them around himself and Katherine, taking care not to disturb Jimmy. Lightly he said, "Good night, Miss Theodopolis."

Katherine rolled onto her side, putting her back toward Blackie, and curled into a ball. He settled behind her in the bed, rustling for comfort, but without coming closer. Then he drew the blankets into place and sighed. The small cabin was silent.

Finally Katherine whispered, "Good night, Blackie."

He didn't answer. Instead, he smoothly wound his arm around her body and drew Katherine back until her bottom was snugly nestled against his hard thigh. His chest warmed her back, and Blackie nuzzled his nose into her hair. He let out a long, satisfied sigh and proceeded to go to sleep.

A full minute later Katherine realized she was light-headed from lack of oxygen, and she drew a ragged breath. Blackie answered it with a husky mumble, but he didn't budge. He slept. He was too exhausted even to tease her.

For a long time Katherine listened to his breathing and imagined that she could also feel the steady thump of Blackie's heartbeat against her shoulder. The darkness enveloped them, and the rhythmic sound of the ocean was lulling. She was glad she had agreed to stay. Tonight was one night she was happy not to spend alone. It was comforting to be held and cuddled. Even Jimmy's presence seemed right.

Though she did not remember falling asleep, Katherine was soon dreaming. Delicious images filled her head and tempted her body. In sleep Katherine allowed herself to give in to the pleasures she usually denied.

BLACKIE QUICKLY QUIETED THE ALARM and dragged himself from the bed in the middle of the night to check the course of *Bobbie McGee*. When he returned to the small cabin, a lovely sight arrested him. The delicate woman who slept in the tumbled blankets looked like a goddess, her hair spilling across the pillow like the black night sea, her skin as milky as moonlight. Even in the meager light thrown from the outer cabin, he could see the pale curve of her cheek, a shine of moisture on her lips, the dusty feathering of her eyelashes. She looked peaceful in sleep, not scared or infuriated or even snooty as a Hapsburg princess. Just sweetly delicate.

The big shirt she wore did not flatter her figure, but it somehow drew Blackie's attention like a magnet. He forgot about how vulnerable she looked. The top two buttons were tantalizingly undone. Damn, she was a beautiful woman. Though not a hint of her breasts showed, a flood of heat filled his loins at the sight of her uncovered skin.

His heart must have been beating like a drum. As if hearing it, Jimmy stirred in the bed beside Kate, then he sighed restlessly and dozed off. In the other cabin the older boys slept soundly, too.

Quietly Blackie slid back into the bed. He gathered Kate close again, loving the feel of her slight body against his. Blowing a dreamy sigh, she snuggled back against him until the sweet curve of her backside rode the one part of his body he could not control. It reacted at once, coming fully erect. She was warm and soft and so soundly asleep that she had no idea what she was doing to him. Blackie felt himself throb simply in answer to her nearness. *So near and yet so far,* he thought, closing his eyes firmly.

But one hot-blooded thought led to another and soon he was wide awake. Blackie wanted nothing more than to take her then and there. The thought of her sleepy smile, perhaps her pliant willingness, only increased his desire. She might not even wake completely before he could sheath himself in her warmth. Surely after tonight she was no longer afraid of him. Surely she would react with passion. Blackie wanted to make love to her, and he was willing to guess that she could be tempted now, too.

But Jimmy lay just inches away. Blackie intended to drive Kate crazy when the time came, and the boy was a definite crimp in an immediate implementation of that plan. Blackie wanted her crying out with abandon, wrestling with him, fighting off the climax until it exploded between the both of them like fireworks. He planned to enjoy her the way men and women were meant to take pleasure in each other. And that wasn't going to happen if a damned kid was in the same bed. Even kids in the *next room* might inhibit things. Kate was definitely the type who needed undivided attention.

No, the time would have to be just right.

With that thought in mind, Blackie tried to concentrate on something else besides the slender woman in his arms. He failed. His body was alert, straining to finish what imagination had started. Grinding his teeth, he felt a sweat stand out on his skin.

What the hell. Without even thinking about what he was doing, he slipped a stealthy hand under the blanket. The shirt buttons parted easily, and Kate did not wake while he accomplished his mission. Finally, cautiously, Blackie's hand sneaked inside the shirt. He nearly groaned when he made contact. Her breast was small, but warm and soft as goose down, fitting his palm perfectly. The flutter of her pulse vibrated against his hand. Cupping her gently, Blackie savored the weight of her rounded flesh.

Kate did not wake. But involuntarily her nipple bloomed against his fingers.

In the darkness Blackie smiled.

It was enough. He put his face against her silky hair and tried again to sleep.

Unfortunately, she woke first in the morning.

She sat up so quickly that Blackie catapulted out of deepest sleep as if he'd been jolted by an electric shock. Dazed, he rolled onto his back.

Katherine's posture was ramrod straight. She clutched the front of her shirt, gasping, then hurriedly began to do up the buttons. She turned to look accusingly down at Blackie with an expression on her face like that of a victimized Victorian lady.

He looked at his hand, which was still warm from her skin. There was no denying that he'd been holding her. In fact, she might have lain awake for a long time before she realized exactly what was going on. Her cheeks were pink, her mouth thinned into an affronted pout. Blackie decided to play innocent and manufactured an abject, guileless look.

"It was an accident," he pleaded, hands upturned beseechingly.

Katherine glared at him. Before she could start a tongue-lashing, though, rescue came in the form of Jimmy. Thankfully for Blackie, the kid chose that moment to wake up. Kate hastily finished buttoning the shirt and turned to the boy, ignoring Blackie pointedly. Her face was on fire.

Jimmy woke up crying, so they didn't have another minute to square things between each other. The boy was hurting, and Katherine immediately fell to tending him. By the sounds of things, the older boys were astir in the outer cabin, so Blackie decided to make his exit before he got his ears boxed. With a final admiring glance down at her bottom as she bent over Jimmy, Blackie sighed and reluctantly slipped past her. Later there would be time to talk.

But the day was busy. While Katherine looked after Jimmy, Blackie and the other boys got *Bobbie* ready for the day. At lunchtime Blackie spread his chart across the table, and the older boys planted their elbows on the edges. Together they confronted the facts.

They were within a day's sail of the Gilbert Islands, where he had promised to drop off his passengers. Blackie described the waters, pointed out the landmarks and described how they would land on one of the islands where he knew the Peace Corps station could help. One call on the radio would alert the people on land that *Bobbie McGee* would be arriving soon. Happily Blackie rolled up the chart.

"If we keep two men on deck around the clock, you can have dinner on land tomorrow night," he announced with a chuckle. "That ought to please all of you. We'll start working in two-hour shifts, all right?"

When he looked around at the faces of the boys, however, he received no snappy, "Yes, sirs."

Letting the chart unroll loosely in his hands, he frowned at each boy in turn. None of them smiled. They stared back at him glumly.

"What's this?" he demanded, puzzled by their change in mood. "You guys getting lazy on me? You want to stay down here and help look after Jimbo or something?"

Peter shook his head. "N-n-no, sir."

"No, sir," Harold mumbled, fingering the binoculars, which were rarely out of his possession. "But we, well, sir, we—"

"We what?" he asked sharply. "You got a complaint about the work load around here, Harry?"

Harold hung his head. "No, sir."

"All right!" Blackie rolled up the chart tightly again with a snap. "This is no pleasure cruise, remember? Everybody pulls his own weight. Two-hour shifts start now. Frick and Frack, you first. I'll be up in a minute."

The twins looked at each other, then got up from the table slowly. With feet dragging, they climbed through the hatchway. Blackie frowned at the two remaining boys. Peter stared at his knees. Harold avoided Blackie's penetrating gaze, too.

Blackie cursed under his breath and got up. What was eating them? He was not going to play cruise director and keep the kids happy every minute.

He worked them hard all day. No way was he going to listen to a bunch of whining kids who suddenly decided they didn't want to work anymore. To keep them occupied Blackie put them through their paces. He was merciless, shouting at them if they made the slightest goof. Frick was near tears because he couldn't keep the tiller exactly in place. After two hours on deck, each shift quickly retired below.

Blackie worked himself into a foul mood, too. Why were the boys turning on him now? At the end of the trip? Had they decided to hate him after all?

To top off the day, Katherine came up on deck once and snubbed him royally. Obviously, she was not going to forgive him for fondling her.

Annoyed at the fickleness of human nature, he skipped dinner and crouched along the rail to make an entry in his journal. He didn't want to be crowded around a table with a bunch of long faces and one up-turned nose. His own words were better company.

To his surprise Katherine appeared on deck about twenty minutes later. He slammed his journal shut and shoved the pencil behind his ear.

"Hello," she said coolly. "I brought you a sandwich."

"Oh." Gruffly he thanked her.

Standoffish, Katherine thrust her hands into the pockets of his rain slicker, which she wore, and stood at the rail with her back to him. Apparently she had no intention of forgetting the episode in bed that morning. Her stiff shoulders told him so. Katherine could harbor a grudge for a long time, it seemed. She was unwilling, however, to leave the deck just yet. Over her shoulder she said brusquely, "I thought you'd be hungry."

Unwrapping the sandwich, he agreed, "I am."

"You were all working pretty hard today."

"Uh-huh."

"The boys are exhausted."

With his mouth full Blackie went to the rail and leaned against it to watch Katherine while he ate his supper. Something interesting was in the wind.

Katherine scuffed her foot along the deck and glanced out at the ocean. "Even Peter is tuckered out."

"Oh?"

"Yes. Harold, too."

"Um-hum." After a swallow Blackie asked, "Is this stilted conversation leading somewhere?"

"No," she said hastily, sending a knife-sharp glance upward before directing her attention to the waves again. "No, of course not. I just—I was making idle conversation, that's all."

"Uh-huh. How's Jimmy?"

"Okay." She shrugged. "He's aching, but not too badly. He's depressed mostly."

Chewing, Blackie looked at her. She could not meet his eyes and appeared to be concentrating rather fiercely on the colors that the setting sun beamed across the water. He swallowed again and repeated, "Depressed?"

She nodded, face averted. "They all are."

Blackie forgot about his sandwich and frowned. "Depressed about what?"

Katherine took a deep breath. She kept her head turned toward the wind, her black hair whipping the smooth planes of her face. "They don't want the trip to be over."

"What?"

"You heard me!" she snapped, impatient suddenly. She faced him, quivering with pent-up energy.

"They're having the time of their lives! They've enjoyed this sailing business more than anything else they've ever done. Naturally, they don't want it to be over. I don't understand how you could have missed the signs."

"I've been distracted lately," he retorted sarcastically, bowled over by her information. "You mean they *like* this?"

"Of course they do!" Her eyes flashed with fire, and her face was suffused with adrenaline-induced color. "They love all of it—the work, the adventure, the excitement and especially being with you. Now you're dumping us all off with the Peace Corps and appear to be happy about getting rid of us."

"I thought they'd be happy about it."

"Well, of course they're not."

"For crying out loud, what do they expect?" Blackie cried, "I'm in a race! Do they want to sail the whole way to *China*?"

Katherine took a big breath. "Yes," she said.

Blackie stared.

"I know I have no business asking," she said rapidly, shaking her head. "It's very rude, not to mention inconvenient, no doubt, so I won't plead with you. I only thought that, well, since you haven't got a crew and you do still want to win this race, you might consider keeping us on while—well, until Guam, at least—"

"Hold it." Blackie dropped his sandwich on the stern seat and put a hand on her arm to pull Katherine around to face him. "You mean that you don't want them rescued now?"

When she glanced at his hand on her arm, her cheeks flushed. She tugged out of his grip. "Well, for heaven's sake, they're safe enough already," she began, her voice querulous. "It's not as though *all* of us need to be rescued from you. And the islands where we're supposed to go are quite wild, aren't they? We might be stranded there for a while until a plane could come, and—"

"I'm sure American diplomats would see that a plane was sent for their kids immediately."

"Oh, probably, yes." Stubbornly Katherine argued, "But they could be easily convinced that a voyage of this nature is safe—not to mention educational. I'll talk to all of them myself." Voice rising, she said, "The boys are so disappointed now! If you would just take a minute to speak with them, you'd see that they really want—"

"What about Jimmy?" he interrupted.

"What about him?"

"He's hurt. He needs a doctor. And you were bitten by a shark, remember?"

"It was only a scratch, and Jimmy just bumped himself. Neither of us is in terrible pain. He'll heal just fine—"

"Bumped himself, you say? Woman, he broke the damned thing!"

"It will *heal*!" Kate insisted. "Besides, he wants to stay as much as the rest of them. He's down there practicing a speech to give to you, hoping you'll let them stay. He thinks it's his fault that you're dumping them."

"I am not dumping them."

"*They* think you are."

"What about you? Do you want to stick around?"

"Me?" She stared up at him and swallowed hard. Her voice wavered. "W-well," she began bravely, "I'll stay with the boys, of course. I'm their teacher. I have a duty—"

"Oh, so you're offering to make a big dutiful sacrifice and stay with your students, right? You couldn't possibly want to stay, too, your ladyship?"

Katherine shoved her hands even deeper into the pockets and sullenly did not answer the question. She eyed him sternly. "I am not about to let this discussion turn into an exchange of personal opinions."

Blackie put one forefinger under her chin and tilted her face until the light of the sunset touched her eyes. He could learn a lot by the signals in her eyes, and he didn't want to miss a single one. Directly he said, "I asked you a question, your ladyship. Do you want to stay or jump ship?"

She tried not to look at him directly; she did not want to slip into intimate territory and so gathered herself together with a herculean effort. Loftily she said, "I—I'll stay with the boys wherever they go."

He shook his head slowly. "Drop the stuck-up teacher routine, Katie. Tell me the truth. After last night are we back to circling like wary tomcats? You're as cold as a Popsicle again."

"No," she said stoutly. "Last night has nothing to do with my acting like a Popsicle today. I—I enjoyed last night, as a matter of fact. You were, well, this morning changed my thinking, that's all. You took liberties, Mr. Lowell."

"Took—" He dropped his hand and exploded, "Judas, Kate, get out of the nineteenth century! I can't help what happens when we're both sound asleep. It was a blasted *accident*!''

"It was *not* an accident!" she accused. "You unbuttoned my shirt."

Ridiculously, he exclaimed, "It's *my* shirt, dammit!"

"While I'm wearing it, I'd appreciate your keeping your sticky fingers off it, thank you!"

Blackie choked. "God's teeth, woman, how do you expect a man to keep his unconscious mind under control when all you've got to wear is one see-through shirt and a pair of shorts that show nearly every inch of your—"

"You cannot see through this shirt!"

"I can see well enough to know you don't always wear a bra."

"I've only got one," she cried in defense. "I have to wash it out once in a while."

"Terrific!" Blackie laughed harshly. "Are you going to survive another couple of weeks with just one bra?"

"Are you?" she challenged sarcastically, arms akimbo.

"I don't know," he growled. "It's damned difficult sometimes."

"What is?"

"Keeping my hands off you, of course!"

Katherine clapped her hands over her ears and spun away. "Oh, my heavens!" she shouted at the sky, furious. "You're such a—a—an unspeakable *pig* sometimes!"

"So sue me!" he bellowed back, following her. "I can't help it, Kate. You're beautiful and once in a while you thaw out and show me what you're really like. Last night I wanted you more than I've wanted any woman since I was sixteen because I thought you were...intelligent and sensitive. You've been troubled and upset about what happened back there, that's all, and now you're getting back to normal. You're a woman and it's stupid to pretend you're a block of wood. Last night I managed—just barely—to keep myself from jumping you like a randy boar because I care about your state of mind. I think I deserve a little credit for stopping myself, even if I did slip up just a little and touch you—''

She whirled around and pointed one accusatory finger at his nose. "So you admit you deliberately unbuttoned my shirt?''

Blackie blew up. "Oh, for God's sake! Hold it against me, if you like. That's just about par for the Queen of Icebergs! Do you want to slap me for it? That's what you highbrow ladies do when you're offended, isn't it? Here! Do it! Hit me! I hope it makes you feel better.''

He stuck his face down where she could reach it perfectly and braced himself for the blow. Katherine seethed. She drew back and let fly, only she missed.

She grabbed the collar of his shirt instead. Teeth clenched, she snapped, "You're such an idiot sometimes!''

And then she kissed him.

It was quick and hard and too rough at first, but then she applied herself, and Blackie forgot about being angry. She was scared and excited and had boiled over like hot soup. He grasped her shoulders and held her, drawing Katherine closer until their bodies were aligned. She didn't fight, but melted into his frame as easily as if she'd done it for years. She slipped her hands around his neck, hesitantly at first, then with poise thrown aside. Gingerly she arched her back, pressing those luscious little breasts into his chest.

A queer shudder shot down through Blackie, startling him. An answering tremor shivered in Katherine, too; he could feel it. She was excited, as charged with tension as he was. He curled his hand into her hair, half to steady her, half to hold her firmly against himself, prolonging the pleasure. His brain clouded. Desire flashed through him like the final, dazzling rays of the setting sun. It was longing so keen that he groaned aloud.

At the sound Katherine's mouth trembled once, a sure sign that her courage was failing.

Blackie relented, but it was Katherine who finally broke the kiss. It had been hers to start. She was in charge.

"There," she breathed, her lips only centimeters from his. "That's how messed up I am right now. I want to crack you across the face, and I end up kissing you. I must be crazy."

"Crazy ain't all bad, lady."

She started to giggle, and he laughed unsteadily, holding her elbows so that their foreheads bumped. Like teenagers they were suddenly shy. Then Blackie brushed her lips once more, teasing, testing. One kiss only made him want more. Katherine made a sound at the back of her throat and parted her lips, accepting him. He pressed deeper.

It was better the second time, for they both explored and enjoyed, surrendering to an instinct more powerful than either could control. Blackie savored her mouth, her taste, her scent, drinking in every nuance of the woman who had tormented him for what seemed like years. Delighted, he found that she was skilled, eager to discover and elicit sensations at the same time. Katherine smoothed her hand up his chest until his breath locked, and he had to tear his lips from hers to gasp a ragged breath. Growling, he sought her throat impatiently, aroused. He pressed one nibbling kiss after another down the tender flesh of her throat, finding the warm spot where her pulse tripped like the wings of a butterfly. Her knees must have weakened, for she caught his shoulders tightly.

Blackie eased back. At any moment the sun would disappear, and he would not be able to see her eyes anymore. Now he wanted to know her thoughts, to understand what she was thinking. He held her off and looked into her face. Languidly Katherine blinked, and her mouth curved into a half smile, a little afraid, a little encouraging. Vulnerable, she was, but sexy, too. At the sight of her, there was an explosion inside Blackie. He felt it as surely as he felt the deck move beneath his feet. What kind of woman did that to a man?

With his thumb he smoothed her cheek, as if testing the delicate quality of her skin. Her softness had always been well hidden. Half of Blackie wanted to let her go on protecting that quality. The other half wanted to make use of her unsteadiness.

She spoke first. Whispering, Katherine said, "You look like there's a war going on inside your head."

He smiled and loosened his hold. "Can you tell which side is winning?"

Katherine slid out of his arms. "Yes. The good side. Good night, Blackie."

She did not want to talk anymore, it was clear. She slipped away. With one backward look over her shoulder and a gimlet-eyed smile, Katherine disappeared down the hatchway.

Blackie gripped the rail to keep himself from chasing after her. It would do no good. The cabin was full of curious little boys, and the chances of making love to her under such circumstances were slim to none.

With an infuriated groan Blackie spun around and stared at the darkening sky. What the hell was going on? Why was his desire for her more intense with every passing hour? And why was it that her brain seemed to make her more and more appealing?

Could he be falling in love? After all these years and all the pain he'd been through? He shook his head. No, no. Surely not. Blackie Lowell would never love another woman in his life.

But that didn't mean he couldn't have her body. And Kate, oddly enough, did not seem so dead set against such a suggestion anymore.

There had to be a way of getting a few hours alone with her. Without boys. With nothing but each other. Maybe if they made love, he'd know for sure.

Yep, Blackie decided. He had to find a way.

CHAPTER TEN

FEELING POSITIVELY Machiavellian, Blackie set out to arrange a seduction.

The boys, overjoyed at receiving a reprieve, did not take notice of his subterfuge. They were delighted to be allowed to continue the voyage. Poor Katherine had spent half a day cajoling worried parents. Finally she turned the microphone over to him to make arrangements for a rendezvous on Guam. When everything was finished, Blackie suggested a party to the boys.

"A party?" Harold inquired, pert as ever behind his thick glasses. "What kind of party, sir?"

"It's a tradition among sailors, Harry, my boy," he explained heartily. "When a sailor crosses the equator for the first time, he has to go through a, well, a kind of initiation."

Peter, more experienced in life, repeated, "A-a-an initiation?"

"Sure." With all the boys gathered at his feet, spellbound and eager to please, Blackie worked at splicing a line and held court. "In the days of pirates, crossing the equator was an event worth celebrating. They used to keelhaul and drink rum, dress in drag and generally misbehave, but we'll tone things down a little, considering we've got a female aboard."

All the boys nodded wisely.

Jimmy, his arm bound in a sling, asked in puzzlement, "How do you dress a drag, sir?"

"Uh, never mind," said Blackie. "The important thing is to plan the festivities. Shall we surprise Kate, men?"

"Oh, yes, sir!" they chorused.

"Excellent," said Blackie, all smiles.

KATHERINE SUSPECTED something was afoot. The boys skulked around the boat, alternately looking angelic or devilish, and it wasn't hard to guess that they were planning something. Since practical jokes abounded, she prepared herself for the worst, but didn't interfere. Harmless fun for the boys, no doubt. Their spirits were high, and that was all that mattered.

After having spoken with all the parents personally by radio, Katherine was doubly aware of her role as teacher and surrogate parent. Not only was she charged with overseeing their education, but she was responsible for their happiness, too. Cavorting with Blackie seemed to make them happiest, she had to admit, so she allowed them to spend as much of their time in his company as they pleased.

As for herself, Katherine was half afraid to be around him.

Not that he was dangerous. On the contrary, he behaved like a perfect gentleman most of the time. He teased her, of course, and laughed with her as before. She wasn't sure of herself anymore, that was all. There were times in his presence when urges sneaked up on her—urges she never remembered experiencing before—and they were disconcerting.

She needed time to sort out her feelings on the subject of Blackie Lowell. Something exciting existed between them, but she wasn't sure what. Was it love? Or some kind of temporary fascination brought on by the fact that they were two adults alone together for an extended period of time in very close quarters? Was Blackie interested in her by virtue of her being the only reasonably attractive female for hundreds of miles?

In addition to being unsettling, his attention was flattering. Blackie watched her. He went out of his way to look after her. He found excuses to be alone with her, even if it meant helping with the dinner dishes or checking the tape binding Jimmy's broken bone. And if he wasn't at Katherine's side, he was on her mind. It was unnerving to be so totally consumed by another person. Was he also daydreaming about her in what few private moments he had?

Thankfully, she had plenty of time to think things over before anything explosive took place. After all, with the boys underfoot constantly nothing dangerous could possibly happen.

On the second night after they passed the Gilbert Islands heading for Guam, Peter came down to the galley where Katherine was puttering with the beginnings of their evening meal.

"Hi," Katherine said to him, tousling the boy's hair as he slouched against the counter. Could it be possible for him to have grown in just a couple of weeks' time? He was bigger, she would swear. She also noticed that he was stuttering less and could look her in the eye when he spoke.

But tonight he sighed wearily. "Hi."

"What's up? You sound exhausted."

"I am. We all are. Blackie says we should come down and rest. He says you should take a t-t-turn at the watch."

Katherine dried her hands on a tea towel, noting that Peter had started to address their illustrious captain by his first name. He was the only boy to start that familiarity so far. "Oh, Blackie does, does he? Can you handle dinner if I go?"

Peter glanced at the stove. "Hamburgers? Sure. Tell me what to do."

While Katherine showed Peter how to cook the meat, the rest of the boys came thumping into the cabin. There were groans and sighs all around, and Katherine's alert ear told her that they were all faking. She pulled one of Blackie's sweaters over her head and, while rolling the sleeves up to her elbows, she regarded the actors. "You fellows look as though you've been through the wringer."

They all groaned and nodded, draping themselves melodramatically on the benches.

"Oh, yes, Miss Theodopolis," Harold mumbled, yawning. "The captain worked us so hard we can hardly stand up."

Wryly she said, "Well, there won't be any dinner if you don't pull yourselves together. I'm going up on deck."

Together they said, "Yes, ma'am, Miss Theodopolis."

Suspicious but willing to play along, Katherine went up on deck.

Blackie was at the tiller, his hair windblown, his jacket flapping around his otherwise bare chest. Captain Blood could not have looked so stunning at the wheel of his ship.

Katherine crossed the small deck to him. "What's going on?"

"Going on?"

"You know what I mean. Is this the Lowell School of Dramatic Arts now?"

He grinned. "Did they overplay it?"

"Terribly. What have you instigated?"

"Wait and see," he promised, taking a moment to slip the collar of her shirt out from under the sweater. Gently he smoothed it around her neck, and Katherine held still under his hand. He said, "They've been planning this since yesterday morning, so give them a big reaction."

"You know I will, whatever it is."

"Yes," said Blackie, looking down into her eyes, a smile playing on his mouth. "You're very good to these boys. You like them a lot, don't you?"

"It didn't start out that way," she admitted, slipping out of his range to lean against the stern rail behind him. "But during the last few months I've gotten pretty fond of all of them."

"Not just Jimmy?"

She looked up. "Of course not. What brought that question on?"

He shrugged, turning his attention to the tiller once more. "Nothing. I—It was something Peter said a while back. Something about you taking the place of Jimbo's mother."

"Oh, that." Katherine put her hands into the pockets of her shorts and hunched her shoulders against the wind as the boat came around on the tack.

She understood what he was asking. Blackie's question was a natural one, she supposed, but that didn't make it easy to answer. She said, "Jimmy's parents are divorced, though they both live on Pago Pago most of the time. His father wants custody of the boy, but the mother is fighting, since Stephen intends to take Jimmy to Guam. It's an ugly situation."

"Stephen," Blackie repeated.

"Yes, well," she said uncomfortably, "I am acquainted with Jimmy's father. We've been friends."

"Just friends?" Blackie asked, putting his face to the wind.

"Good friends," she corrected, with a glance at his profile. "His family situation is too unsettled for our relationship to be anything else."

"Uh-huh," said Blackie, as if not quite convinced.

Katherine grinned. In a rather quaint way he was asking if she were attached to another man. She decided to let him stew about it for a while. Brightly she said, "Jimmy's become very fond of you, I must say. His own father is going to seem pretty dull after this trip."

Blackie glanced at her, and his eyes were direct. "To Jimmy? Or to you, too?"

Feeling like a fool, Katherine blushed.

Blackie put his head back and laughed. "Here," he said when he had pulled himself together. "Hold the tiller. I'll go take in the sail."

Doing as she was commanded, Katherine called, "Why? Are we stopping tonight?"

Blackie was already climbing onto the foredeck. "Yep. For a while at least. It's all part of the plan."

To herself Katherine muttered, "What plan?"

The answer soon came. A whoop sounded from below, a harmonica started to wail and the hatchway was flung open. All five boys boiled up onto the deck dressed in ragtag togas, their faces once again painted with the improvised sunscreen.

The first two grabbed Katherine and quickly tied a rope around her wrists. "You are a prisoner of the gods," growled Harold. "Sit!"

Laughing, Katherine played along. "Oh, help! Savages! Help me, help me!"

Blackie vaulted down onto the deck to the rescue, but he was also captured and bound. Together they were thrust onto the bench at the stern. Harold stood before them, half voodoo medicine man and half dashing warrior straight out of Greek mythology. He waved his finger in their faces. "You belong to us now! Let us celebrate!"

All the boys yelped and sang, dancing around a make-believe campfire and brandishing their weapons—mostly wooden spoons from the galley. Katherine laughed as she watched, and Blackie made himself comfortable beside her, calling encouragement to the boys.

At last Peter ducked into the cabin and came out bearing a tray. In lieu of roasted pig, there were hamburgers and carrot sticks, nuts and apples. Peter bowed low and laid the tray at Katherine's feet. "For the goddess."

Graciously Katherine accepted a carrot stick and then implored, "Please share this feast with me, fierce warriors."

The rest of the boys fell on the food ravenously while Harold took on the role of emcee. "Good evening, lady and gentlemen," he intoned, doing a fair impression of Johnny Carson. "Tonight's show is going to be a corker. We start off the entertainment with a song from the band." He swung the invisible golf club and turned the program over to Frick and Frack.

While everyone else started on the picnic supper, the twins stood up and played a bluesy version of "Home on the Range." They had learned a lot from listening to Blackie's recordings, and they played beautifully. Katherine and Blackie applauded vigorously when the music was over.

"And now a commercial," Harold said.

Jimmy and Peter mugged their way through a commercial for freeze-dried vegetables, the one food both of them had to be coerced into eating at every meal. It was a funny skit, with Peter pretending to be Blackie, who threatened poor Jimmy with dire punishments if he didn't finish his veggies. Everyone laughed, including the actors.

When she had finished her hamburger, Katherine sat back on the seat and relaxed, preparing to enjoy the evening completely. She hardly noticed when Blackie slid his arm across her shoulder.

"Next," said Harold, still trying to be Johnny Carson, "we'll have an interview with Miss Katherine Theodopolis, lately back from a hazardous voyage across the South Seas. Please welcome Miss Theodopolis!"

Frack, dressed in khaki shorts and a white shirt tied in a knot at the midriff, made a hip-swinging entrance from the hatchway. The boys hooted at his imitation of their teacher, and Blackie chuckled heartily, too. Even Katherine had to laugh at Frack's antics, for he batted his eyelashes at Harold and told stories about how exceptional her pupils were.

"Oh, they're all wonderful," he said in a high-pitched voice. "Straight-A students, charming personalities, never a bit of trouble!"

"And now," Harold said when the mock interview was over, "a film clip of a movie soon to be released in theaters near you!"

The skit consisted of Frack, still dressed as Katherine, and Peter, who imitated Blackie as best he could.

"I beg your pardon," Frack said, managing to combine the fake feminine voice with a stuffy accent, "but are you quite all right, sir?"

Peter, pretending to throw up rather graphically, shouted, "No, I'm not all right, your ladyship! I n-n-nearly drowned!"

"In two inches of water?" Frack asked archly, mincing around the deck. "My dear Captain Lowell, did you know you have a shark chewing on your foot? Or are your other extremities as numb as your brain?"

The humor was pure silliness and the acting atrocious, but the boys had a hilarious time, and Katherine found herself rocking with laughter, hugging her ribs that ached more and more with each passing moment. Blackie laughed so hard he had to wipe his eyes finally. The boys delighted in the merrymaking, poking fun at each other and taking the returning barbs without offense. The show closed with the boys standing up in a chorus line complete with high kicks and a song they had composed to the tune of "High Hopes."

Once there was a little old boat
Captained by a big fat dope—

"Hey!" Blackie protested.

When he saw the beach—Eeek!
He-e rescued the teach!
And we have hi-igh hopes,
We have hi-igh hopes
That he won't leave us high and dry-y, folks!
So when you see us comin',
You'd better start runnin'
Cause when we get home we'll know!
Everything he ever taught us, oh,
Everything he ever taught us, oh,
Everything he ever taught us, oh yeah!

Katherine applauded and Blackie clapped and whistled, and the boys milled around looking pleased with themselves. It was a splendid party, and even the setting sun did not signal an end to the revelry. In fact, the party seemed to be just getting under way.

Blackie went below and returned with two bottles of wine.

"Where on earth did you get those?" Katherine demanded, catching sight of the bottles he carried aloft.

"I brought them from New York," he explained blithely, tucking one under his arm and prying the wrapper from around the neck of the other. "I've been saving them."

"You don't intend to give any wine to the boys, do you?"

"I certainly do."

"Blackie!"

Immediately the boys were dancing around her, drowning all her protests with their pleas. "Oh, please, Miss Theodopolis! Please, please! We'll just take a taste, we promise! Please, please! Let us have some wine! It's a special occasion!"

"Absolutely not. Under no circumstances will I allow any of you to—Blackie, put that cork back in at once!"

"Too late," he announced in triumph. "We'll have to drink it. Come on, men, who's first? You, Jimbo?"

In vain Katherine objected again. "This is terrible! These are children! You can't—"

"Put a sock in it," Blackie said pleasantly. "They're just going to try it. Knowing these guys, they won't like it anyway. If they were left alone, they'd choose to live on peanut butter and Kool-Aid. You and I will probably have to drink both bottles ourselves."

"Don't you dare open the other bottle!"

He was oblivious to her voice, and Katherine eventually gave up in a snit. When everyone had a cup of wine, Blackie handed one to her, too, and Katherine accepted it with a glower.

"Cheer up," he ordered, winking. "This is a party, remember? Let's have a toast, gentlemen."

The boys, all offspring of seasoned diplomats, knew all about toasts, so they lifted their glasses to the night sky and chorused, "A toast!"

Blackie raised his wine also. "To a safe and speedy voyage!"

The boys repeated the phrase and drank their wine. All of them took a good taste of it and managed to suppress shudders of distaste. In fact, they were all sparkly eyed and flushed of face, eager to drink some more.

Harold, definitely in the spirit of the evening, lifted his cup again. "To the best captain on the high seas!"

"Here, here," Blackie cheerfully agreed and drank.

"To the b-b-best teacher we ever had," Peter cried, causing everyone to take more gulps from their cups.

Blackie started around the circle with the bottle, plying the boys with refills. "Yes, indeed, men, this has been an exciting voyage! Let me propose a toast to the best crew I've ever had the pleasure of commanding."

"And to the best boat!" Jimmy sang out.

"And the best weather," Frack added.

"And the best fun," Frick suggested.

Before long Katherine gave up trying to stop them. It was useless. Blackie opened the second bottle and passed it around the circle. Each boy poured a healthy slug into his own cup until Katherine intercepted the bottle and hid it under a blanket. Nobody noticed. They were all getting drunk, she realized.

They sang, they told ghost stories. They drank themselves silly and then began to get sleepy.

"Help me put them to bed, Kate," Blackie said when the moon had risen and the frantic pace of the party had slowed to a bleary crawl. "I think they're about to fall asleep in their cups."

He was right. Katherine carried Jimmy to bed, and Blackie supervised the older boys. When they were all bedded down, tucked in and wished good-night, Katherine met Blackie at the hatchway.

"They're asleep already," she said in wonder, listening to the snores that issued from the slumbering boys. "I don't believe it. I thought they'd all be sick."

"Sick?" Blackie objected, voice subdued. "These guys? You've got to be kidding." He took her elbow. "Come on."

"Where?"

"Come on," he urged again, a sly grin on his mouth, "we've got half a bottle of wine to finish."

HIS PLAN could not have gone better. Practically rubbing his hands together with glee, Blackie pulled Kate back up onto the deck where they were going to be alone—he was sure—for the rest of the night. The kids were so drunk they would undoubtedly sleep until noon. Chuckling at the success of his plan, he led Kate to the bench at the stern. The blanket was in place, just as he'd arranged. The moon was high, the night air cool, but not so cold that it would chill any sexual fires.

"Here," he said, picking up the wine bottle from where she had stashed it under the blanket. "How about a nightcap?"

"A nightcap?" she repeated. Warily she tried to hang back.

Blackie pulled her steadily along, high spirits abounding. "Yes, a nightcap. Ever heard of the custom? It's a drink, a sort of good-night libation, a custom in certain parts of the civilized world."

"Like in bachelor apartments?"

"Tch, tch. Kate, you have a suspicious mind." He turned and looked down at her, then couldn't resist a caress along her cheek. "A nightcap is a perfectly in-nocent drink."

"Innocence does not become you," she replied sternly. Her eyes were full of moonlight, though, and her face, upturned to his, looked far from angry. In fact, a smile lurked at the corners of her luscious mouth. What wonders a gentle caress could do when properly executed. She said, "I've never known a man so thoroughly un-innocent until now. You planned this, didn't you?"

He decided to come clean. That might work, too. Smoothing a stray wisp of black hair from her fore-head, he admitted, "Yes. Every last detail. Be-cause—" he paused for effect "—I wanted to be alone with you."

Katherine smiled, but she began to pull out of his arms. "That's flattering, I must say, but please don't get the idea that I have any intention of—of, well, of—"

He followed, catching her hand and teasing, "Of what, Katie?"

"Of having a nightcap, as you call it."

"It's only a drink."

"It is not," she said, trying to be haughty, "and you know it. That word is a euphemism. It means . . ."

When she faltered, he kissed her forehead, just a feathery brush of lips to skin calculated to make women weak-kneed. Diverted, she forgot her train of thought. Indulgently he murmured, "What does it mean?"

She drew an unsteady breath, but didn't push out of his embrace. Instead, she rested her hands along his upper arms. "It—it's come to mean something entirely different, and you know it perfectly well."

"Tell me anyway, Miss Theodopolis." Cradling her easily, loving the feel of her slender body against his, he said, "Think of me as one of your students for a moment. Exactly what *is* a nightcap these days?"

"It's a—" She wavered for only an instant, and that was because Blackie began to nose along her hairline, playfully touching his lips to her skin. Finally she said, "It's a word that implies seduction."

"Seduction!" He couldn't stop a chuckle. "Kate, I assure you that nothing could be further from my mind."

"No?" she asked archly. "Is that why you're holding me like this? And putting little kisses all over my neck?"

"Was I doing that?" he asked, hardly taking his lips from her skin to speak. "Hmm, I'm getting things backward then, aren't I? The drink comes first."

"This—this is making me nervous, Blackie."

"What is? Sitting under the stars and talking with me?"

"We're not sitting. In a minute we won't even be talking."

"Technicalities," he whispered. But she pushed out of his embrace, and Blackie let her go without a battle. He had known it wasn't going to be easy. "What's the matter?" he asked lightly, teasing. "You'll sleep with me in that cramped bunk below, but you won't stay out here for a while? What's the matter? Afraid of me now, Kate?"

"Of course not," she retorted, flustered. There was not enough room on the deck to pace, so she meandered in a small, nervous circle. "I'm just—I don't want you to get carried away, that's all."

"Me? Get carried away?"

"Yes, you," Katherine declared. She stopped circling and faced him. "And me," she admitted. "I don't want to get carried away, either."

"Good grief, could *you* possibly get carried away, Miss Theodopolis? You? I don't believe it!" He folded his arms across his chest and grinned. "What's so different about tonight that you're worried about getting carried away?"

"I'm alone with you!" she burst out. "And all this talk about nightcaps makes me— Oh, I just don't have the boys to run interference, that's all! Without them I'm afraid of what you'll make me do."

That stopped him. There were times to tease and times to be honest.

"Kate," Blackie said softly, suddenly serious. "I won't make you do a single thing against your will. You know that by now, surely."

She turned away shyly. "Yes," she whispered. "I do." In a moment she spoke again, this time so quietly that he could hardly hear her above the sound of the ocean. "Blackie, you're a very desirable man. And I like you for your other—for the rest of you, too. But after what happened back on that island before you showed up, I'm bothered by situations like this. The murder was the worst, of course. But what came before, when he forced me—"

"Kate," he coaxed. "That wasn't anything like what's happening between us. That was violence, pure and simple. This is—"

"It's what?" she asked, facing him, her expression puzzled, but open and trusting. It was a look that made Blackie's heart thump suddenly once. She asked, "Exactly what is happening with us, Blackie?"

He knew what she was asking. Was it love? Or sex? Or something else? Indeed, what was happening?

"I don't know," he said finally, honestly. This was no time to play games. The truth came. "I can't tell you, Kate."

She sighed, not unhappily, and looked at the ocean. "I don't know, either."

Blackie could not stop himself. Logic told him to give her time, to let her work out the problem. But another voice, a wicked one, spoke to him, too. That roguish voice was more persuasive.

Reaching for her hand and with a laugh in his voice, he murmured, "Let's just call it a nightcap."

"Blackie—"

"Kate," he said, "kiss me."

Hesitantly she slipped into his arms. With trembling hands she touched his chest.

He whispered her name again. In response she slowly, cautiously, lifted her head. Blackie descended just as carefully. Their lips met. She tasted sweet. And willing.

He couldn't help himself. She was so warm and pliant, so delicate and alluring. Expertly he eased her lips to part and teased her tongue, then reluctantly retreated, waiting, hoping for her response. Katherine shivered, though he held her snugly against the breeze. Her eyes were stormy and dark. Perhaps eagerness bubbled just inside a strict barrier she maintained? Again Blackie bent and their mouths coupled, tentatively yet searchingly. Softly she made a sound in her throat. With fear? Or could it possibly be relief?

She smelled of the sea and soap and the bittersweet tang of wine, and the combined fragrances filled his head. Urgently he wound his fingers into her tumbled hair. He delved into her mouth, as if seeking the secrets of all womankind.

Then Blackie felt her come alive. Instinctively her body melted into his. Like a cat she arched her back. With a sigh she wrapped her arms around his neck and deepened the kiss.

A rolling swell of passion swept him. She tasted sweet and tart all at once and felt like a purring panther in his arms. Her belly was soft against his, breasts warm. Heady, Blackie found the hem of her shirt and slipped both hands inside. The small of her back was taut, and he smoothed both palms up to her shoulder blades. She wore no bra for him to fight with. Exultant, he broke the kiss and said her name hoarsely.

She laughed—a shiver of excitement, that was all. But she did not refuse him. Blackie began to nibble at her earlobe, the slender cord that ran down her throat and finally the hollow where her voice vibrated ever so softly. All the while he caressed her bare back, learning every vertebra, every sinew. She was breathless.

She yielded. When Blackie pressed one knee between her soft thighs, she surrendered with only a quiet, affirmative sigh. Her flesh felt almost liquid, and Blackie suddenly wanted to be deeply encased in her, to be surrounded by her honey sweetness. Desire tightened his belly, then stabbed lower and quickened to white heat, the kind that needed tending before the final blaze.

She knew it. There was no way to keep his urgency secret, and Katherine displayed no coy shyness. With one hand she found him, touched him and caressed him once, causing a flare of pleasure so vivid that he bit out a harsh exclamation. Kate traced her lips along his jaw, and then she smiled against his mouth. "What did you say?"

All the well-planned speeches flew out of his head. "Kate, I want you," he rasped.

She laughed lightly, breathlessly. "As badly as I want you?"

"Every bit." Blackie found one of her bare breasts under the shirt. Her nipple was hard, and one caress across it elicited a sharp cry from her. He wanted to taste it, take her breast in his mouth and roll her nipple on his tongue. She was ready. Willing.

Purposefully he opened the shirt, heedless of the buttons, determined to satisfy himself.

But she caught his head at the last instant. He was centimeters from laying his lips on her, and she stopped him, her body rigid. "What was that?"

Blackie couldn't hear a thing but the slam of his own heart. "What?"

"Someone called out."

"Kate," he muttered, wrestling her back against the rail for better leverage, "don't distract me."

"I mean it, Blackie!" Kate pushed his chest, straining to listen. "I distinctly heard . . ."

And then he heard it, too. Children crying. Lots of children crying.

Katherine broke away and ran, buttoning her shirt as she went. Blackie slumped against the rail and squeezed his eyes shut in frustration, hoping to get his body under control again. He blew a sigh. His plans were in shambles. "Oh, damn."

CHAPTER ELEVEN

THE BOYS WERE horribly sick. Every one of them upchucked over the side of the boat and lay groaning on the deck. Katherine ran from one to the other, trying to keep them warm, trying to keep them from kicking each other or being sick on the deck. The night turned into a nightmare.

"I want to go home," Harold wept. "Mommy!"

"Where's Mama?" Frick cried.

"I want my mommy!"

It became a chorus from a grisly Greek tragedy. Five boys vomiting and calling for their mothers. Katherine was not sure how she lived through the night.

Though she blamed Blackie completely for every revolting minute, she could hardly criticize him for not helping when the disaster struck. He stuck by her through the whole ordeal, nursing his share of the boys. One after another he dragged them to the rail and tended them as kindly as she would have herself.

It was nearly dawn when Katherine finally began to hope that it was over. None of the boys had been sick for nearly half an hour, and some of them were starting to doze off. She risked putting Peter to bed below, and when that proved safe, she carried Jimmy to bed also. Gradually all the boys settled down.

Katherine staggered up on deck just as the sun peeped out from the horizon. The night was over. She wasn't sure how she'd made it through.

Seeking peace, she climbed onto the bow and crawled forward on hands and knees. She collapsed, exhausted, onto the cool deck and closed her eyes. The newly risen sun was warm on her aching muscles. Turning her face up to the blissful heat, she wondered if it were possible to be too tired to sleep.

Dimly she heard Blackie come out of the hatch after putting Harold to bed. She heard him groan.

Then brokenly he called, "Have you thrown yourself overboard?"

"I'm up here," she mumbled back. "Hiding."

Blackie apparently debated about the safety of joining her. Then he took a deep breath and climbed up onto the bow also. Katherine did not move, but lay like a dead woman, eyes closed, body inert.

"Here," he said, tucking a folded blanket under her head. "A peace offering."

She didn't move. "I should never speak to you again, you know."

"I deserve much worse." Blackie lay down beside her and let out another agonized groan.

Katherine put her hands behind her head and squinted at the blue sky above. No sounds came from the cabin below. Beneath her the surface of the deck was already warming up. *Bobbie McGee* rocked gently against her anchor, and the water murmured against the hull. Otherwise, the morning was quiet. Even the surf, showing white against the sand of a reef just twenty yards away, was silent. Clouds wafted overhead like schooners across an ancient sea. No birds broke the stillness of the air. Only the heat of the sun tingled on Katherine's legs, a lone physical sensation on a morning when she would rather be asleep.

She should have been angry. Or resentful. But strangely Katherine felt nothing.

Eerily she experienced the feeling of being alone on the sea, floating far from civilization and the problems of mere mortals. Nothing mattered here. The boys were safe. The water shimmered in silence. There was nothing to fear, nothing to concern her. She felt alive, wonderfully awake, suddenly tuning in to the world around her. Katherine lay on the deck and absorbed the phenomenon of the boat moving like a living creature, rocking, cradling, stimulating. It felt good.

Katherine found herself smiling lazily at the sky. Why on this, of all mornings, should she feel so pleased with life?

Amused, she rolled onto her stomach and let the sun-warmed deck radiate heat onto her thighs. Blackie was silent beside her, perhaps dozing, and Katherine propped her chin on her hand to study him.

Perhaps he knew she was watching. A minute passed, and then, without opening his eyes, Blackie said, "Kate?"

"Hmm?"

"Listen," he said, "I'm really sorry."

Her smile broadened. "For the wine trick?"

"Yes. It seemed like a good idea, but, well, I got carried away. I am sorry."

He sounded as if he meant it. Katherine stretched and rolled over onto her side to face him. Yes, after seeing him in action as a nurse with the boys last night, she was sure Blackie was capable of feeling sorry for his behavior. He had a heart, there was no doubt. He wasn't simply a rogue male looking for adventure on the high seas. He was capable of tenderness.

She observed him for a while; she wasn't sure how long. He lay on his back. His eyes remained closed. Shirtless and shoeless, his long body looked none the worse for wear. In fact, it looked pretty good to Katherine. His right leg, propped up and relaxed in comfort, looked accustomed to hardest exercise. The sun gleamed on the contours of his powerful chest and stomach. His arms were knit together with the muscle of a working sailor. A more splendid specimen of the male animal surely did not walk the earth, Katherine decided. Even his stubbly face looked rather appealing this morning. And that pirate-rough exterior concealed a man who could hold a sick child in his arms without a complaint.

Katherine touched his cheek with her forefinger, traced a gentle circle and withdrew. "I thought you were going to apologize for starting something you couldn't finish."

Blackie opened one eye slowly. "My brain isn't too keen this morning. What do you mean?"

Maybe she was crazy. Maybe the magic of the morning air had worked a spell on her mind. Or maybe the sun had penetrated her skin and touched places in her body that were not easily reached. Something caused her to smile. Katherine wasn't sure what possessed her. Softly she murmured, "Whatever happened to the nightcap you were talking about last night?"

"The . . . nightcap?"

"Yes, the euphemism we discussed. Remember?"

Surprised, Blackie came up on one elbow. He did it cautiously, as if a sudden move might scare her off. Then he looked at her warily. As if pointing out an elusive scientific fact that would undoubtedly spoil everything, he said regretfully, "It's daylight, Kate."

"Are nightcaps only enjoyed in darkness?"

"Well, customarily..."

She touched the bottom button of her own shirt, toying with it until his voice died out. "I didn't realize that it was an exclusively nighttime activity."

At a loss for words, Blackie watched her hand linger on the button, then raised his puzzled eyes to her face. With comprehension dawning, he gave a soft, half-laughing exclamation. "Judas, woman, are you teasing me?"

"After what you did to orchestrate that nightcap last night," she said, "you deserve to be teased."

Though he didn't move, his eyes sharpened, his muscles flexed and Blackie suddenly had the look of an alert tiger ready to spring. Voice cautiously hushed, he said, "You've been teasing me since you came aboard this boat, you know."

"Then a little longer won't hurt, will it?"

"No," he said, though the syllable was barely audible. "I guess it won't."

She wasn't sure why, but she did it. Perhaps the rising sun turned seductively hot. Perhaps it was because he did not reach for her and prove how much stronger he was. Katherine undid all the buttons, then slipped the shirt off her shoulders and held the fabric against her breasts for a moment.

Half a yard away, Blackie's eyes smoldered, but he didn't move. ''Well?''

For an instant she expected to hear the shriek of common sense in the back of her mind. But the message in Blackie's gaze was unmistakable and she wasn't afraid. He was willing to wait a little longer, she knew. Watching her, he waited for Katherine to make the decision.

So she stripped off the shirt slowly, tantalizing him—and perhaps herself. She felt wanton as she knelt before him in the sunshine. Her heart raced. She could hardly breathe. Perhaps Blackie knew how exciting it felt to be so reckless, for his wicked smile appeared. His eyes sparkled.

Finally he reached and tugged the shirt out of her hands until her breasts were bathed in sunlight.

''You're beautiful,'' he said.

The warmth of his gaze alone caused her nipples to tingle and harden into peaks. Katherine blushed, of course, for she could carry the wanton act only so far, but Blackie grinned like a pirate, enjoying every second. She rushed to cross her arms to hide her breasts, but he caught her wrist just in time.

Then he turned her hand over in his and kissed her palm. His lips lingered on her flesh, his gray eyes held hers.

And Katherine nearly melted on the spot.

He let her go. Softly he said, ''Now stand up for me, Kate.''

She obeyed slowly, uncoiling her long legs and getting to her feet. Standing, she began to unfasten the catch on her shorts, ready to make a gift of herself. Blackie stayed where he was and watched.

But he couldn't be patient forever. By the time she had unzipped the shorts, he was on his knees and drawing the garment down. He grasped her hips, smoothing his palms appreciatively around her pale flesh, almost kneading. Then he bent swiftly and pressed an impulsive, growling kiss into her belly.

Katherine laughed. The sun poured brilliant rays down her bared body like a cascade of liquid gold. Standing in Blackie's worshipful embrace, she tilted her head back, eyes closed to receive the light. She laced her fingers in his hair.

Blackie clasped her bottom, his hands inescapably strong. Cupping her body to his mouth, he began to trace circles on her stomach, teasing and exploring at the same time. She braced her hands on his shoulders, excited yet trembling.

"Mmm," he murmured, "I've wanted all of you for so long!"

She wanted to be his completely, skin to skin and flesh to flesh. She wriggled the shorts down to her ankles, then kicked them aside. When her legs parted, Blackie wasted not a moment. His lips, then his tongue, found a much softer place within her. The intimacy of his discovery caused Katherine to gasp. For a suspended heartbeat she could not breathe and dared not move. It was too fast, too sudden. And yet not soon enough. She felt the sun's rays beat in her veins, as though entering from the point where he caressed her with his tongue. Katherine moved instinctively, mindlessly, obeying him, seeking to draw him deeper.

The caress was too much and not enough. Suddenly filled with the desire to share the wonderful sunlight, Katherine wrenched herself from the brink of an exquisite pleasure. She grasped Blackie's head and drew him back. Caressing his face, she gazed down at his familiar features, his clear gray eyes. A thousand sensations swelled in her heart. Yes, she wanted to share it all with him. And she wanted it to take a very long time.

She smiled. "Come on," she urged in a whisper, "let's go for a swim."

Blackie let her go long enough to strip out of his clothes. When she slid over the side of the boat and into the water, he was right behind her.

She swam lazily, savoring the rush of seawater on her bare skin. Tiny particles of electricity seemed to race around her limbs, stealing into places that cried out for more stimulation. Smooth as an otter, Katherine flipped onto her back, and Blackie was there, gliding in perfect syncopation, close as a shadow, but not nearly as cool. They swam in the dazzling water, floating, diving, dancing effortlessly.

Then he caught her in his arms and stood on the sandy bottom, pulling her body securely into his while the waves eddied around them. The water glistened on his shoulders, throwing the muscles into a breathtaking relief of minute diamonds. His chest was solid against her softer breasts. And Blackie's grin never wavered. He reveled in the magical morning just as much as she. Smiling with him, Katherine wound her arms around his neck, eased closer and found his lips with her own.

His mouth was firm and hot, his tongue not just playful but insistent. Blackie delved into her as if seeking the most perfect, tantalizing oral contact. His

hands stroked her thigh, her waist, cupping and petting, intimate and sure.

At last his touch was more than a tease. With deft
fingers he found what he wanted and cleaved a path
for himself. Katherine threw back her head and
gasped, unable to stop him. Blackie nuzzled her throat
and muttered her name, half pleading, half laughing.
She struggled and he bit her neck lightly. She reacted
with a squeal. The next wave caught him off balance
enough so that she wriggled almost free, laughing. As
breathless as he was, Blackie managed to throw her
backward into the water, and together they plunged
down through the sizzling sea, sunlight dancing in the
explosion of blue-green bubbles.

She burst to the surface, sparkling with excitement,
tingling with fresh adrenaline. Blackie dove for her
and she eluded him, giggling. She thrust off from the
bottom and swam for the reef as hard as she could go.
Blackie grabbed her ankle, but she shook him loose
and plunged away, playing tag.

A wave frothed and threw her forward. Katherine
found her footing and scrambled to escape Blackie's
next lunge. The ocean foamed around her knees, and
she ran clumsily in the surf. She heard Blackie suck in
a huge breath and knew what that meant, but she
dodged too late. He tackled her from behind, and they
crashed into the sea, locked in each other's arms.
Katherine's cry was drowned, his triumphant laugh
quelled by the swoosh of water. When the hissing surf
receded, they were prone on the wet, rough surface of
the reef, rolling in each other's arms, sand shifting
beneath their bodies.

Above her, Blackie kissed Katherine's mouth, then slipped lower to the glistening hollow of her throat. She arched against him, eyes tightly closed to savor the pounding surf, the tilt of the earth. Their legs tangled. Blackie tensed, poised and ready to fill her with sunlight. But in the next instant another wave broke across them.

Katherine choked and laughed, hugging Blackie like a life buoy. Lovemaking on a beach—especially a half-submerged excuse for an island—was more funny than it was erotic. After another crashing wave, she choked and blurted out, "Burt Lancaster!"

He was laughing, too, thank God. "*From Here to Eternity*. Lord, were they this wet?"

"This uncomfortable?"

The next wave nearly drowned them both. When it washed back, Blackie threw a strand of seaweed from his face and gasped, "The boat?"

"Do we dare?" she asked, blinking, trying not to cough and laugh at the same time.

"Come on," he said, dragging her by the hand.

Together they plunged back into the water and swam for the boat. Blackie lunged upward and grabbed the rail. Easily he heaved himself up and turned on the deck, putting his hand down to her. He was strong, and in the next moment Katherine was in his arms. This time there was no laughter. The boys were too close. Quietly, without preliminaries, Blackie laid Katherine across the top of the cabin.

On her back she reached, lacing her fingers with his. "Now," she said, looking up at Blackie. "Let's not wait."

Blackie disobeyed. Bending over her, he touched one kiss to each breast, quiet, almost reverent kisses. He did not thrust into her then, but found her gently so that Katherine arched to meet him, making her wishes known. Watching her eyes, Blackie sank inside her. Together they made a carnal sound, not a whisper, not a moan, but both.

For that split second Katherine was mesmerized by the expression carved on his features. It was a hunter's look, both tense and relieved, satisfied and still urgent, the fierce expression of a man taking his pleasure and giving of himself at the same time. The nakedness of the look snatched her breath away. When he moved within her, though, she gasped.

"Blackie," she whispered, as if naming the act in which he shared his power with her.

"That's it, Kate," he murmured, reading her thoughts. "Give me as much as you want back."

That was his truth. For Blackie, their coupling was not a taking.

After that, it was as if the sun came inside and warmed every nerve ending to the point of bursting. Each time he withdrew, Katherine was sure the ecstasy would end, but each time he returned and found yet another place to set aglow.

Katherine writhed at first, hardly able to match his tempo, but then suddenly she was a part of him. Moving as one, high above the changing tides, filled with the most luminous golden light, they shared a glorious burst of fiery incandescence. It dazzled and remained, hanging in the sky like a nova before diminishing in a cloud of starry particles.

If Katherine cried out, he smothered it with his own mouth. His kiss was hard and rough, but turned gentle when her involuntary sounds stopped. With a raw rasp Blackie slid deep into her softness one last time and relaxed. Katherine closed her arms around him, enveloping the man and drawing him back to earth. The timeless moment passed, and Katherine's thoughts swam.

Perhaps Blackie's did, too. But he soon roused himself and eased her down onto the deck where the blanket lay. With one hand he shook it out and wrapped the cotton folds around her hips, just enough to keep away a chill. They lay quietly then, regaining reality. Around them the boat, the ocean and the sky took shape once more.

After a long while he murmured against her cheek, "All right?"

"Yes," she sighed. "More than all right."

He shifted up on his elbow to look down at her dreamy face. "I meant are you sorry this happened?"

The question might have been unpleasant from any other man. But Blackie understood her. "No," she said. "Not a bit sorry." Katherine opened her eyes and looped her arms around his neck. Her head was filled with delicious numbness, but she smiled. Half to herself she whispered, "Perhaps I'm reassured."

He looked at her quizzically. "Reassured?"

"I—yes. After what happened to me the day we were kidnapped, I wasn't sure that I could—that I ever wanted to be with a man again. But you were right."

He tilted his head again. "About what?"

She touched his face with her fingertips. "That what happened before was violence. It had nothing to do with making love. It sounds silly, maybe, but I was afraid that I'd never want this kind of intimacy again."

He kissed her temple thoughtfully. In a moment he said distantly, "We all need to be reassured now and then."

Katherine fell silent, thinking. Perhaps Blackie needed some reassurance, too. After his wife died, had he doubted his chances for another great love? Had he sailed off on *Bobbie McGee* expecting to cut himself off from people entirely? Was his love for the boat a substitute for the love of a woman?

Bobbie McGee, she thought. Where had the name come from? Why hadn't he called the boat after his wife? Or some favorite book? Or something silly? Was there some significance to the name he had chosen for the vessel that never seemed to carry him home again?

Without thinking, she asked him. "Blackie? Why do you call her *Bobbie McGee*?"

"Hmm?" He'd been half asleep and roused just enough to answer. "Oh, it's a song."

"A...? Oh, yes, Janis Joplin."

"A man wrote it. Kristofferson. 'Me and Bobbie McGee'."

"I remember." Absently she trailed her fingertips down his shoulder, not trying to keep him awake, just enjoying his nearness. He was dozing anyway, no longer listening. Knowing Blackie, he had no intention of discussing his own troubles, not if he could help it.

Staring up at the endless sky, Katherine remembered a line from the song. The words were undoubtedly Blackie Lowell's attitude about life now that he was alone. Freedom, for Blackie, was another word for nothing left to lose.

CHAPTER TWELVE

BLACKIE WOKE and found Katherine gone. He sat up at once and caught sight of her sitting at the stern of the boat, her hands filled with some bit of cloth—a shirt, perhaps. She was sewing, needle in the fingers of her right hand, knees demurely crossed. Her hair, black as Chinese ebony against the vivid blue sea at her back, whipped like silk in the breeze. Her face was perfect, all smooth ovals and delicate skin unenhanced by makeup. Cosmetics could only blur her beauty, he thought. Her dusky mouth was curved into a half smile, and she bit gently at her lower lip with her front teeth, trying to concentrate.

But he must have moved slightly or made some soft exclamation, for she looked up suddenly and saw him. She smiled, her eyes filling with light. Damn, but she was beautiful. That glinting smile of hers, partly teasing, partly joyous, was perfect. Blackie felt his breath leave his body in one great sigh of release.

He rolled to his feet and started toward her, determined to take Katherine's slender body in his arms, to hold her, share her sunny spirit. He wanted her close. He wanted to be a part of her once more. Katherine's female sweetness and her inner fire were pleasures he wanted to experience again and again.

"Blast!" There were kids clustered at her feet. When Blackie stood up, he saw them. Dammit, the boys were awake.

Katherine heard his exclamation and must have seen his expression change because she laughed aloud. He grabbed the cotton blanket and barely missed exposing the proof of his ill-timed desire to everyone aboard the boat.

"Good afternoon, Captain!" she called playfully, watching him approach while trying to keep the blanket around his hips. "There, boys, he's awake. Now you don't have to be quite so quiet."

Peter clutched his head in his hands, as if holding a regiment of noisy drummers between his ears. "Oh, yes, we do, Miss Theodopolis. Please don't let anybody yell."

"Poor Peter," she teased, bending over to chuck him under the chin. "Have you got a hangover?"

"Don't tease me," the boy begged. "I feel horrible."

"Serves you right," she shot back, prim again. "You've learned a valuable lesson, I think. Any pleasure taken in excess is not good for you. Right, Captain?"

Blackie had been about to touch her hair, to fill his hands with the soft strands and bury his nose in it. But her sparkly-eyed appeal brought him up short. "*Any* pleasure in excess?" he asked, a plaintive note in his voice.

"Any," she repeated, sending him a meaningful stare.

He choked on a comeback. She intended to keep her distance while the boys were aboard. If he were read-

ing the signs correctly, Kate had no intention of re-
peating the morning's passion as long as her students
were around.

Blackie eyed her. "Are small doses of pleasure
okay?"

"Very, very small doses." She held her thumb and
forefinger about half an inch apart. "*Tiny* doses."

The boys looked puzzled at this exchange. Clamp-
ing down on his teeth hard enough to keep an explosion inside, Blackie glowered dangerously at the
motley collection of children and wondered if the
sharks could be persuaded to eat them. How was he
going to get Kate back into his arms—and into his
bed—while they were underfoot?

They smiled back at him with adoration shining in
their faces. By the looks of things, they thought he was
Moses and Superman rolled into one package—even
dressed in nothing but a blanket. Kate was right. One
false step could spoil their illusions for good. Somehow she expected him to play a saint.

Naturally, he took out his frustration on them.
Shouting abruptly, he demanded, "What are you nit-
wits sitting around for? We've wasted a whole morning because of your delicate health! What do you
think this is?" he yelled. "A cruise ship? Get below
and clean up down there! Then march yourselves back
up here and we'll get underway! We've lost a day's sail
because of you landlubbers!"

All the boys scuttled to obey. They hustled through
the hatchway, bare feet scrambling, shoulders crashing, heads bumping. If Blackie ordered, they couldn't
move fast enough.

Katherine went on sewing blithely, pretending his bad temper had nothing whatsoever to do with her.

He turned on Katherine and towered over her. But suddenly he had nothing to say. Absurdly, he stood staring down at the woman, feasting his eyes on the curve of her breast that showed in the folds of the shirt she wore. Her legs, those long, slender limbs that had felt like heaven wrapped around his just a few hours before, looked taut and the color of honey. He felt like kneeling down and touching them then and there. Not a single intelligent word came to his mind.

"Do something about that look in your eye," she advised, "before the boys come back."

"Kate," he said hoarsely, "you're not going to do this to me, are you?"

"What? Keep you at arm's length until we get to Guam?" She knotted her thread around one finger, then brought it to her teeth and bit down. Blackie nearly groaned aloud at the sight. His insides ignited like a struck match. Katherine heard his stifled choke and smiled upward. "Yes, Blackie, that's exactly what I'm going to do. You know as well as I do that that's the way things have to be."

He sank his forehead into the palm of his hand and tried imagining how he was going to endure the next several days.

"I'm sorry," she continued, though there was a laugh quivering in her voice. "But we can't set a bad example for the boys, can we?"

"I can," Blackie said. "I have been all along."

She shook her head and put her sewing aside. "No, we're going to behave ourselves."

"Maybe you are," Blackie growled, "but I'm not!"

He snatched her off the bench and pulled Kate into his arms as if she were a helpless rag doll.

She collected her wits and struggled instinctively, biting out his name in a gasp. But his kiss was too much for her, and Katherine's agitation melted like caramel over a hot flame. She molded her lips to his, parted them and gave herself over to the first wave of passion. A soft and urgent sound escaped her throat.

She was perfect—sensual and exciting. Blackie eased back and looked into her eyes. ·

She said, "Don't."

"Kate—"

"I mean it," she insisted, though her voice was hardly a whisper. "Don't do this unless you understand where it leads."

He loosened his grip. "Where does it lead?"

But Katherine shook her head. "You're not ready for the next step, Blackie. Maybe I'm not, either, considering the circumstances. If we make love again, I can't promise that I won't—that I won't do something foolish."

Like fall in love.

A thump in the hatchway startled them both. An alarm in Blackie's brain shrieked, and he dropped her like a hot potato. Katherine staggered, then caught her balance using the railing and started to laugh weakly.

Though he was sure the boys had not seen a thing, Blackie found himself blushing like a teenager with a police officer's flashlight shining in his face.

Kate was right. Love was the next step, and neither of them was prepared for that. This morning was proof of how explosive a physical encounter could be, and if it happened again, Blackie wasn't sure what kinds of things he could be moved to say. He had to keep his hands off her.

So the boys resumed their roles as chaperones, and Blackie had to be content with watching Kate and fantasizing. Sometimes it was almost painful.

But there were good moments during the trip, too, he had to concede. Sailing had always worked magic on Blackie's soul, but having Kate along made an enormous difference. He felt more alert, as though his brain had been dormant too long. She coaxed responses from him on many levels.

The boys were also a balm, he reluctantly admitted to himself. At first they had been timid and unhappy little worms, but the weeks aboard *Bobbie* improved them tenfold. By the end of the third week, they were clambering over the boat like squirrels, chattering, teasing and laughing. Practical jokes became the order of the day. Blackie was treated to a cup of coffee laced with salt one morning, and his outraged reaction sent all the boys into gales of hilarity, to the point of rolling on the deck in hysterical laughter.

Katherine usually watched their antics askance, for she had a fine line to walk with them. She was not their playmate, the way he could be. She was their teacher and their guardian, the adult responsible for their wellbeing. But at times her high-spirited nature could not be restrained. With equal parts of devilment and fun, she helped mastermind some of the more sophisticated practical jokes. It was her fault, for instance, that Blackie fell overboard one afternoon and had to swim half a mile to catch the boat. But her quick thinking fortunately got *Bobbie* stopped; otherwise, he'd still have been floating on the ocean, and they'd have been speeding toward Guam by themselves.

In front of the boys she said she was very sorry, but later she made a much more satisfying apology to him in private. He lost his head and kissed her.

But she allowed him nothing more than that.

If the boys had not been aboard, Blackie was sure the voyage would have become one long erotic encounter. He loved holding Kate in his arms. At the most inconvenient times he imagined making love to her. Her laugh alone, he discovered, was the most powerful aphrodisiac he'd ever known. And his one taste of her body only piqued a voracious appetite. Blackie wanted her again.

She was stronger than he was. Katherine refused to let herself give in to the sexual tension, and Blackie had to be content with a single hour of her undivided company every night. After the boys went to sleep, she stayed on deck with him each evening and they talked. Sometimes by accident they ended up in each other's arms, but never for long. Kate could be a stickler when it came to self-imposed rules.

And what would happen after they reached Guam?

Blackie began to wonder about the future. Could he really drop her off with the boys and never see her again? Should he ask Kate to stay aboard *Bobbie* and take her on some kind of sexual odyssey around the world?

No, Kate was not the kind of woman who could give her body without attaching part of her soul as well. She didn't form casual relationships with men easily, he was sure. Though Kate talked like a sophisticated, worldly woman, she was still a vulnerable girl from

Ohio underneath her stuffy-teacher guise. And Kate deserved better treatment after what had happened to her.

"I can't ask her to go with me," he wrote in his journal one night while sitting under the stars. "She'll misunderstand and fall apart when it's over. My God, she'll expect me to marry her or something!"

And Blackie had no intention of getting married. Not to anyone, not even Kate. All he could remember about marriage was the night Julia had died.

Yes, falling in love with Kate Theodopolis was a bad idea all around. She was a sensitive, quirky young woman who'd been through a pretty miserable ordeal. She needed a man who could take care of her and coax her back to normal, one who would be tender with her wounds. What she did not need was a man as thoroughly messed up as Blackie was. He couldn't get entangled in another marriage.

"I don't like putting my heart on the line," were the last words he wrote that night before hiding the journal in the navigation desk. "To be safe I'm going to have to break this off before it gets started."

So he decided to pick a fight with her.

It took a while to figure out which button he could push that would make her angriest. Not until the day before they sailed into Guam did he find the right opening. Blackie steeled himself to carry out the plan, knowing it was for the best.

Katherine worked hard at keeping the boys' spirits up, for they were all on the verge of another depression with the end of their trip on the horizon again. She bustled around the boat, making preparations for landing. For crying out loud, she was doing *laundry*.

"You're going to look like gentlemen if it kills me," she lectured the boys. "It took a lot of fast talking for me to convince your parents that it was all right for you to come along on this trip, and if they see you looking like a tribe of hooligans, I'll be in big trouble! Peter, go take off that shirt. It's torn and I'll fix it for you."

"Aw, Miss Theodopolis!"

"Now, mister!" she ordered. "And bring up Blackie's shirt, too. The one that's hanging on the door."

Grumbling, Peter said, "Yes, ma'am."

Blackie, having overheard the exchange, said over his shoulder, "You don't have to fix my shirts."

She smiled at him, squinting against the afternoon sun. "I want to."

He took a deep breath, bracing himself. "What are you trying to do?" he asked roughly. "Be my mother, too?"

She blinked, startled by his tone. "Of course not. I only thought it would be nice—"

"Hey," he interrupted, rude and brusque, "you can play motherhood games with the boys, but don't start on me."

Katherine did not answer.

Blackie concentrated on executing a tack and did not look at her face. For good measure he added, "I don't need you to do these little wifely tasks."

"I am not being wifely," she said, her voice dangerously quiet.

"No?" He gave a short derisive laugh. "It sure looks that way to me—sewing, cooking, cleaning up—"

"If I could sail as well as you, I'd do my share of that, too," she explained sharply. "But I can't, so I figured I'd pull my own weight by helping out in ways I know."

Another chuckle, full of macho condescension. "I figured you were proving your femininity or something. Trying to impress me, Katie girl?"

At that, of course, Katherine exploded. Who could blame her? Never mind that the boys were wide-awake and within earshot. She blew up like a Roman candle. "If being feminine means doing the cooking, what does that say about you, Captain Know-It-All? You were alone on this bilge bucket for weeks before we came along and did your own damned cooking and cleaning! Does that make you any less of a man—"

"Hey, hey," he said, wheeling on her, half anxious that he had pushed too hard and yet determined to see the argument through. "Watch your language, your ladyship."

She bridled magnificently, eyes flashing with fury, fists braced on her hips. "Oh, does a little cursing make me too unfeminine?"

"I was thinking of the boys and—"

"Get this straight," she commanded, jamming her forefinger straight into his chest. "I know we've been playing stereotypical roles right from the beginning, but it's only because I don't know how to do the things you do. I'm working as hard as the next person because I want to do my fair share of making this horrible little boat livable!"

"Not to show us what a good little girl you are?"

Perhaps he had gone too far. Staring at him in amazement, Katherine asked, "What's gotten into you, Blackie?"

He shrugged and turned back to his task. "Look, maybe you've got to work through a few problems. Some guy roughed you up and you fought back pretty hard. Now you're not sure what kind of woman you are, right? Go ahead and play house if that's what makes you happy, but don't expect me to—"

"Why, you arrogant, self-satisfied slob!"

"Boys," said Blackie, "maybe you'd better go below."

"Is that what you think I've been doing?" she demanded, oblivious to the awestruck children. "Trying to fit into some straitlaced Victorian idea of what a woman is because of what happened to me? I suppose you think I deserved to be raped, too? By virtue of the fact that I'm not old and shriveled?"

"Lady," he snapped, hoping to put an end to it, "don't dump your screwed-up problems on me—especially not with impressionable kids listening to every word. Work them out on your own time! I've got enough of my own!"

"You're telling me!" she retorted sarcastically. "What's the matter, Blackie? Am I getting under your skin too far? Are the boys and I making you feel too human these days?"

She was smart. Her brain worked faster than his most of the time, and her insight was usually deadly accurate. Blackie looked at her narrowly and warned, "Don't start on me, Kate."

"*You* started it!" She stayed on her side of the deck, watching his face with a shrewd frown. "You're pick-

ing on me all of a sudden because you're afraid I'm
going to ask you for something, aren't you? You don't
want to get mixed up with me for fear something scary
will happen—like you might join the living again!''

Blackie didn't like the direction of the argument.
Defensively he snapped, ''Don't drag me into this.
You've got a problem, and you've used me to get over
it. Isn't that enough?''

''I—'' Outraged, she glared. ''Just exactly *how* did
I use poor you?''

He forgot the boys. ''You were scared to death to be
touched,'' he blurted out. ''And I was simply a tool to
get you over that phase.''

''I don't believe it,'' Katherine said, staring at him.
Her face was white and her mouth had stiffened into
a line. She was not going to cry. From the beginning
Katherine had always been able to control herself.
Voice tight, she said, ''You are an absolute pig,
Blackie Lowell.''

He returned her look coolly. ''You found me to be
a useful pig, though, didn't you?''

''You found me useful, too.''

He faltered. ''What?''

''I won't give you what you want, so now you're
miffed.'' Katherine spun away, furious and proud. ''I
think I know what's going on here. Get us to Guam as
fast as you can, Mr. Lowell. I'll be glad to get out of
your life!''

Not thinking, Blackie shouted after her. ''Kate!''

But she slammed through the hatchway and did not
come out again.

All the boys stayed riveted to their spots, silent and
shocked. The looks on their faces were accusing. In

one glance Blackie could see whose side they were on. And it wasn't his.

Peter came up on deck. His expression was stormy, and he could hardly speak for the anger boiling inside. He clenched his bony hands at his sides. "What d-d-did you d-do to her?"

"Nothing that she didn't have coming," Blackie snapped, angry with himself as much as with Katherine. A horrible taste soured his mouth, and he felt mean.

In the next second Peter flew at him, fists flailing. Blackie caught the boy just in time, but took a surprisingly hard punch in the ribs. He gasped and fought Peter off, grabbing the boy's arm and pinning it behind his back. Peter struggled, kicking. "You s-said you'd be n-nice to her! You s-said you'd stop!"

"Take it easy," Blackie panted, just barely managing to subdue the furious teenager.

"You're rotten!" Peter shouted. "You're as b-bad as the other man was! M-making her feel small!"

Blackie shoved the boy off. It felt good to hurt someone. Peter skittered across the deck and slammed into the opposite rail. He whirled around and faced Blackie bravely, though, his face screwed into an expression of furious resentment. Blackie couldn't find a thing to say in his own defense. Peter was right.

"Get to work," he ordered tersely, ashamed of himself for acting like an animal. Damned if he was going to apologize now. Hadn't he achieved what he set out to do? Turning his anger on the boys, he snapped, "Stop whimpering about your precious teacher and help get this boat back on course. The sooner we get to Guam, the better! I've had it with the lot of you!''

CHAPTER THIRTEEN

TUMON BAY, the harbor at Guam, looked like Fifth Avenue at lunch hour to Katherine after weeks in the company of only six other human beings and nothing to look at but open water and sky. She forced herself to notice every detail of civilization as they sailed into the company of other boats. The seaside resort was colorful and busy. High-rise hotels, powerboats, palm trees waving in the afternoon breeze, bathers splashing in the azure water—the place could have been Monte Carlo.

Fiercely Katherine concentrated on the sights. She was determined not to make a fool of herself this morning. Alone in the forward cabin the previous night, with the boys asleep and Blackie pacing around the deck above, she had buried her face in the pillow and wept like a sniveling fool. *Why?* she had asked herself. Why cry over insults so obnoxious they were beneath contempt? Or was she crying because Blackie had turned out to be such a jerk, after all her hopes that he was a gentleman in disguise?

No matter. It didn't matter a whit anymore. She knotted her fists and rested them on the rail. In a few minutes Katherine would say goodbye and never see the man again. After today she could erase John

Blackford Lowell from her memory and get on with her life. She could pretend he didn't exist.

Lined up beside her, the boys were strangely quiet also. Even the busy harbor seemed to hold little interest for them. They stared sullenly at the other boats and waved desultorily when sailors on passing crafts hailed them. Harold fingered the ever-present binoculars, not bothering to put them to his eyes to scan the beach and countryside. His mind was elsewhere.

"There," said Blackie, pointing from his position at the tiller. "That's the slip they radioed about. Pull down the sail, Peter."

Slowly, and without acknowledging the order, Peter obeyed.

As *Bobbie* swung around, the boys became alert finally. They tensed, necks and heads straining up like those of pert eager puppies. They hung onto the rail and leaned out to see who could catch the first glimpse of waiting parents.

"Hey!" Harold yelped. "It's my mom!"

Frick and Frack cried out simultaneously, "Daddy! Mom!"

And Jimmy hopped on one foot and tugged at Katherine's newly mended but still ragged skirt. "There he is, Miss Theodopolis! There's Dad!"

The dock was clustered with well-dressed adults, standing with their hands upraised to shade their eyes from the blistering sun. A few handkerchiefs fluttered and anxious voices called out. The boys began to shout back in excitement, bouncing around Katherine like a litter of wolf cubs. Katherine felt a lump rise abruptly in her throat.

For her, the reunion was exciting, but painful, too. As *Bobbie* drew close enough and the faces of the boys' parents came into view, she experienced the first jab of dismay. She was about to lose the boys. They'd become her purpose in life during the voyage, and suddenly she was aching inside, as if they'd already been snatched from her arms. She hadn't expected to feel so awful about losing them.

It wouldn't do to get emotional now. After all, she'd be mediating their squabbles in the classroom soon enough. She ought to be thankful that they weren't her sole responsibility anymore. Trying to muster some energy, she waved weakly at the crowd on the dock. Then she stopped, her hand frozen in midair, when Jimmy's observation registered. Standing at the head of the group was Stephen Monahan.

Her first impulse was to look over her shoulder at Blackie. She couldn't stop herself. But Blackie watched the bow of the boat, frowning, hands braced on the tiller, legs spread for balance, oblivious to the people on land. A hundred details crowded into Katherine's mind: the sunlight beaming brightly on the shoulders of his light jacket, his eyes squinting against the glare, his brown hands moving once, gently, to steady the boat. And his hair, mussed by the breeze, was burnished with highlights from the sun. But Blackie did not notice Katherine's surveillance. He seemed to be concentrating on making a perfect landing and barked another order at Peter.

Why did each nuance of his appearance seem suddenly vital in that split second? Hurriedly Katherine spun around, putting her back to Blackie. This was goodbye, of course. She wasn't going to see him again.

Some part of her unconscious mind wanted to pre-
serve a last picture of him, she supposed. Determinedly she lifted her hand and waved again to
Stephen. Soon she wouldn't have to worry about
Blackie Lowell.

Bobbie McGee bumped the padded wharf once,
causing everyone aboard to lurch and laugh. Ashore,
the parents laughed, too. Blackie, alone in ignoring the
nervous excitement of the moment, leaped to the
dock, snubbed a line around a post and threw his
weight on it, pulling the boat to a stop. *Bobbie McGee*
eased against the dock and bobbed once. Immediately the boys boiled over the rail and into the arms of
their parents. Cries of joy filled the air. A lone cam-
eraman intently snapped photos of the reunited families.

Blackie strode back along the dock and stopped,
putting his hand down to Katherine in silence. Word-
lessly she accepted his help, avoiding his eyes, and
stepped from the boat onto the dock. She was immediately surrounded by parents.

"My dear Miss Theodopolis!" trumpeted Mr. Frick
and Frack. "I can't say how pleased we are to see you
and the boys looking so well! Quite an adventure,
eh?"

"Oh, yes, quite an adventure," Katherine agreed,
blushing foolishly as she accepted his hearty handshake. Her patched skirt and borrowed white shirt
must have looked astonishingly out of place to the
parents, who knew her as the prim and proper teacher,
always flawlessly turned out. Her shoes had been ruined, and she had no choice but to face them barefoot. For the first time in weeks, Katherine felt the

constraints of high society come crashing down. An urge to hop back aboard the boat seized her.

"Good to have you back," added the twins' father jovially, releasing her hand. He looked from her to his chattering sons as they hugged their mother. "The boys look splendid. So do you, Miss Theodopolis."

"Thank you," Katherine said faintly, rubbing her palms together.

Then Stephen loomed. The sight of him brought Katherine's heart to her throat. Stephen Monahan, slender, blond and as aristocratic as Ashley Wilkes, wore an immaculately pressed white suit, perfect for the tropics. Stephen's wardrobe was extensive, and Katherine could only imagine how long he must have deliberated before deciding what to wear to the reunion. To Stephen, clothes made the man. He was careful to orchestrate his outfit for every single occasion and was rarely seen without a silk tie knotted at his throat. His pencil-thin mustache fairly twitched with excitement, however, and when he pulled off his aviator sunglasses, his pale-blue eyes seemed genuinely full of pleasure.

"Katherine! Darlin'!"

In the next second Stephen swept her into a quick hug—quick so that he did not muss his suit, but hard enough to convey his delight in seeing her. His honey-thick southern gentleman's accent sounded more pronounced than ever when he exclaimed, "Darlin', are you all right?"

Extricating herself, Katherine said, "Yes, Stephen, certainly I'm all right."

He held her hand and didn't let go, obviously pleased to have Katherine in his possession. "I had to see for myself," he pronounced, smiling. "Hearing your voice on that blasted radio wasn't enough. My word! Look how sunburned you are! Poor thing! Is it painful?"

"No. I'm used to it now."

"Well, you look quite fit in spite of it. Except for your clothes, of course. What a ragamuffin you are today!" Stephen chuckled, nipping the shoulder of her white shirt between his slender fingers. "Heavens!" He laughed, wrinkling his nose. "Katherine, you even *smell* just a bit!"

Jimmy scampered around his father and piped, "Those clothes belong to Blackie, Daddy!"

"Who?"

"Uh," Katherine began, clearing her throat, unable to put off the inevitable, "Stephen, there's someone you ought to meet."

It was impossible to ignore Blackie, who stood just six feet away, calmly winding a length of nylon line and watching everything with that blasted eagle eye of his.

Blackie was several inches taller than Stephen and forty pounds heavier, certainly. Size was not the only attribute that made him conspicuous, however. All the parents had unconsciously edged away from him, as if he were an infamous pirate who had gunned his way into their midst. Blackie did nothing to alleviate the tension. Scowling, he looked Stephen up and down, and one eyebrow shot up derisively. Katherine intervened before they could speak to each other.

"Stephen," she said hastily, "this is Blackie Lowell. Mr. Lowell, may I introduce Stephen Monahan. This is Jimmy's father."

"Hello," Blackie said curtly, and he took Stephen's hand in a grip that could crack walnut shells.

"My word," Stephen said, attempting to smile politely after a glance from Blackie's scruffy beard to the less-than-spanking pair of khaki shorts he was wearing. Stephen blinked and inquired, "Lowell, is it? You're an American?"

"Yep."

"I see. Racing this boat, Katherine tells me?"

"Yep."

"I see," said Stephen, clearly not sure what opinion he should adopt on the subject of a yacht racer who looked as if he might be happy in the Bowery with a bottle of muscatel in a paper bag. Blackie was not about to demonstrate his good breeding, so Stephen accepted him at face value. He said, "Well, I'm glad to meet you, Lowell. You really own this boat, do you?"

Blackie, looking even more disgusted, did not bother to respond to the inanity.

Before he could make a wisecrack, Katherine spoke up swiftly. "He's competing in a race to China, Stephen. The longer we keep him here, the farther behind he gets."

"Oh!" said Stephen, still making an effort to be cheerful. "Well, we wouldn't want to be the cause of your losing the big race, would we? Not after all the help you've been in rescuing our children. Perhaps we can offer you a reward before you go? It looks as though you could use some extra cash, Lowell—"

"Stephen," Katherine warned, seeing the sudden fire in Blackie's eyes.

"Oh, hush, darlin'. The man deserves to be repaid for what he's done. How about a hundred dollars, Lowell? Does that sound good to you?"

Appalled, Katherine grabbed Stephen's hand as he pulled his wallet from the breast pocket of his white suit. "Stephen, *please*, let's just go!"

With a wink at Blackie, Stephen said, "You know how nervous ladies get when it comes to monetary transactions, Lowell. I'll see you later on this matter, all right? Let me run Katherine over to my hotel first, and I'll be back to settle up with you. Darlin', I've got a suite of rooms waiting, and I'm sure you're thinking about a long soak in the tub, right?"

"All right," she snapped, her face hot with a conflict of emotions, all of them embarrassing. "Let me make sure all the boys are taken care of before I go, Stephen."

"Darlin'," he said, dropping his voice and taking her elbow, "I hate to hurry you along, but my wife—I mean my ex-wife, sorry, darlin'—may be showing up here at any minute. I'd rather confront her under less public circumstances, if you know what I—"

"Are you still fighting over Jimmy?"

Stephen sighed. "Fighting is not the word, Katherine. We've escalated to atomic warfare. She's here in Guam, and I purposely told her the wrong time to come to the dock, so—"

"Stephen! That's not fair! She must be frantic about Jimmy."

"Listen," he hissed, suddenly pinching her elbow. "I've got to do what I think is right for my son. Now will you come along, please?"

Katherine disengaged her arm. "All right," she said, trying to remain calm, though she was disturbed by Stephen's vehemence. The custody battle for Jimmy was a mess she had hoped to stay out of. "But let me check on the boys before we go."

Blackie was still standing there, and from the suspicious look on his face, he had overheard at least part of her whispered exchange with Stephen. He chose to ignore what had been said. "Everybody's taken care of," he reported bluntly, "except Peter."

Katherine scanned the departing crowd and her heart sank. She hadn't even had time to say goodbye to the boys properly. The twins were being borne off by mother and father and a little sister. Harold's mother and aunt were gushing over their charge using four-syllable words. Peter alone stood sullenly apart from everyone.

Katherine crossed to the boy at once. "Peter?"

"It's o-okay," the boy said stiffly, sliding back into his stutter. "My m-mother couldn't come. She sent her s-s-secretary, that's all."

A nervously sweating, blue-suited young man from the governor's house on Pago Pago stood aside from the group, waiting expectantly and mopping his forehead with a limp white handkerchief. Katherine knew him, and he recognized her at once also, though his eyes scanned once down her bare legs in surprise before snapping up again. "Hello, Miss Theodopolis."

"Hello, Henry," Katherine said, walking over to him. "Have you come for Peter?"

"Yes, ma'am," Henry reported, stuffing his handkerchief into his trouser pocket. "Mrs. Dodd sent me on a chartered plane yesterday. She's been tied up all week with a complicated development, so I'm standing in. My instructions are to take Peter home as soon as possible."

"I see," Katherine murmured, biting her lip.

Blackie arrived and caught her elbow before she could speak. Authoritatively he spun her around and led Katherine to the edge of the dock. Putting his head down to hers, he said, "You can't let this happen, Kate."

She clenched her teeth and did not look up at Blackie. How dare he tell her what she could and could not do. One glance into his face would surely undo her, however, so Katherine avoided glancing up and kept her voice rock steady. "Exactly what can't I let happen, Mr. Lowell?"

"Don't send Peter off with this bureaucrat. The kid is depressed enough as things are."

"Whose fault is that?" she inquired.

Blackie sucked in a breath and expelled it shortly. "Okay, so it's my fault he's mad at the world at the moment."

"I'm amazed that you noticed."

"Look, you can be as angry as you want with me, too," Blackie said in an undertone, "but just devote a little sensitivity to Peter right now, will you? The kid doesn't want to go with that clown."

"That clown," Katherine pointed out, her poise fiercely held in check, "has been sent by the child's mother to take him home."

"Peter's no child," Blackie muttered, "and he doesn't deserve to be treated like one."

"Since when do you care about how anyone is treated?"

That nearly did it. Blackie moved suddenly, as if to grab her arm, but he caught himself. He froze, perhaps counting inside to calm down. Then he said, "It only takes one look at the kid to see he's unhappy. Do something, will you?"

Katherine folded her arms across her chest and continued to avoid looking at Blackie. "Since you're such an expert suddenly, just what do you suggest?"

"Take him yourself," Blackie said promptly. "He needs a friendly face, and if you wipe that snide expression off yours, he might just go with you. Or—" Blackie interrupted before she could retort "—are you planning a few days of rest and relaxation with the Ambassador of Ooze over there?"

Infuriated, Katherine threw up her head and glared. "Stephen is his name! You have no business calling anyone names, buster!"

Blackie's gaze was as stony as hers, but something flickered briefly, something quite frightening. Then it disappeared. "Okay, okay," he said without apology. "What about Peter?"

"What about him?" Katherine demanded stubbornly. "The boy is already—"

"For God's sake, Kate! You've taken care of him like a mother hen up until now. Why can't you keep it up a little longer?"

Full of sarcasm, Katherine snapped, "Oh, but I'd hate to *use* the poor boy for working out my own problems! After all, that's what I did with the bunch of you aboard that boat, isn't it? I shouldn't continue to mother anybody, should I?"

"Damn you," Blackie muttered. He shoved his hands into the pockets of his shorts and executed a half turn away from her, shoulders hunched. "Damn you," he repeated, shaking his head. An instant later he said, "All right, I'll take him myself."

"*You?*" she repeated, flabbergasted. "Are we talking about the same Blackie Lowell who—"

"Shut up!" His tone was enough to stop her words, and his glare was just as poisonous. Blackie jerked his head toward Stephen. "Run along with Mr. Belvedere and have a good time, your ladyship. Maybe he'll buy you a hundred dollars worth of decent clothes. After all, you'll have to match his sartorial splendor after you get out of the bathtub."

"I'll return this shirt to you when I get to the hotel," Katherine snapped. "Will I have time to have it cleaned before you leave? Or do you intend to weigh anchor and get away from us as fast as possible?"

"I'll stay until tomorrow," Blackie returned. "But you can keep the shirt. Burn it, if you like."

Furious, Katherine began, "You are—"

"—an unspeakable pig," he finished, amazingly unruffled at her seething anger. Taunting, Blackie said, "Go play with your stuffy boyfriend, Miss Theodopolis. The two of you look as if you deserve each other."

There was nothing more to say. Katherine made a stiff about-face and stalked back to Stephen. She was trembling so hard that she was afraid her voice was shaking, too. "Jimmy, say goodbye to Mr. Lowell, please. And thank him for taking care of all of us."

Jimmy heard nothing amiss in her tone, and he was the one boy who did not appear to hold a grudge. He stepped forward like a jaunty little soldier and bravely put out his good hand to Blackie. "Goodbye, sir," he said. "And thank you for everything."

Blackie hesitated, towering over the tight-faced but eager little boy for a moment. Then he relented and put down his hand. "Goodbye, Jimbo. Have a good trip back home."

Jimmy tilted his head up until he could look at Blackie's face. He smiled, but his voice caught when he spoke. "Will—will you be going home when the race is over, sir?"

Blackie tried to smile, but failed. "*Bobbie*'s my home, son."

"But—" Jimmy frowned and glanced at the tied boat, empty and silent. "But you'll be all by yourself now, sir."

For a moment Blackie didn't answer. Then gently he said, "That's just the way I like it, Jim."

The boy pondered that idea, but could not quite grasp all the angles. Still puzzled, he said, "Well, I hope—I hope you win. And then I hope you have a good trip at least, sir. Wherever you're going."

A ghost of his old grin crossed Blackie's face, and he touched the boy's taped shoulder. "Thanks, Jimbo. You, too. Take care of yourself, hmm?"

He spun the boy around, and Jimmy scampered to his father, who put a protective, perhaps possessive, hand around his son's back. Stephen eyed Blackie curiously.

Blackie returned the look with a blank stare.

Katherine felt light-headed suddenly. Whether it was anger or the heat or some emotion she did not want to examine just then, she wasn't sure. She groped for Stephen's hand and pleaded, "Let's get out of here, please. I can't stand this."

But there was one more obstacle to overcome. Katherine had been so concerned about Blackie and Stephen that she had not noticed the small crowd still gathered on the dock just a few yards away. When she turned to hurry away from Blackie before a deluge of unexplainable tears burst from inside her, she realized there were men in uniforms waiting. She hesitated, uncertain about the platoon that confronted her.

One man separated himself from the pack and stepped forward smartly. He wore a short-sleeved United States Air Force uniform, and there was a gun strapped to his hip. An MP armband was the next detail that Katherine's dulled mind noted.

He sketched a salute. "Miss Katherine Theodopolis?"

Puzzled and weak, Katherine said, "Y-yes."

"State Department employee? Teacher at The American School on Pago Pago?"

What was this all about? "Yes," she said, frowning.

"See here," Stephen objected, stepping forward. "I thought we agreed to postpone this unpleasantness until Miss Theodopolis had a chance to rest."

"What's going on?" Katherine asked, mystified. "Stephen?"

The MP avoided Stephen, glanced warily at Blackie and then devoted his full attention to Katherine. "Miss Theodopolis, the government of the United States has asked me to take you into custody."

"What for?" Blackie demanded dangerously.

"Concerning the murder of one Alfred Torres, a man who died—"

"Judas," said Blackie, and he caught Katherine as she stumbled backward, blown away by the shock.

CHAPTER FOURTEEN

THEY TOOK HER AWAY. Helplessly Blackie watched the military police haul Kate away like a criminal. He remembered only one other occasion that he felt the rage and anguish of being incapable of making a difference. It didn't feel good the second time around, either.

"Good heavens," said the pasty-faced squirt who was supposed to take Peter home to his mother. He stood beside Blackie and stared up the street, mildly surprised and cheerfully curious. "Is Miss Theodopolis really a murderess? I'd never have guessed."

The logical thing to do was to grab the man's throat. Blackie throttled him and demanded, "Who the hell are you?"

The squirt gasped and wiggled and turned purple and finally squeaked, "Henry Halsey, s-sir!"

Common sense began to return, and Blackie loosened his murderous grip. This pip-squeak might be capable of providing information, at least. "And who the hell is Monahan? A lawyer or something?"

"Oh, yes, yes, sir!" Henry Halsey sputtered, eyes bulging. "Yes, sir, he's a lawyer. One of the best. He'll take care of her, sir."

"You sure about that?" Blackie roared, squeezing the man's windpipe again.

"Oh, y-yes, sir! Yes, sir! P-please, don't hurt me, sir!"

Blackie finally became aware of Peter hanging on his arm like a bullterrier.

"Blackie," Peter said, panting with the effort to stop him from strangling his mother's secretary, "we've got to help her!"

Breathing heavily, Blackie shook off both Peter and the Halsey squirt and glared after the uniforms who were marching Katherine up the street. It took a monumental effort to get his brain working again, but gradually his powers of thought returned. Blackie assessed the situation, pacing up and down the dock like a caged beast. Finally he stopped. "We need a lawyer."

"Mr. Monahan *is* a lawyer," Peter objected.

"Mr. Monahan looks like he couldn't even *carry* a law book by himself, let alone understand one!" Blackie wheeled around and headed for *Bobbie* and the radio.

Peter stumbled after him. "Where are you going, sir?"

"To call Pointy Hargraves."

"Is he a lawyer, sir?"

"You bet," Blackie snapped, and he vaulted over the rail of the boat.

Henry Halsey, scampering to keep up, said, "You don't mean Pierpoint Hargraves, do you?"

"The one and only."

"Oh my," said Henry Halsey. "The famous one from New York? I've heard of him. Oh my, yes! Everybody's heard of Mr. Hargraves."

Blackie radioed Pointy from the boat. From the beginning of the race, they had set up a method of communication, and Pointy answered cheerfully. "Where are you, Blackford? Gone back to Rio to coax your lady friend back aboard?"

"Shut up, Pointy," Blackie said. "I need *you* now, not a woman."

"Good heavens," said Pointy, laughing across waves of static. "Forgive me if I sound nervous. This is my first experience in this kind of thing, Blackford. Be gentle with me, will you?"

"Just get to Guam as soon as you can," Blackie commanded, in no mood for jokes. "I've got a problem to take care of. A legal problem."

"Blackford, you know I'm not exactly eager to—"

"Blast you, Pointy, I don't care what kind of personal crisis you're going through at the moment. I'm asking you as politely as I know how to put it on hold long enough to help me."

There came a silence. Finally Pointy asked, "Is this a ploy to get me to lose the race?"

"Dammit, I'll forfeit the stupid race! Just get here!"

Pointy began to laugh. "One question, Blackford. This isn't a paternity suit, is it? Those are so dreadfully boring."

The question didn't deserve an answer, not the way he was feeling just then. Blackie terminated the call without responding. Then he turned to Halsey, ready to get down to business. "Okay," he ordered, "tell me about Guam."

"Guam?" Halsey repeated, startled.

"I don't know a damned thing about this place. Who do I have to go see? What can you tell me?"

Peter stepped forward. He was smiling.

Blackie looked narrowly at the boy. Then he sat back in his chair, folded his arms and said, "Okay, Peter. What did Kate teach you about Guam?"

Peter snapped to attention and began to recite. "Guam, where America's day begins, is a U.S. Trust Territory, sir, governed by an appointed governor who lives in Agana, the capital city, which is about ten miles from here, if this is Tumon Bay."

"It is," Halsey put in.

Peter nodded and continued the history lesson. "The island was first discovered by Magellan in 1521 and later became a supply base for the Spanish galleons that transported gold around the world. Neat, huh? At the end of some war—the Spanish-American one, I think—Guam became a part of the United States. Now it's a 'free port.' That means all kinds of foreign merchandise can be bought and sold duty free, so the island is a real popular resort. For American and Japanese tourists, plus American military personnel. Several military facilities are located on the island. Andersen Air Force Base is one, and—"

Blackie interrupted. "That's where they'd take her? The air force base?"

Halsey nodded. "Probably."

Blackie got to his feet. "Let's go. Peter, keep talking."

FOR KATHERINE the afternoon passed with the excruciating pace of an execution by torture. After a blistering-hot van ride to a military base, she was taken to a low featureless building and secluded. For hours she sat in a windowless room with two chairs, a table, an aluminum can of Diet Coke and a sleepy air force sergeant while Stephen dashed off to argue with the base commander. Essentially she was alone with her thoughts. And fears.

She should have known it would happen. The events of that night on a South Sea island were not imaginary, and she could not ignore them. The voyage with Blackie had almost obliterated what had happened from her mind, but she should not have let it. She was guilty, after all. Wondering how she ought to be punished for her crime kept Katherine occupied until her head was one tangled mess of fact and fiction.

When the sergeant left to see if he couldn't "rustle up some supper," as he put it, Katherine was left alone. She tried to relax, putting her head down on the table and closing her eyes wearily. After days and days surrounded by a boatload of noisy little boys, the room was eerily quiet. She was almost relieved when the door finally swung open again. Even the down-home humor of her air force companion was preferable to solitary confinement. Katherine got to her feet.

It wasn't the sergeant. Or even Stephen.

"You!" Katherine backed up until she collided with the table. "I thought you'd be on your way to China by now."

"I should be," said Blackie, glancing quickly around the unadorned room. His face was grim and unfriendly, and he put his hands into his trouser pockets. "But I'm not. This isn't exactly the Ritz, is it? Are you all right?"

Katherine gulped and ran her hand through her tangled hair. She was exhausted and hungry and emotionally raw, and if Blackie couldn't see that, he was slipping. Couldn't he leave her alone? Unwillingly she allowed herself to look into his eyes, and Katherine saw that he knew exactly what she was going through. Ashamed of herself for feeling weak, she turned away from him. It was unsettling to be able to communicate so clearly with anyone, let alone a man she had decided to dislike.

"Forgetting your manners?" Blackie asked lightly, keeping his distance. "You're supposed to invite me to sit down, I think. Even in jail."

"This isn't jail," Katherine replied, trying hard to sustain the anger she'd mustered against him since their argument aboard *Bobbie McGee*. "It's—I'm in temporary custody, that's all."

"So I hear."

Katherine stole another look at him. He was fully dressed for one thing, which seemed odd after their long weeks of sharing a wardrobe. He wore a pair of his usual khaki trousers, a shirt, a pair of boating shoes and even a navy sport jacket, one he must have kept in the zippered garment bag in his cupboard.

Blackie drew up the chair that the sergeant had vacated and turned it around. Straddling it backward, he sat down and rested his forearms across the back of the chair. Blandly he continued, "The only way I could talk my way into seeing you was to point out that you haven't been charged with a crime yet. After the inquest I suppose it'll be—"

"Inquest?"

"Hasn't Monahan told you anything?" he asked, his voice laced with impatience.

"He's been gone since I got here." Katherine crossed to the table and rested her hands on the top to keep herself from rushing closer. Blackie knew something. He was a source of information. Eager for news, Katherine forgot her irritation and asked, "What's going on?"

"That's some lawyer you've got," Blackie remarked, eyebrows cocked.

"Just spare me your personal opinions, please! Are you here to make things worse? Or to tell me something?"

Blackie didn't apologize. "There's going to be an inquest," he began, speaking without inflection. "Probably tomorrow, if they can get all the information together. The men who were with the guy you killed are pressing charges."

"*What?* They kidnapped us in the first place!"

"Take it easy," Blackie soothed. "Kidnapping isn't as bad as murder, and the fellow that you—the victim, that is—is apparently a distant relative of an important man here in Guam. He was a local, a native of the islands, and the family is not keen on Americans, so they're hoping to prosecute you as an example of some kind of imperialist—"

"Oh, dear," she whispered, sinking into the other chair. Things were worse than she had imagined. Much worse.

Blackie paused. In the short silence he studied her. In a different tone he suddenly asked, "Have you eaten anything?"

Katherine shook her head. She couldn't manage to speak.

With a carefully drawn breath Blackie reached into his jacket pocket and pulled out a wrapped sandwich. He tossed it onto the table between them. "Here. Ham and cheese on white bread. Best I could do." When she did not reach immediately for the food, Blackie pushed it across to her. "Go on. You'd better eat something. This is going to be a long haul, I'm afraid."

Numbly obedient, Katherine reached for the sandwich. Maybe she was exhausted, or maybe it was sitting so close to him that made her light-headed. A part of her wished that Blackie hadn't come.

"Come on, Kate."

Not speaking, she unwrapped the food, her fingers trembling.

Blackie continued to talk as if not seeing her distress. "Monahan's having a meeting with the powers that be, hoping to convince them that you should be released to him until the trial—assuming there's going to be one. You should probably get sprung from here tonight, considering that your plea will be self-defense. The sticky point is that the local authorities are wrangling with the air force about who gets the pleasure of prosecuting you. According to something called the Status of Forces Agreement, the American military and the civil government must agree on who tries the case. You're an employee of the State Department, and you were doing your assigned duty when the incident took place. The air force thinks that entitles them to run the show."

"Is that good?"

Blackie rested his linked hands on the table and nodded. "Personally, I think you'll be better off getting tried by the air force. That will keep you away from the local politics at least. But instinct tells me the civil authorities will be handling the inquest, anyway."

All afternoon she had felt as though a storm were bearing down on her. The clouds had been gathering, the breeze had picked up. Now the wind and rain were nearly upon her. Katherine's troubles loomed like the first signs of a hurricane. Blackie was right that the whole ordeal was going to be a long haul. Katherine sighed unsteadily. Her first bite of the ham-and-cheese sandwich hadn't been too bad. Now her stomach rolled, though, and she doubted if she could swallow any more.

"The first order of business, in my opinion," Blackie continued, "is for you to dump Monahan."

Katherine jerked her eyes up to his, her brain stirring. "What?"

"You heard me." Blackie returned her look without a waver. "Monahan's not doing you a damned bit of good, Kate. Maybe he's the next best diplomat since Winston Churchill, but he hasn't practiced litigation since law school. You should fire him."

She shook her head. "No, I won't do that."

"Why not?" Blackie asked testily. "Because he's a friend? Kate, this is a pretty big mess you're in right now. You need a real lawyer, not a kid who—"

"Stephen is not a kid."

"Well, he's no Clarence Darrow, either."

"How should you know? You're a—an *art* dealer, for heaven's sake! And not very often, I might add!"

Trembling, she said, "I'll be the judge of my own legal counsel, thank you."

Blackie's glare intensified. "I've already called a friend of mine."

"You..." Outraged, Katherine exploded, "How could you do such a thing?"

"It was easy," he retorted. "I figured you'd be the first and last case Monahan ever took before a judge, and I didn't—"

"This is none of your business!"

"If I hadn't interfered in your business once before," Blackie snapped, "you might still be back on a deserted island, your ladyship!"

"All the more reason for you not to get involved now." Galvanized by anger and desperation, Katherine scrambled to her feet, throwing the sandwich down on the table. "This matter does not concern you, Blackie Lowell. Why did you have to stay on the island?"

"Because," he shot back, as if it made perfect sense, "Harold took my binoculars."

"Harold...?" Katherine stared at him. He couldn't even give her an honest answer. Fury flared up inside her, as if a match had been struck against dry tinder. She clenched her hands. "How does a pair of stupid binoculars," she shouted, "bring you clear out here to me?"

Blackie got up then, too, as though the force of her voice drove him to a standing position. He wheeled away from the table and began to pace, trying to patch together an argument that she might believe. He said quickly, "I had to stay on the island a little longer anyway. Leaving you with Monahan wasn't, well, I might as well have let the sharks get you as leave you in his incapable—"

Katherine snapped, "You had nothing to do with that shark incident! I took care of that myself, and I can do the same now. I don't want you here."

"Well, I'm here anyway," he growled. "Looking after you has become a habit."

"Break it! I don't want you involved anymore, Blackie. You saved my neck once already, and I don't—I don't want to be indebted to you anymore."

"*Indebted* to me?"

"You know what I mean. I have—because you helped me before I had to—you made me feel—"

Blackie put two and two together. "Like you had to sleep with me to say thanks?"

"No!" Katherine burst out. "I didn't mean that! I only—oh, damn, I felt weak and dependent on you, that's all. And I don't want to feel that way anymore! It made me do things I shouldn't have done."

He froze, eyeing her dangerously, and his voice dropped to a menacing growl. "We are talking about the day we made love now, aren't we?"

Steadily she said, "All right, maybe. Maybe I shouldn't have let you—"

"If I remember correctly," Blackie snapped, "*you* did the seducing, not me. Don't make it sound like I forced you because you owed me something."

"You didn't force me," Katherine agreed hurriedly. "I just—it was—" Desperately she cried out, "I felt like a helpless woman with you."

"You," Blackie said roughly, "are anything but helpless. You might be vulnerable, but you're not helpless."

"I can't control the way I feel."

"I can't, either. Both of us were vulnerable out there."

She stared, not sure she had heard correctly. "What?"

He turned away, agitated and explosive. "Dammit," was all he said.

He had closed the barrier. "Once again," Katherine said loudly, "we fall into stereotypical roles. I'm supposed to admit my problems and work through them, but you're allowed to keep everything bottled up inside for as long as you please. You didn't like being vulnerable, did you, Blackie? As soon as you told me about your wife and little girl, you wanted to take it back, didn't you? It put us on an equal footing, and that made you uncomfortable."

He swung around, face white with anger. "Right. You're absolutely right."

"So imagine my position, please. Once again I've got to give you a share of my problems. If I accept help from you, it'll make me feel more vulnerable than ever before. I don't like it any more than you do. I want to take care of myself."

He moved uncontrollably. "Kate—"

"So leave me alone," she insisted, backing away from him. "Let me take care of myself this time."

Blackie stopped. "You're being stubborn at a time when you shouldn't."

"Maybe so. But this is *my* problem, and you made it abundantly clear that you'd prefer we keep our problems to ourselves. The price I'd have to pay you for helping me again is too high."

"What price? What do you think I want from you?"

"You want me to bare my soul and give you everything I have."

"Love?" he demanded, full of skepticism. By the tone of his voice, he might have said a disgusting word.

"I think so," she agreed, trying to appear composed while a tumult raged inside. He turned his back to her, and she said, "That's what you want, Blackie, but you don't like to admit it. And you won't give any love in return because it's not in your character to be vulnerable with another person. You want to play by your own rules."

"*Your* rules are the same," he said, not turning around. "You're not going to admit that anything happened between us, either, are you?"

"Nothing happened between us," Katherine said, "except a release of some tension during—at a time when both of our defenses were down. It was an emotional time for both of us."

"It was an accident, then? The morning we made love?"

She nodded stiffly. "It never should have happened."

Blackie kept his back turned. He walked slowly to the door. For a split second Katherine was afraid he was going to exit without another word. She held her breath, wondering if this was the last she was going to see of Blackie Lowell.

But he glanced over his shoulder, one hand still on the doorknob. His eyes were cold, and his face was controlled. His voice, however, contained a sound that was almost a rasp. He said, "It will be a relief to wash my hands of you, but there's something in me that won't run away from a fight like this. If you want me to stay and see what I can do to help, I will."

Katherine shook her head. Her throat was too tight to allow words to pass. She shook her head fiercely.

Blackie nodded and opened the door. Simply he said, "All right, I'll go."

He didn't say goodbye. He left and closed the door, and his footsteps sounded in the hall outside. Not until she was sure he had gone did Katherine allow herself to cry.

CHAPTER FIFTEEN

WHEN BLACKIE GOT BACK to *Bobbie*, it was dark and he was feeling poisonous. He wanted to put as much distance between himself and women in general as could possibly be accomplished in one night. He also wanted a drink.

Bobbie was quiet, and it felt odd to jump aboard and not hear the murmur of childish voices below. There was no bickering over some inconsequential slight, no scuffle of bare feet and no smell of cooking. No laughter rang out, no silly giggles. The boat was empty. Yep, a drink would suit his mood exactly.

Blackie shouldered the hatchway open and thumped down into the cabin.

Like a flushed grouse a figure started up in the darkness. "Sir!"

Blackie stifled an exclamation and fell back against the hatchway. Then, heart hammering, he squinted in the darkness and recognized the skinny shape that wavered before him. With a grope he found the lamp next to the radio and switched it on. "Peter! What the hell are you doing here?"

"I—I stayed, sir. I told Mr. Halsey I wouldn't go with him tonight." Peter hesitated in the middle of the cabin, blinking in the light. "I hope you don't mind. I—I didn't touch a thing, sir. What happened?"

Blackie grunted. He ripped off his jacket and threw it into a corner. Finding Peter aboard was strangely comforting, but Blackie was too filled with annoyance to say so. He headed purposefully to the galley. "Nothing happened. Zilch. They're keeping her, and Monahan is about as effective as a caterpillar. What does she see in him, anyway?"

Peter tagged after him. "I d-don't know, sir. Perhaps he's going to defend her?"

Blackie snorted. "They might as well break out the guillotine right now in that case."

With a noisy gulp Peter whispered, "Oh, n-no. Oh, what are you going to d-do, sir?"

"Nothing," Blackie said, not looking at the boy. Peter was stunned and frightened, and Blackie was in no mood to comfort the kid. He reached into his locker with one hand, rooting around in the dark until he found the flask of brandy. Exactly what he needed. Standing up, he said, "I'm not going to do a damned thing, Peter. Except get out of here."

Stupidly the boy repeated, "Out of where, s-sir?"

"Out of Guam. Away from people again." Impatient, Blackie snapped, "Away from that crazy woman and back to my own life, that's where! I need a glass."

Peter handed him a coffee mug. "But, sir, you can't leave yet." As if explaining a vital fact to a simpleton, he explained, "They've arrested Miss Theodopolis, sir."

"I know that," Blackie snapped, exasperated. He snatched the cup and peered into it, making sure it was clean. Half to himself, he mumbled, "They haven't arrested her precisely yet. They're going to, of course, and she deserves it, but there's nothing I can do about it. At least nothing that she wants me to do.''

''But—'' Peter watched in amazement while Blackie poured brandy from the flask into the waiting cup. ''But, sir—''

''She told me to butt out, Pete. And that's exactly what I'm going to do.'' Blackie knocked back the first slug of brandy. It hit his throat and burned a path down to his stomach. He squeezed his eyes shut and concentrated on the sensation he knew would follow. Numbness. Delicious numbness.

''Sir?'' Peter asked softly, breaking across the moment of silence. ''Are you sure?''

Blackie refilled the cup and took it with him to the door of the forward cabin, nodding. ''Yep, I'm sure. The bitch wants me to leave her alone, to let her fight her own battles. So—because I'm always the gentleman when it comes to polite requests from a lady—I'm heading for China in the morning. After I get good and plastered tonight.''

Peter stood in the middle of the cabin, his bony arms hanging limply at his sides. His face was naked, full of dismay and childish disappointment. Blackie found himself feeling most annoyed because the kid's sunburned nose was peeling again. He turned away from Peter.

''Don't look at me like that,'' Blackie snapped, yanking his shirt off. It was one that Katherine had worn, and he was sure he could still smell her on the fabric, which was dumb since she'd washed every scrap of clothing before she left. He threw the shirt onto the bunk—the bunk where she'd slept since he'd found her. Glaring down at the rumpled blanket, it occurred to Blackie that he'd missed a lot of chances in that bunk. Cripes! Everywhere he looked, there was something to remind him of the prissy Popsicle.

"Prissy Popsicle," he mumbled. "That's what she is, Peter."

"Sir?"

"Most of all she hates to melt," he muttered, glaring down at the bunk. The brandy was starting to perform, all right. A few ounces on an empty stomach was working its way very rapidly to his head. Already Blackie could conjure up the sight of her—the curve of her hip as she had lain in the blankets, her limp hand upturned and still. She'd slept with her nose buried in the pillow and her silky hair all over the place. And that unbuttoned shirt could have aroused a monk. With eyes half closed Blackie remembered every detail of the vision she'd presented that night, snuggled into his bed with little Jimmy beside her. Both of them had looked like angels. Awake, though, it had been a different story. Blackie drank the rest of his brandy in one swallow.

"She always looks like an angel," he said aloud when the booze had seared his insides again. "She's a beautiful woman, I'll give you that. But she's got armor on all the time, let me tell you, Peter. She's cold steel. She's tough."

Behind him Peter said, "She's not t-tough."

Blackie laughed and swung around unsteadily, heading for the flask. "Oh, yes, she is. You wait till you're a little older, Pete, my boy. Kate is a *queen* among tough ladies. I'll tell you all about her someday when I'm good and drunk."

"Like in about ten minutes," said Peter. "I don't think you'd better drink anything else, sir."

"Don't mother me, kid." Blackie swiped the flask off the counter in the galley and chuckled mockingly at himself. "That's what set her off, remember? I told her to quit mothering me. Man, that technique worked even better than I figured it would."

"Technique, sir?"

Pouring, Blackie recited in his best Shakespearean voice, "The best-laid plans of mice and men, Peter, often screw us up completely." With a long look into the cup, he said, "I did everything I could and some things that I shouldn't have done. Now she's fired me from the team, Coach, and I'm heading for the locker room."

Peter pried the flask from Blackie's left hand and said, "I think you'd better have something to eat. And some coffee."

"Like hell," said Blackie, and he let loose a ferocious bellow. "Let the woman rot in jail, damn her!" To the ceiling of the cabin, Blackie yelled, "She wants to fight her own battles, let her try! I'm heading for China!"

"I'll make some sandwiches," said Peter, pushing him gently. "Maybe you'd better go find a sweater, sir. It's getting cold."

"Damned right," Blackie muttered, heading for the forward cabin. "'S been damned cold since the night she got on this bilge bucket. Good riddance to her, I say."

THE NIGHT PASSED, but he wasn't sure exactly how. All Blackie did know was that he woke in the morning with a headache that would put the neutron bomb to shame and a foul stomach that was so empty it hurt. He recognized the sensation in his abdomen as an ache resulting from dry heaves. If the signs were the same, he'd experienced a bender of a night. Blackie rolled over on the bunk and heard a heart-wrenching, pathetic sound. It was his own groan.

A face appeared above him—a clean, perky, clear-eyed face connected with a squeaky-clean voice. "Sir? Are you awake?"

Blackie squinted. "P-p-p?" His throat was so dry he couldn't get the word out.

Peter nodded. "It's me, sir. Shall I make some breakfast?"

The mere mention of food had a surprisingly galvanizing effect. Blackie's empty stomach rolled, and just to be on the safe side, he scrambled out of the bunk, shoved past the boy and headed for the deck, planning to upchuck over the rail if it came to that. One step out of the cabin stopped him like a bulldozer, however. The blinding sunlight caused a lance of pain to pierce his skull, and he staggered back through the hatchway without another thought to throwing up.

Peter was smiling. "I think you're better."

"Better?" Blackie croaked, trying in vain to hold the halves of his head together with both hands. He closed his aching eyes and sank gingerly into the chair at the radio console. "How bad was I?"

"Well, you didn't bay at the moon, sir."

Blackie sighed. "Thank God."

"Not until you chased Mr. Halsey away again, at least."

Blackie opened one eye and regarded the kid, looking for signs of smugness. Peter seemed matter-of-fact, though. He wasn't holding a grudge or, worse, playing holier-than-thou. Blackie was relieved to be spared that, at least. There was, on the other hand, a new directness in Peter's gaze, a sudden confidence that the kid exuded. And he hardly ever stuttered anymore. When had the boy grown up? Blackie wondered. He had been such a baby at the beginning.

"I was just making coffee, sir," Peter added, unaware that he was being studied. "Want a cup?"

"Sure." Blackie nodded cautiously. "Just keep the noise down, huh?"

"Right, sir." Busying himself at the stove, Peter did not speak again. He moved capably around the galley, though, knowing exactly which cupboard held the pot, finding the coffee just as easily and measuring the grounds as expertly as if he'd been doing it all his life.

Massaging his temples, Blackie asked gruffly, "When did you learn to do all this, kid?"

"Oh, Miss Theodopolis taught me," Peter said promptly. "She made us all take turns helping in the galley, sir, just the way you made us work up on deck. We learned a lot of things."

In the interest of self-preservation, Blackie let the air out of his lungs slowly. Gently he said, "Let's not talk about Kate this morning, all right, kid? My bet is we talked about her a great deal last night."

"No," Peter said carefully, keeping his back turned while he worked at the stove. "You mostly talked about Julia."

Blackie sat very still and did not speak.

Peter glanced over his shoulder briefly. "Your wife must have been just as nice as Miss Theodopolis, sir."

Blackie couldn't say a word.

Peter continued to busy himself in the galley. "She sounded really great, the way you talked about her. You missed her an awful lot, I guess. Heck, even I started wishing she was still around. And your little girl, too. I'm really sorry that accident ever happened to them." He put the coffeepot on the stove and frowned while he adjusted the gas under it. "I guess you really needed to be alone for a few years, right, sir? To kind of find a way to be around people again without, well, without feeling angry about what happened."

Abruptly Blackie got up and went out the hatchway. The sun was brilliant, but he didn't mind the pain in his head anymore. He welcomed it. How could he have allowed himself to talk to Peter like that? He must have told the kid things he couldn't even tell himself.

He braced his hands on the rail and looked down at the water as it slapped *Bobbie*'s sides. The sandy bottom of the bay was as clear as if just a few inches of water covered it instead of several feet. Two fish, slivers of shadow and light, flashed once before they cruised under the hull of the boat.

What had he told the boy? The same things he'd admitted to Kate? Or more? Had he told Peter about Julia's sweet laugh? The way her brows twitched when she concentrated on some household project? The way her hair smelled after a day at the beach?

Or was it Kate's hair that smelled so wonderfully tangy? Was it Kate's laugh he heard in his head now?

Looking down at the water of the bay, Blackie saw his own reflection, and he looked at it carefully. The gentle waves distorted the picture, mixing all his features into a shivering pattern. He couldn't make out his own face. Abruptly he wondered if he could put Julia's face together in his imagination now. Or would she be distorted, too, her memory getting mixed up with the vivid reality of another woman?

For Kate was every bit as vibrant as Julia. She was fiery and clever, funny and sensitive. Proud, too. Kate was more gallant than Julia had ever been. Julia was softer, perhaps, more pliant. But Kate was a fighter, determined to do things her own way.

He wasn't sure how long he stood there, looking down at the water and letting his mind stumble over thoughts he had purposely avoided for so long. No conclusions occurred to him, just impressions.

And then Peter arrived and pressed a mug of coffee into his hand. His voice was wary. "Here, sir."

Blackie took the coffee and walked to the stern of the boat, sure he didn't want Peter to see his face just then. He put one foot up on the seat there and leaned on his knee.

Waiting in the hatchway, Peter said, "Any breakfast, sir?"

"No," said Blackie. Then, more harshly, "Did you turn off the gas?"

"Yes, sir." Peter came up on deck. A minute might have passed, or five. Then he said, "You promised that you'd help her, sir."

Blackie gulped coffee and didn't ask for elaboration.

Peter said, "You told me that we'd look after her, remember? That night we talked up here—"

"I remember," Blackie interrupted, recalling exactly what he'd said to the boy on the night Peter had confronted him about his teacher's welfare. Shaking his head, Blackie said, "That was before she told me to get out of her life, Peter. I can't do anything now."

Peter came to the stern of the boat. Reproachfully he persisted. "That night you said you'd be nice to her. When I told you about them hanging her, you said you and me and the—the rest of the fellows would take care of her. You promised, sir."

"Peter, I can't help her if she won't let me."

"You're stronger than she is," Peter insisted.

Laughing once, Blackie said, "Don't you get it, Pete? That's what she doesn't like about me the most. I'm too strong for her delicate sensibilities. She doesn't like me bullying her around."

"You don't understand her," Peter said, quiet and fierce. "But I've known her a lot longer than you have. She's—"

"I understand her well enough," Blackie snapped. "I understand that she asked me to leave her alone. What she wants is some bleating character like Monahan around who—"

"N-no," Peter said. "She might think she wants Mr. Monahan, but she really needs something else. You're both the same, you know. It's obvious."

Blackie glared. "What's obvious?"

"You're still sad about Julia, and she's too—too upset about everything that's going on right now to figure everything out." Angrily Peter blew up. "You ought to be *nicer* to each other!"

Blackie might as well have been a bull that had just had a red flag waved in its face. His hangover intensified the anger, and he turned away before it exploded.

Peter followed. "You know, you can say a lot of nice things when you're drunk, but you can't come close to saying them when you're sober! You like her, but you won't tell her. How is she supposed to know what you think if you keep acting like a jerk? That's stupid."

"Oh, for God's sake," Blackie muttered. "What are they teaching you kids in school these days?"

"Miss Theodopolis taught us a lot of good stuff."

"Yeah?"

"Yeah," Peter shot back. "Not just numbers and words and stuff, but things like loyalty. And honor. And duty."

"Oh, Judas," Blackie said prayerfully. "Don't start on me, Peter."

"I'm not q-quitting," Peter replied, "until you change your mind. You should stay and help her get out of this mess. You promised you would. You're smart, Blackie. I know you can figure a way to get her out of here!"

"Get her . . . ?" Blackie stared at the kid. "Boy, do you know what you're saying? She's being held by the United States Air Force. How do you expect me to get her away from them? Go in and ask politely? Or—"

"I don't know," Peter said stubbornly. "That's your department. I'm just going to help get her away."

"Help get her away!" Blackie repeated. "You and me and what army?"

"*You* figure out a way!"

Blackie stormed away from the boy, too tempted to commit an act of violence to remain close. The kid was crazy. He'd seen too much television. What miracles did he expect from Blackie? Some kind of jailbreak with helicopters and automatic weapons? A riot staged so they could whisk Kate out a secret tunnel or something? It was ludicrous.

Drinking a mouthful of hot coffee, Blackie thought over the situation again. Kate was in big trouble, of course. But the worst problem was that she knew she'd killed the man, and she was not the kind of woman to lie on a witness stand, even if it meant saving her own neck. Did they still hang murderers in these islands? Surely not. But Blackie wasn't positive.

If it came to an execution, what else could be done? Blackie's imagination began to turn. Rescuing damsels in distress had always been a favorite fantasy of his. What stunt could he really pull off?

Peter broke into his plans. "Sir? Here comes Harold, sir. With somebody."

The somebody turned out to be Pointy Hargraves.

"Blackford!" Pointy stood on the dock and stretched out his hand jovially. "By God, you look miserable!"

Blackie summoned a grin. "Morning, Pointy. You're dapper as ever, of course."

Pointy Hargraves, Manhattan lawyer *extraordinaire*, was short, but imposing nevertheless. For tropical lawyering he had dressed in immaculate white trousers, white suede shoes, white shirt and a silk ascot, and a natty blue blazer complete with yacht club insignia. He was trim, fit, handsome in miniature, and he possessed an air of supreme confidence. The sharkskin briefcase he clasped under one arm looked official and expensive. But more than a month at sea had dulled Pointy's normally razor-sharp appearance. He had not shaved in a while and was sporting a recently trimmed beard that did not look entirely out of place, Blackie decided. It gave him a certain rakish quality. Perhaps a few weeks of relaxation had worked its magic on Pointy's soul as well. He seemed ready to get back to legal battles.

Pointy smiled benignly, though his eyes were sparkling with excitement already. "I believe you have a case for me to consider, Blackford?"

"I do," said Blackie. "Come aboard. Harold, I thought you had run off with my binoculars. Where are they?"

Harold Pickney, looking inquisitive and alert as ever, snapped a salute. "Good morning, sir! Peter called me last night for assistance, and I've been on the job ever since, much to my parents' dismay. I've escorted Mr. Hargraves around the island while you slept it off, sir. I haven't had time to get the binoculars."

Pointy jumped aboard *Bobbie* and landed lightly, his smile broad. "You've got quite a band of merry men working for you, Blackford. There are little boys all over the island at this very minute—all readying the defense of one Katherine Theodopolis, who is, may I say, a rather lovely eyeful."

"You've seen her?" Blackie asked eagerly.

"In a photograph," Pointy corrected. "The local newspaper is full of the story. I gather from the boys that she's in a spot of trouble."

"You're working on the case already?" Blackie asked, hoping against hope that Pointy had reached some definite conclusions about his misfired legal career.

"Some of us," Pointy began sternly, "do not spend our evenings getting drunk and our mornings sleeping it off. I rose early to get started on the business at hand. Are you awake enough now to contribute?"

Blackie ignored the smirks that Harold and Peter exchanged. "I'm awake," he said belligerently.

"All right," said Pointy. "Then brace yourself. Things are worse than they were yesterday."

A blow struck Blackie in the solar plexus. "Worse?" he asked.

"Yes. The men who allegedly kidnapped—"

"Allegedly! Wait a damned—"

"Shut up and listen, will you? The kidnappers have gotten together and manufactured a story that they think will ruin our self-defense plea. They claim that Miss Theodopolis deliberately seduced the man she—"

"That's a lie!"

"Blackford," Pointy said patiently, "of course it's a lie. But it's their word against ours, and we only have five little boys to tell our side of the story. They've got adults who have powerful relatives. We've got a weak case, Blackie."

Blackie tightened his jaw. The time had come for drastic measures. "Okay, Pointy, I've got an idea."

Pointy smiled. "Good. I was hoping you might. Shall we all have some coffee and discuss the possibilities?"

CHAPTER SIXTEEN

IT WAS THE SILENCE, Katherine decided, that she minded the most. Stephen had finally convinced the air force to release her, and she was settled at the Hilton in a top-floor suite the likes of which any sane woman would have adored. But Katherine couldn't get used to the silence.

It wasn't just the noise of the sea that she missed, she thought. It was the constant turmoil of having five youngsters and one overgrown boy underfoot constantly. There had been precious little privacy aboard *Bobbie McGee*, but it had been oddly comforting to know that other people were just a whisper away.

"For heaven's sake," she murmured to herself, standing on a balcony of the Hilton that overlooked the beach and tennis courts. A hot wind fanned her face, and her hair streamed around her shoulders as she shook her head at her own foolishness. "I miss them."

From inside the room Stephen called, "What did you say, darlin'?"

"Nothing," Katherine replied over her shoulder hastily, feeling guilty. "Just mumbling."

Stephen sauntered out onto the balcony and put his arm around her from behind. He kissed her ear lightly.

"You're having a rough time," he soothed, drawling. "You're allowed to talk to yourself, I think."

Katherine smiled wanly, but didn't answer. Stephen's words weren't comforting anymore. She sensed he was making conversation by rote, following all the directions for polite responses. Stephen had no spontaneity, that was it. He said the right things as if he'd practiced them before a mirror first, the way he checked his clothing before going out. Blackie never stopped to think what he was going to say. He just said it.

Stephen let her go and neatly tugged the starched cuff of his shirt out from under his coat sleeve. "I have to run to a meeting now, Katherine. I'm seeing the governor this afternoon. After that, unfortunately, I have to meet with my ex-wife."

Katherine roused herself. "Oh, Stephen, I'm sorry that situation is not improving."

"Not improving?" he asked, giving a bitter smile. "I had him, Katherine. Jimmy was mine until she took him last night. Can't she see how much I want him, too?"

"You can't arrange some kind of agreement?"

Stephen pulled a face. "We are having the same old argument. I hope to get a fairer share of my son's time, and she wants him with her constantly. Even you see more of him than I do. I keep thinking she'll listen to reason, but—" He stopped himself and grinned, then lifted his hands to cup Katherine's shoulders. "Well, my problems are nothing for you to worry about. I'll be back in time to take you to dinner tonight, I promise."

"Stephen, if there's anything I can do to help the situation with Jimmy..."

He laughed gently. "There you go. Offering to help me when you're in a bit of a fix yourself. Don't spend a minute thinking about it today, all right? Just rest. I'll come get you later. Will you be all right by yourself until then?"

Katherine nodded. Though she couldn't think of a more horrible way to spend the afternoon, she had no intention of going out in public once her picture had appeared in the newspapers. Solitary confinement was making her nerves raw, however. Her nightmares had come back, and images had even begun to haunt her during her waking hours, too.

Stephen kissed her forehead. "You're such a brave trooper, darlin'. Keep your chin up. I'll be back as soon as I can."

Listlessly she said, "Bye."

She stayed on the balcony, her face turned to the breeze again, straining to smell the ocean. She heard the door close. Then, sighing, she gazed out at the ocean. Being released into Stephen's custody was better than jail, but what she wouldn't give to be back out on the waves with nothing to look at but the open sky!

Staring at the sea from a hotel room only depressed her more, she decided. Slowly Katherine went back into the suite. Stephen had thoughtfully provided some new clothing, food and glossy magazines, but she couldn't work up an interest in any of those diversions. To please him she had dressed in a powder-blue linen sheath he'd bought for her in the hotel boutique. Katherine had not even glanced at her reflection after she put it on.

As she paused in the doorway to the balcony, the telephone rang in the empty room. The sound startled her, and she realized how long it had been since she'd heard the signal. Civilization wasn't so civilized after all. Anyone at all could interrupt.

Katherine picked up the receiver reluctantly. "Yes?"

"Miss Theodopolis? This is Michaels at the main lobby desk. There's a gentleman here to see you. A Mr. Blackford Lowell?"

Katherine gripped the phone with both hands.

"Miss Theodopolis? Are you there?"

"Yes," she said weakly.

"Shall I send him up?"

Adrenaline coursed through her body. Blackie was supposed to be on his way to China by now.

"Miss Theodopolis?"

"Yes," she whispered finally, caution thrown to the wind. "Send him up."

The clerk hung up before she could snatch back the words.

She panicked. Katherine had only enough time to comb her hair and splash her face before she heard him knock softly. Blackie must have taken the express elevator because he was at the door in less than two minutes. Her heart was tearing out of control, but she hesitated on the other side of the door, terrified, for some reason, to open it. Peeking through the security glass, she could see the broad line of a man's shoulders encased in a white shirt. No doubt about it. He was Blackie, all right. Cautiously she unlocked the door and opened it.

Blackie turned around. A navy blazer was slung over one shoulder, and his other hand rested in a trouser pocket. He looked handsome, so startlingly so that he took her breath away.

"Hello," he said.

Speechless, Katherine stared back.

"I deserve a hello, at least."

Slowly she said, "Hello."

Her response was not enough. Blackie's expression clouded and grew taut. Roughly he said, "I deserve a hell of a lot more than a hello, now that I think about it."

He moved fast. In an instant he stepped inside the room, whipped the door closed and pinned Katherine against the wall, his hand grabbing her upper arm in a bone-breaking grip.

Katherine gasped. "What do you think you're doing?" she demanded, writhing against him, her anger instantly overriding the shock. "You big ox! If you're here to—"

"I'm here for a lot of things," he snapped, holding her effortlessly. "But now that you're so close, I'm damned if all my reasons haven't gone clean out of my head. You're beautiful, all right, Kate."

"Stop ogling me!"

He laughed, slightly breathless. "Soon, your ladyship. I've got something to say first."

Heaving against him, Katherine raged, "I hope it's goodbye!"

Blackie's face tightened, and his eyes turned slate gray.

Just watching the light drain from his face caused a sensation as powerful as a kick in her stomach. She'd actually hurt him with her cutting retort. "I'm sorry," she whispered at once, relaxing her struggle against him. "I didn't mean that."

He tilted his head, eyes cold, his mouth a taut line. "Really?"

She gulped. "R-really."

"You want me to stay?"

What was he up to? Katherine met his eyes and was mesmerized for a moment. She felt afraid, but not of Blackie, she thought. It was the way her heart hammered in her chest that was scary. She couldn't breathe, either. Suddenly her self-control seemed distant and unattainable.

Blackie didn't wait for an answer. Perhaps he saw that she was incapable of speech just then. His face was shuttered, but in a voice that was surprisingly husky, he asked, "Did you miss having me around last night?"

"Maybe," she whispered.

He bent closer, closer. "I missed you, Kate. Much more than you can imagine."

Katherine stared up at Blackie, not sure she had heard correctly, yet wildly hoping that she had.

Blackie kissed her then, and Katherine forgot to fight him. Joy leaped inside her. He felt wonderfully familiar and exciting, and she closed her eyes to drink in every detail of his nearness. His lips were full of fire, searing his soul to hers for a timeless instant.

Yes, she'd missed him, she wanted to cry out. Every shred of her had subconsciously yearned for a moment just like this. When he released her, she wound her arms around Blackie's neck. His body was hard and powerful, but it was magically good against hers. Katherine moved to make the contact perfect. With a groan Blackie slid one arm around her waist. He hugged her tightly to his chest, his lips pressed to hers, savoring, reveling, foolishly demanding the sensations they'd both denied.

At last she broke the seething contact. "Blackie—"

"Don't say it," he said, just as urgently as she. "Just don't say anything."

They were both scared. Terrified of giving up, of giving in. Katherine slipped her hand behind his head, weaving her fingers into his curling hair, and her once rigid legs parted and then surrounded his thigh until their limbs were intimately molded. She could feel the first stirrings of his pleasure and couldn't help laughing breathlessly against his mouth. It would always be this way between them. Desire first. Consequences later.

As if she'd said it, Blackie started laughing, too, cradling Katherine and smoothing his palm down her back to the curve that most tempted his hand. He broke the kiss, smiling, then returned as if drawn by magnets, brushing her lips, parting them, stroking them with his tongue. He nipped her chin and growled with the onrush of physical need.

"Good Lord," he muttered, caressing her cheek with his nose while inhaling her scent, "I wonder why it's this way with you? You, of all people."

"Are we such opposites?" she whispered.

"Whatever we are makes the sparks fly, that's for sure," he said. Reality was forgotten. Nuzzling her throat, he chuckled ruefully and mumbled, "I suppose I should have asked first. Is your pal Monahan around?"

She laughed, drunk with being in his arms. Common sense had flown away. How could self-control get so far out of hand? Exhilarated, she hugged Blackie's head so that his lips never left her skin. "No," she whispered, "Stephen's gone."

"Good." He took a deep breath and held it. "I came here for a totally different reason, Kate, but—"

"Yes?"

He pulled back and grinned, holding her gaze with his. It was his dark angel look, one that sparked a tremor of anticipation in Katherine. He caressed her with his eyes. "I haven't had time to case this joint yet," he said, voice low. "Is there a bed?"

Her courage wavered like a fire deprived of fuel. "Blackie—"

"Don't," he said roughly, returning to kiss her mouth once, twice, rekindling the flames. "Don't get scared now," he urged. "Once before we got carried away like this and nothing terrible happened. Katie, love—"

"All right, don't talk," she said swiftly, holding his shoulders so hard that her fingers whitened. She knew her eyes must have reflected the same passion and excitement she could hear in his voice, so she squeezed them tightly shut. "If we talk, we always fight."

"Remind me to pick up the argument with that point," he said, "when I'm finished."

She laughed again, light-headed and euphoric. She wanted to stop pretending, to give up fighting the attraction. She wanted to give in.

Blackie was all man, muscle and bone and supple sinew, all tuned to her with a precision so exact it could only be nature's way. If Blackie, who could stand calm in the face of hurricane winds and man-eating sharks, was reduced to a male animal trembling with urgency and homed-in on her alone, there must be something right between them. The rest of the world would have to wait.

Katherine wrapped her arms around his neck. "Make love with me, Blackie."

"Monahan won't burst in?"

"No. We have all day." When he gathered her into his arms, she nearly said the rest. *We have the rest of our lives.* But that wasn't true. There was only the moment, the hour, the afternoon to be taken.

He carried her to the bed gently, as if she were a priceless treasure he didn't want to scratch. Solemnly he laid her down, stroking her thighs, her flanks, kissing her mouth until she whimpered with the tension. Giving way to mounting urgency, he dragged her clothing off and threw the new dress on the floor. No ceremony, just pure desire.

Katherine wasted not a moment in stripping him, either. She wanted him naked, to sweep his body with her eyes and feast on his male beauty. She wanted to touch him everywhere again, to memorize the contours of his muscles, the texture of his skin. There wasn't time, though. Blackie was too quick, too determined to have her. No games were played this time. And when he pressed inside her, Katherine wasn't surprised to find that she was ready. At the first sight of him in the doorway, she had been ready to receive him.

Though she could hold Blackie at bay in all other matters, Katherine could not deny him the pleasures he took in her body. Gift became possession, and

Katherine was powerless to halt the crescendo in him or in herself. Blackie shouted and fought, trying hard to control his own tensile strength, but the effort became impossible. He drove her into the bed until Katherine felt a universe of sensations streaming in her blood, pumped by a heart so beyond control that she could not even breathe except in wild pants. The rhythm, the pounding of sea and heart and sexual desire throbbed so deeply within her that she called out time and again until the surf broke and washed her senses clean. Then, trembling, rocking still on the beach on which he anchored her, Katherine felt the second wave crest and explode, sending a foam of effervescence shimmering along her nerves like a dazzle of stars. Blackie thrust one last time and found his own climax just as the bright stars winked and dimmed.

He twisted inside her, growling like a wild animal released.

Afterward, tumbled together and shivering with exertion, still stroking each other, though with weakened fingers, they shared a long, uneasy gaze.

"I don't know," she whispered, "if we should have done that, but . . . I feel so alive with you."

He touched her cheek with one finger and traced its curve tenderly. "I didn't hurt you?"

"Of course not."

On a different note he said, "I don't ever want to hurt you, Kate. Honestly I don't."

She turned in his arms and settled her back against his chest. It was still easier talking to Blackie when they didn't have to see each other's face. Nestling in his arms was enough. Murmuring, she said, "We have gotten into the habit of saying things that hurt."

He sighed and nosed through her hair to press a small kiss to the back of her head. "It's a habit we're not going to break yet. I've got things to tell you, Kate."

Uneasy, she tensed at once.

Blackie hugged her. "No," he said, lips touching her earlobe. "Don't start objecting yet. Listen, will you?"

Cautiously she asked, "What is it?"

Blackie expelled a long breath as he decided how to begin. "I trust you, Kate," he finally murmured. "You know that, don't you? During the past couple of weeks, I've learned a lot from you. Nobody could coax me out of exile until you came along. Do you understand?"

She was afraid then. There was more coming, she could sense it. Tears were clogging her eyes, her throat tightened and Katherine could not speak for fear Blackie would detect the evidence in her voice. She nodded against the pillow and clasped Blackie's two hands against her naked breasts.

"All right," he said, soothing her. "I'm asking you to trust me now in return. Will you? Will you do something for me? Without asking too many questions?"

"Wh-what is it?"

He turned her onto her back and used his thumb against her cheek. His smile was gentle, not wicked or teasing. Lightly he kissed her mouth. "I want you to play along with the boys and me."

She blinked and forgot about crying. "Play along? What are you talking about?"

"The inquest. It's going to take place tomorrow or the next day, we're sure. That's when the judge will decide whether or not you should stand trial for murder."

Katherine stared. "What are you going to do?"

"Get you off, if we can. You must have heard that the kidnappers have concocted some kind of story against you that's pretty convincing. Pointy thinks—"

"Pointy?"

"My sailing friend, the lawyer from New York. He's absolutely the best, Kate, and Monahan—"

"Wait," she said, bracing her hand against his shoulder. Anxiety drained away to be replaced by pure suspicion. "I thought we already discussed this matter."

Blackie hesitated, eyeing her. "Don't get stubborn, Kate. Not now. We're going to get you off the hook, but it means ditching Monahan early."

Calmly she objected, "Stephen is my friend, Blackie. I can't just—"

"Stephen can go to hell," he snapped, releasing her entirely. "You don't owe him a damned thing—not when your freedom is at stake!"

Katherine sat up and reached for the sheet. "I may not owe him anything, but—"

Blackie thrust away from her, glaring. Harshly he accused, "You don't imagine that you're in love with him, surely?" His eyes glittered suddenly. "Judas, Kate, you're not sleeping with him, are you? In this bed?"

"No, of course not," Katherine said quickly, gathering the sheet to her body. Her throat became horribly dry, almost painful as she tried to explain. "After you and I— Well, Stephen and I decided on separate beds, naturally. He's staying in the other room. But he and I care for each other, Blackie, and he wants to help—"

"My God! The man's an idiot when it comes to law! I think you must *want* to go to jail!"

"What?"

A beat of silence passed. "That's it, isn't it?" Blackie stared at her. "You're feeling guilty about this murder thing and you *want* jail!"

"Of course I—I'm feeling guilty! Blackie, I *killed* a man!"

He grabbed her wrist in a grip so hard she cried out. His face was white, his jaw tightened dangerously. "You were attacked, dammit. For all you know, he could have planned to kill you when he was finished with his fun and games." Blackie shook her. "For crying out loud, Kate, it was self-defense!"

"We don't know for sure!" she cried. "Maybe he didn't mean to hurt me, maybe he—"

"Oh, stop it! You told me yourself the night it happened! He had his fingers in your mouth, didn't he? Does that sound like a man who was worried about how you felt?"

"N-no, but—"

"Look," Blackie cut in, "you're upset. You're a nice girl from Ohio who's got a strict idea of what's right and what's wrong. Kate, you're in the right this time! Just because you cracked some maniac's head with a rock doesn't mean—"

"Don't!" she cried, hugging her ears to stop the words. "Don't try to talk me out of this, Blackie!"

"Good Lord, that's it, isn't it? You really think you deserve to be punished, don't you?"

The look on his face was shocked, disgusted and angry. Katherine couldn't hold herself together anymore. Her own feelings of revulsion swept up like the black waters of a vortex. She gave up fighting. She lost control. "It was horrible!" she cried, her voice breaking with a sob. She turned on Blackie and blew up. "I did a horrible thing, Blackie! I hated him and I killed him! I had his blood all over me! On my hands, in my eyes . . . you saw it all over my clothes! He'd be alive today if I hadn't hit him!"

"And you might be dead."

She put her hands over her face. "Maybe so," she choked, too upset to get a grip on herself. It felt good to surrender finally. "Maybe so. I can't stand it. Maybe you can—you're different from me. You don't mind being bad sometimes—you even seem to enjoy it. But I—it's too awful for me. I enjoyed myself on the boat when I should have been sorry for what I did."

Blackie cursed softly and rolled out of bed.

She looked after him, tears streaming down her face. "I was having fun with you and the boys, enjoying myself when that man's body was—was rotting or—or—"

"Don't torture yourself," Blackie snapped.

"I can't help it!" Katherine threw herself back down onto the bed. Further explanations were futile. How could he understand the way she felt? Desperately she cried, "It's the way I am, Blackie!"

"Then what was this all about?" he demanded menacingly, gesturing at the bed with a sweep of his hand. "You were eager just now, Kate. You made love like a—" He caught himself and stopped, staring. "My God, was I supposed to be some kind of last cigarette for you? One last wrestling match before you go to jail?"

"Maybe," she said dully. "Maybe that's what it was. I don't know. I just—I wanted you, that's all."

"Me? Or anyone? Would Stephen have fit the bill just now? Could any man have pounded you into the mattress hard enough to satisfy your desire for punishment?"

Katherine could not answer. She was not sure why she had allowed Blackie to bring her to the bed. It had been pure impulse . . . or instinct. Punishment hadn't entered her mind. But the sensuality they enjoyed had helped somehow. Sharing the most carnal intimacy with him had made her feel alive when she wanted to be reminded of life's power. And Blackie represented the most powerful force that had ever entered her life. No, he was not punishment. He led her to high places where good and bad did not matter.

But Katherine did not try to explain to him. She wasn't sure she was capable. And Blackie would not understand if he were angry.

There was silence after that. Then she heard Blackie getting into his clothes. *Let him go,* she thought. She lay still and did not try to get herself under control again. The tears flowed from inside her without sobs, spilling in hot spurts across her cheeks.

Finally Blackie spoke again. His voice was cold. "We have a plan," he said, "and it's going to work whether we've got your cooperation or not. Are you listening? All we want is for you to keep quiet at the inquest. Don't volunteer any information, and for God's sake don't argue with us."

Katherine put her head against the pillow and covered her other ear.

Blackie said, "I want you to trust me, Kate. I know what's best this time. Until now you've made the rules. This time it's my turn. You've got to trust me."

She sucked in a deep breath. "Blackie—"

"No," he interrupted. "I won't listen to any more sermons from you. You were right to kill the son of a bitch, and nothing will change my mind about that. You're going to go free, understand? I've just spent the last eight years of my life in a prison I made for myself, and I won't see you go through the same experience."

Though she did not respond, Blackie returned to the bed. He drew the sheet up to her shoulders and tucked the blanket around her legs. Bending close, he kissed her cheek and tasted the tears. Finally he touched her thoughtfully with his fingertip, drawing a line through the slick wetness.

"Goodbye, Katie," he said.

CHAPTER SEVENTEEN

THE COURTROOM WAS AIR-CONDITIONED to a temperature so cold that Katherine shivered in her sleeveless linen dress. She sat in a hard chair beside Stephen at a polished table near the front of a long room crowded with the local press corps and curious spectators. Stephen made frantic notes on a yellow legal pad, offering no comfort. Katherine was nervous, too. And frightened.

Across the aisle was the prosecuting attorney, looking smug and resolute in an Italian-made suit. The smell of his musk cologne traveled for yards. Beside him sat the Torres brothers. Katherine recognized the pair immediately as two of the men who were involved in the kidnapping. Like a terrified rabbit she could hardly tear her eyes from them.

There were only two of them today, both swarthy, muscular little men with flat black eyes that reflected no personality. They might have been stone statues, for they were motionless and devoid of expression, ignoring both the crowd and Katherine. One of them had glanced her way when she arrived, and his eyes had flicked down her bare legs before the lawyer had touched his arm and made him turn away.

An inquest required no jury, of course, so the judge came out alone and called the noisy room to order.

Stephen sat up straighter, pulling himself alert. Katherine did not bother. Her head was filled with a numbing buzzing. She only wanted the procedure to be over with.

The judge laid down some rules for the attorneys. He was an elderly man, but his vitality was not impaired by his age. His face was tanned, and his right arm, bare to the elbow under his flowing robe, was hard with tennis muscle. Though his hair was white, the judge looked alert as a boy. When he studied Katherine from behind bifocals, she noted how keen his gaze was.

He began the inquest by requesting that the prosecuting attorney come forward to explain the circumstances. "Mr. Barto?"

Barto, oozing confidence as well as cologne, got briskly to his feet and stepped before the bench to speak. He was interrupted immediately.

A commotion at the back of the room caused everyone to turn around and look. Katherine put one hand to her mouth and gasped.

It was Blackie, of course, but he looked appalling. His dramatic late entrance only made his scruffy clothes more obvious to the courtroom. He had not combed his hair, and his beard was rough. There were great circles under his red-rimmed eyes. One look informed everyone that he was recovering from an all-night binge of drinking and carousing. His trousers were encrusted with salt, and his grungiest sweater had been torn around the neck, perhaps in a fistfight. He looked dangerous and predatory. Rasputin entering the czar's grand ballroom could not have caused a greater stir.

The biggest reaction to his arrival came from the rear of the room where, Katherine realized, all the boys had been sitting together. They must have been requested by the court to postpone their return home. A collection of parents sat nearby. Peter, Harold and the twins perched on a bench in a neat row, dressed in clean uniforms, complete with straight bow ties. Their faces were scrubbed, their hair trimmed and tidy. They all stared at Blackie with huge eyes, looking almost frightened.

Blackie took no notice of them. He swept the room with contempt until he laid eyes on Katherine, and then a bolt of electricity might have passed between them. Katherine was too stunned by the real power of his gaze to move.

Then the moment broke and Blackie strode down the aisle, still the object of everyone's attention. Noisily he scraped his chair across the floor until its position suited him. Then he sat down, propped one leg up on the chair in front and relaxed, tipping back his own seat and folding his arms across his chest, ready to listen.

The judge cleared his throat with disapproval, frowning over the rims of his glasses at the spectacle Blackie had made of himself. With an annoyed wave he directed his attention to the prosecuting attorney again, ready to continue. "Proceed, Mr. Barto."

"Thank you, Your Honor. We're here to discuss the death of one Alfred Torres, a father, husband and community leader, who died as a result of a head trauma on the night of the twelfth day of last month. His body was transported to the morgue on Pago Pago, but he was shipped here, Your Honor, last week. It is our contention that Mr. Torres died during a scuffle with the woman Katherine Theodopolis. I think we should start with the coroner's report, sir.''

The judge accepted the stapled papers and glanced through them briefly. "I'll study these later, Mr. Barto. I may want to hear from the coroner also."

"He's ready to testify, Your Honor. In the interest of getting all the pertinent facts out in the open as quickly as possible—knowing that Your Honor does not like to waste time—I'd like to call Mr. Joseph Torres to speak.''

The judge nodded.

The older of the two Torres brothers got to his feet and shuffled to a raised chair beside the judge's bench. He was overweight and wore too-snug, bell-bottom blue jeans with a white shirt hanging out, the lowest two buttons unfastened to allow for the bulge of his stomach. Though he wore no tie, the man's neck had begun to sweat, discoloring his collar, which was already stained. Katherine couldn't help but think that it was hard to imagine such a disreputable-looking character could be a pillar of any community.

Perhaps he sensed that the gathered crowd was against him already. When he was seated and sworn in, Torres took out a crumpled handkerchief and began to wipe his face. He manufactured an expression of a noble man about to do his duty.

From behind her Katherine heard Blackie snort.

"Mr. Torres," began the prosecuting attorney, "will you tell us the events of the day your brother died, please?''

"Sure," Torres said, his voice thick. He coughed to clear his throat and rolled his handkerchief into a ball between his palms. "We, uh, we picked up some passengers from another boat, an' she was with them."

"Who was with the other passengers?"

Torres pointed. "Her. The bimbo."

Stephen stood up. "Your Honor, I object to—"

"I agree," said the judge. "Mr. Torres, in my courtroom you're going to have to refrain from making crude remarks about anyone, understand?"

Katherine sat back in her chair, wishing she had brought a sweater. She was freezing. She closed her eyes and tried to concentrate on staying warm.

Mr. Barto got his witness back on the right track.

"Okay," said Torres when he understood what was expected of him. "We were out on my brother's boat, an' she started making passes at all of us. You know, batting her eyelashes, showing us her legs. She was hot, let me tell you." Torres laughed uncertainly, then sobered and picked up the thread of his story with haste. "There was a storm coming up," he continued, "so we went into a cove on an island to wait it out. She kept it up the whole time—you know, making suggestions an' that kind of stuff. My father decided to take her up on her offer, so they went onto the beach. Next thing I knew, she was yellin', an' we, well, we all went down to the beach an' found him lying in the sand with blood all over. We looked for her, but she was gone. It was her, all right. Nobody else was on that island. We looked all over it that night."

"I see," said Mr. Barto. "Now, just to be sure of your role in these events, Mr. Torres, perhaps we should back up a bit. Will you tell us why you picked up Miss Theodopolis and the other passengers on that day?"

"Okay," said Torres, clasping his hands on his lap. "We were hired to find a boatload of kids. They were taking a—an excursion trip, we was told. We were supposed to find a kid named Jimmy Monahan."

It was true, Katherine remembered. They *had* asked for Jimmy. How could she not have realized? Katherine sat up, startled. "Jimmy?"

Stephen jumped to his feet. "Your Honor!"

"Yes, Mr. Monahan?"

"Your Honor—" Stephen's voice squeaked with nervousness, "—I don't see what this has to do with the matter at hand. If—"

The judge interrupted sternly. "You're stepping into my territory, son. This is an inquest, not a trial. Go ahead, Torres. What about this boy you were supposed to find?"

"Well," said Torres, "we were supposed to snatch the kid. I don't know the details. But there were a bunch of kids on that boat, and the bim—the lady wasn't very cooperative, and the kids were so scared they couldn't talk. So we decided to take the bunch of them and figure out later which one was the one we were supposed—"

"I see," said Barto. "Can you tell us who hired you, Mr. Torres?"

Torres shrugged. "My father made the deal. I don't know for sure."

"But you heard him say...?"

"Yeah, he said that the kid's father wanted him snatched. He paid my brother to keep quiet, too. But we haven't seen a nickel. There was a deal to take the kid away from his mama."

Voices erupted. The courtroom was suddenly vibrating with commotion. The judge called for order, but his voice was drowned by the babble. Barto smiled and Torres began to daub his face with his sodden handkerchief.

Katherine said coldly, "Stephen."

He turned to her, anxious and sputtering. "Katherine, th—this was not supposed to come out. Really it wasn't!"

She stared at him as if seeing the man for the first time. Perhaps she should have put the pieces together long ago. Her friendship with Stephen had clouded her thinking. His face was white, his mouth trembling. Stephen looked frightened. She said, "This can't be true, can it?"

"Well," he began, swallowing twice before he could explain. "Well, Katherine, it wasn't supposed to happen the way it did. I had to buy some time before I could explain. I love my son, you know, and I—"

"My God," she said, feeling faint.

"I was desperate. I wanted to get him away from my ex-wife. You know what a stickler she's been about letting me—"

"Stephen," Katherine exploded. "You caused the whole thing!"

"Katherine!"

She was on her feet suddenly and shouting at him, crazy with anger, mindless of the roomful of people watching. "You idiot! You jeopardized your son, don't you see? We could have all ended up hurt or worse all because you wanted to kidnap your own child from your—"

"I didn't have any more choices!" Stephen cried helplessly. "I couldn't help that it got out of hand! I hired those men because I—I heard they could handle a job like— Well, I never thought they'd hurt you! Please, I—"

She yanked out of his reach when Stephen made a feeble swipe for her hand. "Don't you touch me!"

"Please, Katherine, you must understand that—"

"Your Honor," called a stentorian voice from the audience, "may Miss Theodopolis make a change in representation?"

The judge shouted, "Anything! Just get this room in order again."

Pointy Hargraves appeared behind Stephen and tapped his shoulder. "May I cut in?"

Stephen shrank back from Katherine, his face pleading. Even his perfectly cut suit and white shirt could not disguise his terrible error in judgment. "Katherine, I hope you can forgive me. It was all a huge mistake, you know."

"She knows," said Pointy, dropping his briefcase on the table. "Now run along, old fellow," he said kindly. "Let me see what I can do, all right?"

Stephen gave up trying to be convincing. He knew when he was beaten. Gathering his papers hurriedly, he promised, "I'll talk to you later." Pointy pushed him out into the aisle, and Stephen said desperately. "I'll explain everything, I promise."

"Order, please," the judge commanded. "Let's get this train running on time again, gentlemen. Who are you, young man?"

"Pierpoint Hargraves, Your Honor," without taking offense at the judge's deliberate attempt to address him as if he were a child. "I'll represent Miss Theodopolis now, sir."

"Hargraves...Hargraves?" The judge pursed his lips. "Do I know you, son?"

"I don't believe so, sir. May I have a moment to speak with my client?"

The judge reached for his water pitcher. "Why not? Just make it snappy, boys. I want this mess cleared up quickly."

Katherine was cold and numb. She couldn't think, but she allowed Pointy to ease her into her chair once more. He sat down beside her and began to wrap something warm around her shoulders. Katherine was only partly aware of his ministrations. "Here," he said, voice soft but urgent in her ear. "Pull yourself together, my girl. Are you all right? Need a sip of water?"

Katherine managed to shake her head. "N-no."

"All right, listen up." Pointy touched her chin, forcing Katherine to look him square in the eyes. "I want you to keep quiet from now on, all right? This is going to get rougher before it gets better, understand? Don't say a word—promise me? Don't open your mouth, no matter what happens."

Dully she nodded, huddling under the woolly garment Pointy had wound around her shoulders. Stunned, Katherine recognized it as Blackie's sweater. She touched the sleeve. He'd known she was cold, of course. Blackie knew everything.

Pointy was on his feet, and Katherine forced herself to listen to what he was saying.

"We want you to understand how little my client knew about the events that took place around her,

Your Honor. And I must respectfully claim that most of the story Mr. Torres just told us is a complete fabrication.''

The judge was grouchy by that time. ''How do you intend to prove that, Hargraves?''

''By asking one of the witnesses of the events to come forward and tell his side of things.''

''Who?''

''Harold Pickney, Your Honor. One of the boys taken by the Torres family on the afternoon of the alleged murder.''

Harold obeyed the summons by standing up and marching down the aisle like a little toy soldier, though he carefully skirted Blackie's relaxed leg where it was stretched out in his path. Importantly Harold took the seat by the judge's bench and sat alertly there, his eyes alive, hands folded precisely on his knee.

''Now, Harold,'' Pointy began, when the oath had been recited, ''how about telling us exactly what happened?''

Harold's voice sounded childish, but eager. ''Starting where, sir?''

Pointy frowned thoughtfully. ''How about starting backward, Harold? Does that make sense? Tell us why you haven't spoken up about these events until now.''

''Nobody asked me, sir.''

Everyone laughed and Pointy looked amused. ''Of course. But something else was bothering you, wasn't it, Harold?''

Harold did not answer. He blinked uncertainly behind his thick glasses.

''Come, come, Harold,'' coaxed Pointy. ''You're perfectly safe now. Nobody will harm you. In fact, if you tell the truth, the person who has threatened you will be arrested.''

Harold bit his lip.

"Who threatened you, Harold?"

Harold swallowed and squeaked, "Mr. Lowell, sir."

"Lowell?" interrupted the judge. "Who's he?"

Harold turned eagerly to the judge. "He's the man who picked us up on the island, sir. After we escaped the men who kidnapped us, Mr. Lowell took us prisoner."

Katherine sat up again, alert and frightened. *Now what?*

"Go on," said the judge.

Harold wiggled in his chair until he could have a private conversation with the judge. "Well, Your Honor," he began ingenuously, "we were kidnapped by those men in the motorboat, and they tried to hurt Miss Theodopolis. She didn't encourage them at all, sir, but they were, well, they pulled at her clothes some. The one man dragged her onto the beach. She escaped from him, and we jumped off the boat, too, but another boat came. Mr. Lowell's. He made us get on *his* boat, and then he went after Miss Theodopolis, too."

"Went after her?" the judge asked.

"Yes, sir. He fought with the other man to see which one would get her."

Katherine struggled to her feet. "Harold!"

Pointy flew to her side, his face white with tension. He shoved her back down into her chair again and pinned her there. "Go ahead, Harold."

The boy nodded and proceeded to lie as if he had been born a con artist. "Well, sir, Mr. Lowell wanted

Miss Theodopolis to come with him because he said she was pretty. He intended to ransom me and my friends, but he wanted to take our teacher along, too. I don't know why, sir."

The judge nodded grimly. "I can imagine, son. Go ahead."

"Well, Mr. Lowell was awfully mean," Harold glanced warily into the courtroom. Apparently frightened, he turned back to the judge and lowered his voice, "He used to beat us, and he hurt Miss Theodopolis, too. He made us work on his boat, and he wouldn't give us enough food or water. It was terrible, sir. Just like *Treasure Island*."

Horrified, Katherine glanced over her shoulder. Blackie was still sitting in the crowd, and he met her eyes above the heads of the people between them. *Trust me,* he had said.

"Back up, Harold," said the judge gently, drawing Katherine's attention once more. "Back up to the night on the beach. What happened between Mr. Lowell and Mr. Torres?"

"Oh," said Harold, widening his eyes innocently. "Miss Theodopolis didn't kill anyone, Your Honor. You should believe me. Mr. Lowell did it. He hit the other man and killed him."

Katherine closed her eyes and moaned.

"You see, Your Honor," Pointy said, still resting his hands on her shoulders to hold her steady, "my client is perfectly innocent. She was kidnapped twice and thoroughly abused all along the line—mentally and perhaps sexually. She's the wrong person to be accusing at this inquest, sir. We should be arresting Blackford Lowell."

Someone screamed. A crash sounded at the back of the room, and Katherine jerked around, a cry leaping to her throat. People milled around, then suddenly split apart, making room. In the middle of the crowd was Blackie, on his feet, eyes flashing. "Stand back!" he shouted.

Katherine cried out. Blackie had grabbed Peter and pinned the boy against his own body. There was a knife at Peter's throat in Blackie's powerful hand. He looked absolutely capable of violence, too. His face was hard, eyes piercing. The crowd backed away from him.

"Stay away," he warned again. "Nobody's going to arrest me!"

The judge shouted, "You can't get away with this, young man!"

Blackie laughed rudely and hitched the knife dangerously higher. Peter gasped and froze. Snarling, Blackie said, "I will get away with it. You'll see. Anybody lays a hand on me, and this kid dies. Got that? Now back away from the door. I'm getting out of here."

Slowly the crowd of people nearest the door gave him room. Blackie backed toward the exit, holding the knife perilously close to Peter's tender skin. Peter walked with him, but his thin legs were unsteady.

Suddenly a door opened behind the judge.

"Get him!" someone shouted.

Katherine saw a uniformed man leap from the judge's chamber. There was a gun in his hand.

She had to do something. It came to her mind at once, and she screamed. Sweeping the table, she fell sideways, pretending to swoon and making as much noise as she could in the act. She knocked over her chair, which hit the floor with a crash, and papers went flying everywhere. Pointy shouted and dove down as if to help her. Harold shrieked. The crowd burst into hysteria again. All hell broke loose.

"It's all right," Pointy said finally, pulling Katherine to sit up. "He made it. He's gone."

Katherine was too weak to stand, too undone to speak. She hugged Pointy, and he wrapped one arm around her. Patting her back, he said, "It's all over. You're in the clear. It's over. He'll get away."

POINTY HARGRAVES THEN PROVED he was a man of action.

After the judge had dismissed them, he hustled Katherine out of the building and into a car that had been waiting. He whisked her to the Hilton and ushered her into the elevator without speaking. Katherine clutched Blackie's sweater around her shoulders and allowed herself to be bullied.

When they were alone in her suite at the hotel, Pointy said, "Now straight to bed before you faint, young lady."

"No," she said. "I couldn't sleep, Pointy."

"Then I'll call the house doctor. We'll get you a sedative, and—"

"No, please," she insisted, shaky but determined. "You must tell me everything. Is this what you intended to have happen? Is this the plan Blackie came to tell me about?"

"Sort of. I admit we were caught off guard by the Monahan wrinkle. My word, he really orchestrated the kidnapping of his own son, didn't he? I couldn't believe our luck."

"Luck!"

"Yes, of course. We weren't sure how we could explain that whole side of the story. Why the Torres family kidnapped you in the first place was the mystery. Now we know. They were hired."

Katherine sank down onto the sofa, mentally exhausted. "By Stephen of all people—mild-mannered Stephen Monahan."

Pointy lounged against one of the stools at the bar and folded his arms, smiling and satisfied.

Katherine came out of her reverie. "Never mind about Stephen, for heaven's sake. Where is Blackie now?"

Pointy laughed and shrugged. "Out on the ocean, of course. He had to clear out of here as fast as possible, or he'd be in jail next. Quite a clever plan, don't you think?"

"I don't know," she said uneasily, hugging herself. "I have a terrible feeling about this, Pointy."

He chuckled and came toward her. "Now, now. Blackford warned me about your high ideals, Miss Kate. He said to get you out of the courtroom as quickly as possible, or you were liable to ruin everything by blurting out the truth."

"What if he gets caught?" Katherine appealed to him honestly. "All he's done is substitute himself for me. Pointy, if Blackie returns to Guam, he'll be arrested immediately!"

"He won't come back," Pointy assured her kindly. "Don't worry about Blackford. Despite everything he's been through, he always comes out alive. He'll manage this time, too."

Katherine prayed that he would. Blackie deserved to come out alive. He'd been through hell, and she'd caused part of it. Holding his tattered sweater in her fingers, she wished he was safe. She wished he was with her.

The phone startled both of them. Pointy crossed to it, asking, "Shall I? Hello? Yes."

Katherine waited, holding her breath. Was it Blackie?

"Oh, Lord," said Pointy, and he quickly spun around so Katherine could not see his face. "What do you mean?"

Katherine stood up, trembling with fear. "Blackie? Is he all right?"

Pointy waved his hand to calm her. "Don't make a move, Harold. I'll come right away. Yes, good boy. You did exactly the right thing. Are you all right? Not sick? Atta boy. Hold on. I'm coming."

"What's wrong?" Katherine demanded, when he had hung up.

Pointy sighed explosively. "I don't believe it."

"What?"

"They've got the wrong body."

Katherine stared. A light-headed sensation swept her like a wave, and she sat down unsteadily.

"I mean the wrong Torres," Pointy corrected, running his hand across the top of his head and trying to make sense of everything. Sounding astonished, he said, "It's not Alfred who's dead at all. Someone just turned him up on the Gilbert Islands—alive and kicking."

"Alive?"

Agitated, Pointy began to pace. "The judge ordered Harold taken down to identify the body in the morgue. The kid took one look and nearly threw up, but he made the ID. It wasn't Alfred you killed, Kate. It's his father who's dead."

"His father?" Katherine cried. "The old man? Pointy, he didn't come near me all night! I swear it was Alfred that I hit."

"Then you didn't kill him," Pointy snapped, already heading for the door. "The man you hit is still alive." With a harsh laugh he said, "My heavens, Miss Kate, you might have been suffering all this time for no reason. I don't think you killed anyone! They're trying to frame you." Making a U-turn, he came back to her. "My dear, will you be all right if I leave?"

Stunned, she nodded.

"You're sure?" Pointy insisted, bending over the arm of the sofa to touch her hand. "Blackie will kill me for leaving you like this, but I've got to run. You'll stay here? I'll send the hotel doctor up at once, all right?"

She wasn't sure if she answered. Katherine sat on the sofa and didn't move. She didn't hear Pointy go, and she didn't speak. For an eternity she sat in silence.

Was it true? Had the man lived? She hadn't killed anyone?

Where was Blackie? He'd know for certain. He could tell her the truth. Not thinking, Katherine got up again. With his sweater around her shoulders, she left the suite, not even stopping to lock the door. She rode the elevator to the lobby and walked out into the fading sunlight. The sounds around her blurred. She was blind to the busy sights, the color and laughter of tourists. Her brain was a muddle. Walking, Katherine headed for the bay. She would find Blackie aboard *Bobbie McGee*, and they could sail away together.

She had been in shock, Katherine decided later. Her mind had ceased to function on a conscious level.

It was Stephen who found her wandering on the dock after dark hours later. He took her back to the hotel. Katherine was too upset to even recognize him. Stephen treated her like an invalid. Somehow, before he even spoke, she knew something was terribly wrong.

"I'm sorry, Katherine," he said, once the hotel doctor was present. "You'll have to learn eventually."

She fought like a mad woman, and it took both men to subdue her. "Tell me, Stephen," she begged, trying to fight off the pill the doctor offered. "Where's Blackie?"

"I'm sorry," Stephen said, sounding very far away. "The boat blew up. Something to do with propane gas in the galley. Lowell is dead. The boy, too."

CHAPTER EIGHTEEN

THE NIGHTMARES RETURNED. Even though she knew that the murder was no longer real, Katherine dreamed the same sequence again and again. Only when the horror was finished, when she'd struck the blow and felt a man's blood on her own flesh, only then did she see that it was not Alfred Torres who lay lifelessly on the beach. It was Blackie Lowell.

She woke weeping, disoriented and sweating, but too exhausted to drag herself from the bed. She had killed him. Certainly she had sent him to his death. Trying to save her from undeserved punishment, Blackie had made a mistake with *Bobbie*. He had slipped just once and he'd died. For her.

Katherine knew she should take comfort in knowing that he'd been with his precious boat when it happened. For that, Blackie was probably smiling in heaven—or maybe hell, knowing his propensity for being wicked when he chose. But Katherine couldn't be happy about the circumstances of his death.

She couldn't feel anything. Not anger, not outrage, not frustration. Only a terrible oneness. Katherine had never felt so utterly alone. That kind of grief was pain she wasn't sure she could bear.

So she took drugs. She swallowed the pills and drank the water and slept. The nightmares were punishment she was willing to suffer. Blackie had said she wanted to be punished, and he was right.

Stephen tried to help, and in her state, she soon grew weary of telling him she never wanted to see his face again. She should have given him credit sooner. When he denied her the sleeping pill, she screamed at him like a woman gone over the edge of sanity. He gave in that night, terrified by her fury, but the next day, when she finally opened her eyes in mid-afternoon, he stood firm.

"No, Katherine. Sleeping through this isn't the way to cope." He brought her clothes to the bed and thrust them into her hands. "Get dressed. I owe you this much after what's happened. Get up and I'll take you out."

"I won't go."

"You can't stay here and sleep anymore. You need food and sunshine. My God, you wouldn't suffer this much if they'd sent you to prison! Now get up!"

She wanted to refuse. But the mention of sunlight tempted her. Maybe standing in the sun and listening to the ocean would bring him back, at least for a few moments in her imagination. Weak as a colt, she slid out of bed and accepted the clothing. Yes, she would go into the sunshine.

Despite her protests, Stephen forced her to walk to the bay where the sailboats were tied up. She looked carefully at each boat, trying to find one that reminded her of *Bobbie McGee*. But the boats were all new and gleaming, rich men's boats with sleek lines and layers of expensive paint. Not one looked like gallant, grubby, little *Bobbie*. Each beautiful boat caused Katherine even more intense pain.

At last they came upon a long, lovely boat with flags flying and party lights strung along her timbers. The sun was resting on the horizon, turning the sky pink as the inside of an oyster, and the fine mahogany finish of the craft glowed warm above the waterline. She rode gently on subtle waves. Her name was painted in calligraphy on her bow. *Nightcap.*

Katherine spoke for the first time all evening. "That's Pointy's boat."

Stephen brought himself up short. "Hargraves's? I thought he left days ago."

"He did?"

"Yes, the day—when we heard about Lowell's accident. The air force spotted some wreckage, and he went off to see if he couldn't find, well, anything. I guess he's back."

The urge to run away clawed at her. Katherine did not want to see anyone. But Pointy was one man who no doubt had known Blackie better than she had. She strained forward.

Stephen released her hand. "I can't go," he explained, understanding her intention before she said it aloud. "I've humiliated myself enough already. To face such a respected member of my profession— Well, you go talk to him alone. I'll come back and get you later."

Katherine nodded. She walked away from Stephen.

Nightcap was a beautiful boat for beautiful people. Katherine was not surprised to see Pointy lounging on her deck with a glass of wine in one hand and a beautiful woman sitting close by. He looked tired, though. His face was turned up to the sun as if for nourishment. When she appeared on the dock and her shadow fell across his eyes, he tipped his head forward, saw her and smiled. Without hesitation Pointy put aside his drink and got up.

"Kate," he said and came across the deck with his hands outstretched. Helping her down to his level, he kissed her cheek warmly. "I'm glad you came. I was going to come get you tonight."

A kiss was not enough. Katherine hugged him. "Oh, Pointy!"

"Hey!" he called softly, putting his arm around her. "Crying? This isn't the Katie I've heard so much about, is it?"

"I'm sorry." She let go and tried to smile and choke back tears. "I've been such a mess. Are you—did you just get back?"

He kept his arm around her back and kindly led her across the deck to a camp table where a portable bar had been set up. "Yes, we arrived just half an hour ago, in fact. Kate, this is Marjorie Donnell, my, well, a friend of mine. She's my crew, I guess you could say."

Marjorie was taller than Pointy, blond, slender and nearer fifty than thirty. Even dressed in a bathing suit and terry cover-up, she looked elegant and wealthy, a suitable partner in life for Pierpoint Hargraves III. She had a natural smile, though, and warmth in her brown eyes. Her handshake was firm. "Hello, Kate. I'm delighted to meet you. You'll stay with us, won't you?"

"I—"

Pointy interrupted. "I haven't had time to ask her yet, but I'm sure she will."

"Pointy—" Katherine began, but her voice broke. He was so kind, so generous. It had not even entered his head that his friend was dead because of her. She felt the tears start again.

"Now, now," said Pointy, patting her back. "Don't lose that formidable control of yours completely, my dear. You'll spoil all my preconceived notions. We have a lot to talk about."

She tried to smile. "I think I'd like that, Pointy."

He beamed. "Then it's settled? You'll spend some time with us?"

Why not? Katherine knew she didn't want to go back to teaching—not yet, anyway. Perhaps someday she could face the boys again, but not now. The memories of the man who had brought them even closer together would be too painful. Some time spent with Pointy might be the best medicine. She looked at Blackie's good friend and said, "Yes, Pointy. Thank you."

By then Pointy was positively chuckling. "Good girl. Why don't you go below and tidy up first? Wash your face, calm down?"

Marjorie began to protest, "Oh, Pointy, that's—"

"Go on," Pointy said, and he gave her a push. "You'll thank me for suggesting it. Some other people will be coming by any moment—a party of sorts, though it sounds heartless when I call it that. It's the best idea, I'm sure. We'll all feel better when we're together. Run along and fix your face."

Hating the idea of behaving like a fool in public, Katherine obeyed.

The hatchway was much larger than the narrow door leading to *Bobbie*'s cabin. And the interior of Pointy's boat was luxurious in the extreme. Only an Arab sheikh or a Manhattan trial lawyer could afford a boat like *Nightcap*. She hesitated in the middle of the saloon, for unlike Blackie's boat, this cabin was lined with doors that clearly lead to sleeping cabins or storage. Which was the head?

Her question was answered. Water swished, a door opened and he came out with his head in a towel.

Katherine didn't move. She felt her heart stop beating.

Blackie stared back at her as if he'd seen a ghost, too.

Maybe she said his name, but suddenly the light seemed to dim, and she wasn't sure if she was dreaming.

Blackie saw her start to fall. He dropped the towel and lunged for her, catching Katherine just before her knees gave out completely. "Kate! Good God, it wasn't supposed to happen this way! Katie, my love, don't faint. It's all right. It's really me."

She blinked her heavy lashes, fighting to stay conscious, and caught his shoulders with weak hands. "Blackie?"

He laughed and swung her into his arms. "Didn't recognize me with a shave, huh?"

As if a white-hot needle had injected stars into her heart, seething energy filled her veins. Katherine seized him, clawing handfuls of his shirt. "Blackie!" she cried. "Are you—they said you—"

"I'm here," he said, his eyes clear as diamonds and just as full of sparkle. "I wasn't sure I was going to make it a couple of times, living on a rubber dinghy with nothing to eat but chocolate syrup, and the sharks—"

He gave up trying to make light of the moment. No amount of teasing was going to lessen the impact of his miraculous survival. Blackie took a deep breath and hugged her tightly to him, squeezing Katherine as if he never imagined he'd have the chance to do it again. "Oh, Kate."

It was heaven to be in his arms. Joy coursed between them like the pulsing rays of a brilliant sunrise.

When his embrace finally slackened, Katherine opened her eyes and clasped Blackie's face between her hands, wanting to be certain. For a glorious instant there was nothing in her universe but Blackie's radiant eyes, his wicked grin, his wonderful presence. She couldn't believe it. He was alive, here, in her possession. Katherine's throat contracted, and her own eyes were swimming with tears. "Blackie," she said, voice breaking, "I was so unhappy, so sorry—"

"It's all right," he said gently. "I'm here."

She tried to smile, but couldn't manage. "Peter?"

Blackie laughed once, lightly. "He's fine. Here with me, sleeping in that cabin over there at the moment, but otherwise healthy. I looked after him as carefully as you would have. I even radioed his mother. She's coming to get him personally this time."

Relief felt like a fresh breeze across an open sea. Katherine sagged weakly. "Thank God you're both safe."

Blackie carried her to a fold-down couch and eased her onto the cushions. He sat beside her and smoothed a wisp of dark hair back from her temples. He smiled, but Katherine felt a tremor in his fingertips. "I'm sorry," he murmured, his eyes smoky with understanding. "You weren't supposed to go through all this."

"I—I thought you were dead."

"I know. My love, I know exactly how that feels, and I wish I could have spared you the last two days. It couldn't be helped."

She clasped his other hand tightly. "Will you tell me what happened?"

"Of course. I—Pointy was supposed to explain the whole plan to you, but he said he had to go rescue Harold and straighten things out with the coroner."

"You know about that?"

"That the man you hit is still alive? Yes. And I know that after I picked up you and the boys that night, the Torres brothers turned on the old man and killed him for not sharing the payoff equally. When they realized they'd actually killed him, they decided to try to pin the blame on you. Pointy and I didn't know that part, though. We only knew we had to get you off the hook somehow. So the boys and I cooked up the scene in court."

"Harold lied under oath, Blackie. That's—"

"No one is going to prosecute a kid his age, especially not a kid whose father has just been appointed ambassador to Japan. Besides, I forced him to say what he did, and I'm dead now, aren't I? It was our only choice, Kate. I took the blame for everything, then sailed off into the sunset. We calculated that Pointy had to follow me out to sea no later than three hours behind me, so we could make the rendezvous. That's why he had to leave before explaining all this to you."

"What rendezvous are you talking about?"

"After we sank *Bobbie*."

"Oh, Blackie." With dread she asked, "*Bobbie* is really gone?"

He touched her face, smiling gently. "Yes. I blew her up off the Volcano Islands."

Katherine could not speak. The enormity of his sacrifice overwhelmed her. She wept.

"Don't cry," Blackie murmured and bent to brush the tears with his lips. "Don't cry for a boat." Softly he explained, "It was the only way to convince the authorities that I was dead. They didn't figure out the Torres's scheme until later. I didn't want to spend the rest of my life as a fugitive, so this was the easiest way we could think of. Peter and I sailed her out and turned on the gas. We bailed out and shot a flare into the cabin. After a few too many hours in the dinghy, Pointy finally picked us up and brought us—"

"But, Blackie," Katherine argued miserably, interrupting the explanation, "you loved her! How could—"

Blackie touched his fingers to her mouth, stopping the discussion. "Kate," he said solemnly, "I love you much more."

Katherine looked into his face and knew that Blackie was not a man to say those words lightly. He seemed sobered by the finality and depth of that declaration. His voice was husky.

"I do," he said. "I have for a long time, but I was— the past has haunted me, Kate. It's kept me from truly living in the present. I didn't realize how much I cared for you until you tried to throw me out of your life. I couldn't go. I couldn't leave you. Brave, sensitive, beautiful Kate," he murmured, "I'm in love with you."

For an instant Katherine was transfixed by his words, his face, his presence. A burning intensity radiated from Blackie, the man who knew her mind and her body as well as she knew it herself. He was larger than life, a fiery pirate, full of a kind of vigor that most men could only dream about. Inexplicably Katherine felt afraid.

Perhaps he saw it, for he took both of her hands in his and pressed them together, kissing her fingertips before speaking again. "I've been a pig, I know. I've treated you crudely and taunted you from the moment we met. It was stupid—"

"You were troubled," she intervened, whispering.

"Yes," he said steadily. "I had a lot of thinking to finish. You'd imagine that after eight years I could have worked through the way I felt, but I haven't quite. I may never come to terms with losing my wife and our daughter. But with you, Kate, I've learned to stop dwelling on it. With you I've learned that I can love someone without fearing that I'll be punished for the way I care."

The tension in his face was more than she could bear. Katherine said, "I love you, Blackie. So much that it frightens me."

He frowned, puzzled.

She said, "You've destroyed your boat and risked your life for me. I understand why. When I thought you were dead, I'd have given my life for yours without a second thought." Katherine gazed into his eyes, seeking the truth. "I'm afraid of such fierce love, aren't you?"

He said, "For me, that's what love has to be."

"Because you hold yourself responsible for your wife and child." Katherine shook her head. "Blackie, I don't want you to sacrifice yourself for me. I couldn't live with that. Do you understand?"

Softly Blackie asked, "Will you marry me?"

She shook her head. "Not until we reach an understanding. I can't mean more to you than your own life."

"Will you sail away with me?" he asked tensely. "And we'll try to work this out?"

With a smile Katherine touched his hair, petting him back to good spirits. "Will we be alone?"

He laughed then. "Without a platoon of little boys to keep us on the straight and narrow?"

"I love them dearly, and I can't cut myself away from them completely, but a vacation wouldn't hurt."

"No," he agreed. "It wouldn't hurt a bit. We'll visit them from time to time. For now, though, I want to be absolutely alone with you, so we can make love day and night. Whenever and wherever I choose."

"Why, you sound like a frustrated man, Blackie Lowell!"

"Frustrated nearly to the breaking point. Weren't you?"

She smiled benignly. "Wait and see."

"I can't wait," he murmured, dipping closer to press a warm kiss on her throat.

"There's just one problem," Katherine cautioned, though happiness and excitement swelled inside her like sails filling with brisk winds. She put her arms around his neck and sighed. "We haven't got a boat, my love."

"On the contrary!" Blackie said, pulling back and laughing with his old verve once more. He spread his arm to indicate the luxurious yacht around them. "My illustrious competitor has decided to forfeit the race. Pointy's flying back to New York tomorrow to marry his crew and get back to work."

"Forfeit the race! But you destroyed your own boat—"

Blackie tousled her hair and laughed. "A technicality. But Pointy's been cleansing his soul, too, my love. He lost a big case not long ago, and it's taken some soul-searching before he felt capable of going back to work. Your case just piqued his ambition once again. Now he's anxious to go home. And he needs someone to sail this—"

"This bilge bucket?"

"Exactly." Blackie laughed and gathered her seductively into his arms again. "He wants someone to sail it back to New York for him. And he doesn't care how long the voyage takes. It's a bigger boat than I'm used to, of course. I'll need a crew to help—just one inexperienced sailor should be enough. Would you like a new job, Miss Theodopolis?"

"We could take our time?"

"We'll drop anchor every night," he promised, coming so close that his lips touched hers. "And sleep until noon. This boat is *Nightcap*, you know."

"How appropriate." Smiling, Katherine kissed him once lightly, then a second time with more concentration. Her senses swam deliciously. Mouth against his, she murmured, "It will take months to get to New York, you know, if we anchor every night."

"I certainly hope so." Blackie deepened the kiss and slid his hand to the back of her dress, smoothing it down her body. "After that, we might even explore the Great Lakes. What do you think? Sail into Cleveland and see what's new with the Theodopolis family?"

"Would you like that?"

"Certainly. I'd like to see what kind of family turned out a woman like you."

Thoughtfully Katherine said, "I think I would, too. I've learned some things about myself lately, you know. Maybe it's time I went home. Just for a visit, of course."

He winked. "And by the time we get to New York, we may have worked out a few things about us, don't you think?"

Voice equally low, Katherine said, "I'm sure we will. I love you, Blackie."

Blackie grinned. "Tell me true, your ladyship. Did you ever imagine you'd say those words to me?"

She laughed. "Are you going to tease me like this forever?"

"Of course," he said. "I'm an unspeakable pig, remember?"

Harlequin
Superromance

COMING NEXT MONTH

#222 THE LONG ROAD HOME • Georgia Bockoven
Jennifer Langley becomes Craig Templeton's link to
the prominent Kentucky family that had long given
him up for dead. Suddenly love and destiny conspire
to change their lives forever....

#223 CHOICES • Jane Worth Abbott
In this spin-off to Superromance #192, *Faces of a
Clown*, Sara Fletcher finds herself falling in love with
a younger man. And the unexpected object of her
affection is Evan McGrath, the man who is turning
her workplace upside down!

#224 MEANT TO BE • Janice Kaiser
When Diana Hillyer attempts to rescue a teenager
forced into prostitution in Honduras, she discovers
that an American soldier, Cleve Emerson, holds the
key to the girl's freedom. His stubborn refusal to
help infuriates Diana, but she finds his allure
irresistible....

#225 UNTIL NOW • Sally Garrett
Old maid schoolteacher. That's how Kathryn Keith
figures the townsfolk refer to her. All except John
Brasher, that is. The towering lumberjack is out to
change her reputation—with a marriage proposal.

Harlequin "Super Celebration"
SWEEPSTAKES

NEW PRIZES—NEW PRIZE FEATURES & CHOICES—MONTHLY

1. To enter the sweepstakes, follow the instructions outlined on the Center Insert Card. Alternate means of entry, NO PURCHASE NECESSARY, you may also enter by mailing your name, address and birthday on a plain 3″ x 5″ piece of paper to: In U.S.A.: Harlequin "Super Celebration" Sweepstakes, P.O. Box 1867, Buffalo, N.Y. 14240-1867. In Canada: Harlequin "Super Celebration" Sweepstakes, P.O. Box 2800, 5170 Yonge Street, Postal Station A, Willowdale, Ontario M2N 6J3.

2. Winners will be selected in random drawings from all entries received. All prizes will be awarded. These prizes are in addition to any free gifts which might be offered. Versions of this sweepstakes with different prizes may appear in other presentations by TorStar and their affiliates. The maximum value of the prizes offered is $8,000.00. Winners selected will receive the prize offered from their prize package.

3. The selection of winners will be conducted under the supervision of Marden-Kane, an independent judging organization. By entering the sweepstakes, each entrant accepts and agrees to be bound by these rules and the decision of the judges which shall be final and binding. Odds of winning are dependent upon the total number of entries received. Taxes, if any, are the sole responsibility of the winners. Prizes are not transferable. This sweepstakes is scheduled to appear in Retail Outlets of Harlequin Books during the period of June 1986 to December 1986. All entries must be received by January 31st, 1987. The drawing will take place on or about March 1st, 1987 at the offices of Marden-Kane, Lake Success, New York. For Quebec (Canada) residents, any litigation regarding the running of this sweepstakes and the awarding of prizes must be submitted to La Regie de Lotteries et Course du Quebec.

4. This presentation offers the prizes as illustrated on the Center Insert Card.

5. This offer is open to residents of the U.S., and Canada, 18 years or older, except employees of TorStar, its affilliates, subsidiaries, Marden-Kane and all other agencies and persons connected with conducting this sweepstakes. All Federal, State and local laws apply. Void where prohibited or restricted by law. Winners will be notified by mail and may be required to execute an affidavit of eligibility and release which must be returned within 14 days after notification. Winners consent to the use of their name, photograph and/or likeness for advertising and publicity in conjunction with this and similar promotions without additional compensation. One prize per family or household. Canadian winners will be required to answer a skill testing question.

6. For a list of our most recent prize winners, send a stamped, self-addressed envelope to: WINNERS LIST, c/o Marden-Kane, P.O. Box 525, Sayreville, NJ 08872.

No Lucky Number needed to win!